HUDSON

THE BILLIONAIRES OF WHISPERS
BOOK 2

SAMANTHA SKYE

ISBN: 978-0-6486083-4-9 (E-book)

ISBN: 978-0-6486083-3-2 (Paperback)

ISBN: 978-1-923258-02-0 (Alternative Paperback)

Cover Design: Angela Haddon

Editor: Nice Girl Naughty Edits

Proofreading: Kimberly Dawn

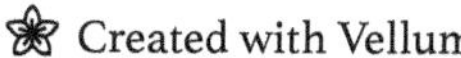 Created with Vellum

1

───────

LACY JONES

My back aches. Is that normal for a twenty-three-year-old woman?

"What's wrong?" My mother's voice is terse as she assesses me from where she sits in the living room. Perched up in her large, worn-out armchair, I've already fluffed her pillow, refreshed her water, and made sure she has her book and phone nearby.

"Nothing," I tell her, my smile small and a little forced as I continue wiping down the kitchen counters and cleaning up from breakfast. I feel like I'm forgetting something as I run through the mental checklist in my mind over and over again. I need to triple-check Mom's medication for today and make sure her phone is charged. The washing machine beeps, indicating the end of the cycle, so I also need to hang the laundry before I go. No time to stop, no time to slow down.

"You're tired, Lacy," Mom says and I catch her still looking at me. She's right. I'm exhausted. But I have a lot on my plate, and being exhausted during the day is my only antidote to trying to stave off the nightmares that come for me in the darkness. Sometimes it works, but most of the time, it doesn't.

"Don't worry about me," I tell her, trying to placate her worry as I make my way over to where she sits in the living room. I grab the small blanket nearby and place it over her knee. As I do, I notice it getting a little threadbare, and I add another mental note to go to the cute homewares store in town and see if I can find another one for her.

"Stop your fussing. I'm doing well. I can walk around and get my own things," she snaps at me, and I jolt upright at her bark.

"I just want to make sure you're settled before I go to work," I explain, for what feels like the hundredth time, while my eyes flick to her dwindling library book stash next to her. I frown, trying to remember what the opening hours are at the library, knowing I need to get there before she runs out of books this week.

"Honey, you need to relax. I'm more than capable." Her voice changes to that low, caring octave she sometimes gives me. The one that makes me pause and swallow hard. She's right. She is good. And while we are not out of the woods yet, this is the healthiest she's been in years.

"I know." I continue to fluff her blanket some more, needing to do something with my hands. Mom is capable. *At the moment.* Signs are good, but her health ebbs and flows. Sure, some days are better than others. Some weeks are great, others abysmal, but I'm all she has, and I need to take care of her. That's why I can't stop, I can't slow down. I need to be on top of things, I can't let anything slip.

"You work too hard looking after me. You work too hard at the distillery. You should be young and free and dating, meeting men, and living life," she says whimsically, obviously reminiscing on her own past. I snort. *Dating, what is that?*

"I'm fine right where I am, Mom." Most young people itch to leave the small towns they grew up in, but I feel content being home. Happier still because I landed the job of my dreams right here in Whispers, and I get to care for her in her times of need.

"Sure you are, but if you are not careful, honey, life will completely pass you by. You need to slow down, smell the roses."

I look at her and sigh. She's right, of course. Always is. But there is no one else here to manage things, and if I slow down, then I might forget something or make a mistake and with Mom's health, I can't afford to make that kind of mistake.

"How is work going at the distillery?" she asks, watching me carefully.

"It's busy, but I love it." My answer obviously appeases her because she smiles.

"You do, don't you?" she asks, her tone one of relief. She looks good today. Lots of color in her cheeks and her eyes sparkle.

"I do. I mean, it's everything I could ever want and everything that I've been aiming for," I admit. "None of my friends from college have had the opportunities I have." Never in my dreams did I think this job was remotely possible, especially here in our small town. But here I am, the marketing manager for Whiteman's Whiskey, working on bringing the whiskey brand to life. I'm new to the role, so while the salary is good, it's still a little bit tight some weeks. I have the two of us to look after. I have medical bills, home expenses, not to mention the basic living expenses like food and medicine. There is always something to be paid.

"I feel bad for bringing you back here. I still don't know why you left college early to come home. That was your ticket out of here, and now I've pulled you away from that dream," she says, a little melancholy. A shiver runs through me. College is almost a distant memory, which is where I want to keep it.

"It was easy to just do my final six months remotely from here. That way, I could be here with you and finish my degree at the same time." I tell her the same story I always have. She doesn't need to know anything different. "Besides, it's turning out alright, Mom. You and me always, right?" I say our little slogan, and I see it eases her concerns. "We're a team. Nothing but blue skies for us." Feeling the need to instill some positivity into this conversation, I leave everything else buried, if for no other reason than to see her smile. There's too much to unpack, and now isn't the time. She needs to focus on healing, not on me.

"Speaking of jobs, I need to get going. I'm working with Connor on the next new release today. Bottle samples are supposed to arrive." I find it hard to contain my excitement as I triple-check all her pills and vitamins to make sure they are in order for her to take today.

"Don't forget, I have an appointment at the hospital this afternoon," Mom says, and I pause midway between her and the laundry to sort it out before I go. I had forgotten about her appointment. My brow crumples, wondering how I forgot something like that. I'm usually on top of all her appointments. "Susan's taking me," she adds quickly.

"Susan?" I question. It makes sense. Susan Hamilton is one of Mom's oldest friends and is always popping over to help, which has been a godsend for me, really. But I usually take Mom to all her medical appointments. I feel bad that I didn't have today's appointment written in my schedule, and even worse about the fact that it wasn't on my radar at all. The familiar feeling of failure creeps up my spine, making my stomach curl.

"You need to stop trying to look after me all on your own. We have a good community here, and lots of friends. It's just a checkup, and I'll be saying goodbye to the doctor. I didn't tell you because I thought it might give you a break," she says, fixing her blanket with a proud smile on her face.

"Goodbye?" My brow furrows deeper as I wonder what else I have missed. *Hell, where has my brain been at that I seem to be missing so much lately?* I think briefly to my nightmare last night, knowing exactly where my mind now lives. The smell of gasoline is still one I can't stomach.

"He is finally retiring. Going traveling before settling down in Florida, where his grandchildren are." Mom saying the information only adds to my confusion. The washing machine beeps again, reminding me that I need to tend to it.

"What? When did that happen? Why didn't I know..." I start to say, my chest feeling tight. Sure, he's at retirement age, but I didn't know he was leaving so soon. "What will happen with your care?" I ask, concerned, my body starting to tingle with panic. I need to speak to the doctor. I need to sort out Mom's medical care moving forward. If we need to travel farther to appointments, then I'll need to pencil that in, move things around in my work schedule.

"Lacy. With everything that's going on at work for you, not to mention, you are working through your own things, I just didn't need you to worry about me too."

There goes my stomach. Feeling heavy like it's weighing me down, yet simultaneously wanting to empty. I quickly look at the bathroom, like I might need to dash.

"I'm fine, Mom." I feel like my words are on repeat as my shoulders tighten, and I try to tamp down my insides.

"I know. You're doing so well with your therapy, and I'm so proud of you. But I'm okay too. Susan will take good care of me today. Besides, she was keen to see the hospital one last time before Hudson comes back. Apparently, he wants to make lots of changes once he is here," Mom says, and just at the sound of his name, I'm on high alert, my heart back to racing.

"Hudson?" I ask cautiously. I feel like the dots are starting to connect in my brain. Hudson Hamilton is Susan's son and a billionaire doctor from the city, a man who screams wealth, who grew up here, and is best friends with my boss. He is also the man who rescued me from certain death six months ago. Held me close and promised to keep me safe, and I believed him. Pity my panic attacks prove otherwise.

"Hudson is coming home. He's going to run the hospital. Susan is so glad to have him and her grandson coming to live in Whispers, she is beside herself. It's all she has been talking about for weeks." Mom huffs with a small smile dancing on her lips, filling me in on the local gossip.

I swallow harshly. I knew my boss, Tanner Whiteman, was trying to get Hudson to come back to manage the hospital, and even though Tanner runs this town and is good friends with Hudson, I never thought he would accept the offer. Hudson lives in LA and is one of the country's best doctors. Having invented some unique medical testing equipment while he was in med school, he earned his billions from selling his prototype to the country's larger medical company, and even though he could retire young and live a life floating around the Mediterranean, he doesn't.

If Hudson is, in fact, coming back, our billionaire count in Whispers will rise again. Our little quiet patch of the country already has many, Hudson's brother Huxley also living here part-time. I'm quiet for a beat. Shocked, really. I first met Hudson months ago when he came to Whispers to spend a few weeks at the hospital to try it out. I remember his eyes following me around the bar in town when I worked the night shift and whenever he would come past the distillery to see Tanner. We shared smiles, a few harmless flirtatious moments. They were brief, yet butterflies swirled every time he was near. But after the incident, he left pretty quickly. He sent me text messages almost every week for a month before they stopped—probably because I never responded. I was healing, both physically and mentally, and he's a billionaire dad, who lives in LA, so far removed from my day-to-day that my dreams of being swept off my feet are well and truly just that. Dreams. I never thought I would ever see him again. I guess I was wrong.

"Lacy. Lacy?" Mom says, grabbing my attention, and I shake my head.

"Yes, Mom?" I ask, just as the washing machine beeps for a third time, making my shoulders inch upward to my ears.

"You need to get to work. You will be late, honey."

With that, I shove Hudson to the back of my mind and run to the laundry, pulling out the wet clothes and throwing them into the dryer, the outside breeze not one I have time to utilize today before I quickly gather my things.

Mom is right. I'm busy. Busy with my new role, busy being her primary caretaker, busy trying to sort myself out, manage the house, manage our finances. It leaves little time for anything else.

Men and dating included.

2

HUDSON HAMILTON

My son runs around the empty house, arms spread out wide, pretending to be an airplane. His fascination with planes started when we took a trip in the jet back to Whispers a few months ago. Now he can't get enough of them.

"It looks so big!" he exclaims as he zooms past me, my smile wide as I watch his delight.

"He's right. This house is so empty, our voices almost echo," my friend, Sutton, says as he takes a swig of his morning take-away coffee. I look around. The walls that were once covered with my multimillion-dollar art collection are now bare. My Dali and Picasso are now in safe storage. The polished marble flooring makes the house feel cold and uninviting, instead of warm and welcoming. Family photos that lined the wall up the stairs are all packed away, as are all our other things. The time has now come.

"Your place echoes," I huff to him, knowing his Hollywood Hills mansion is decorated well, but has no life.

Like me, he works too hard, although instead of a busy city hospital, he's always off on a movie set somewhere.

"True. Maybe I need a new decorator?" he murmurs, obviously bored already and needing something new to focus on. Perhaps his new leading lady is yet to make an appearance. While I played the field in my youth, that side of me is long over. However, Sutton Silvers puts us all to shame. He has a different woman on his arm at every event.

"You need to enjoy life and stop working so hard. If anything, these past few years have taught me that," I try to explain and ignore the small empathetic smile he gives me. I prefer his wide Hollywood grin, the one where his teeth are so white they are almost blinding.

"Well, I won't keep you. I need to head to Cannes for the film festival this afternoon. I think my jet is parked near yours at the airport, actually. Tell Sawyer I said hello." Then my best friend surprises me, pulling me close and slapping my back as we hug. His brother Sawyer spends a lot of time in Whispers these days due to his work with Tanner Whiteman, owner of the local distillery, quasi-mayor of the town, and one of my best friends.

Not much happens in Whispers without Tanner's hand, including me being placed as their new full-time resident doctor. It was always in the cards. I don't work for the money anymore, but the deep-seated need to continue to help people through medicine runs through my veins and is what pushed me through my medical degree. After selling my prototype for new medical testing equipment years ago, my life is all financed, as is that of my son and grandchildren, should I have them. With money not an issue, I can do life on my terms, and for a long while, that was city living and working to help people in the busy city hospital. Now my pace in life has changed and back home in Whispers, closer to friends and family, is where I want to be.

"I will see you across socials, no doubt. Come visit, yeah?" I ask him, and he gives me a cheeky grin.

"I heard the country girls are nice?" he says slyly, wiggling his eyebrows as he starts to walk backward toward the door. I swallow roughly as I think about my small town and the one woman I think about often. Lacy and I shared a significant night. And she hasn't left my thoughts, even though she hasn't responded to any of my text messages. Just the knowledge that I'll be seeing her again has me both nervous and hopeful.

"I won't be telling you a thing," I say, smiling devilishly. I've been single for the past few years, preferring to keep my life without strings attached, trying to balance single parenting with work and not really succeeding very well. I need a fresh start and can't wait to get to Whispers just to breathe.

"Hudson, so glad I caught you," my sister-in-law, Melody, says breathily as she sweeps through the open front door, interrupting us. She acts like she has run from the car, yet nothing about her is out of place. Just like my late wife Amanda, she is prim, proper, blond, blue-eyed, plumped and primped and boringly perfect.

"That's my cue," Sutton says, giving me a jovial salute and walking past my new guest, giving her a wink.

"Bye, champ." Sutton fist-bumps my son before he picks him up off the floor and squeezes him tight.

"Bye, Uncle Sutton." Harvey giggles uncontrollably as Sutton tickles him and then places him back on his feet and waltzes out the door. It must be nice to not have a care in the world. I can't remember those days.

"I keep forgetting your best friend is a movie star," Melody mumbles as she watches him go.

"What's up?" I ask, giving her a small smile. She is a doctor herself. A cancer specialist. The two of us worked day and night to treat my wife of the terrible disease she suffered, but to no avail. Her cancer was a shock and aggressive and, in the end, untreatable.

"Hi, Aunt Melody," Harvey says, and I smile at his manners.

"Hi, Harvey. All set?" she asks, eyebrows raised expectantly.

"I can't wait!" Harvey's barely able to contain his excitement as he jumps from foot to foot; his little legs can't stay still for long.

Even though moving to Whispers was always in the cards, taking Harvey away from his mother's side of the family is a battle I wasn't sure I could master. But my former in-laws are both professionals who never had much time for their daughters, and that ended up being the same story when it came to their grandson. Since Amanda's funeral, I've hardly seen them these past few years. My former father-in-law, especially, as he's a man whom I don't really enjoy being around for no other reason than he is just a pompous asshole who thinks he is better than everyone else.

"Yes, well, I would prefer you both to stay here," I hear her murmur, and I give her a soft smile. I know she is sad to see us go, but Whispers is amazing. Fresh air, open fields, small, yes, but also quaint.

"We are both excited," I confirm, and she gives me a tight smile. "What can I do for you?" I ask, wondering why she's here. I see her around the hospital on rare occasions, but she's been coming by to see me more and more since I told her of our decision to move.

"I just wanted to say goodbye." She looks at me with a face full of hope that I will change my mind.

"We said goodbye yesterday..." Harvey and I spent the day with her and her mother, having lunch together. I wanted to do the right thing.

"I know, but that was so... impersonal."

"Impersonal?" I frown, unsure what she means.

"It's just. Mom and Dad are still in mourning..."

I take a deep breath because I don't believe that for a second. It's true the death of my wife hit everyone hard. Her diagnosis during pregnancy, then starting treatment after birth meant that she didn't get onto the disease straight away, and after a long year of battle, it finally won. But it has been years now and we all need to move forward. Her parents are more about appearances than anything real.

"And well, we went through so much together." Her own eyes glass over with tears. This is why I have to leave. I loved my wife. We met just as I was finishing my residency and sold my medical testing solution, dated for a short amount of time, then fell pregnant unexpectedly. I did the right thing and put a ring on her finger, and we had a shotgun wedding. It all happened so fast, including losing her. I have officially been a widower longer than we even knew each other, but if I'm to have any chance of moving on, then I need to leave here.

"We all need to start moving forward. It's what she would have wanted," I tell her sister, resting my hand on her shoulder to give her some comfort. I try to be empathetic. The two of them were close. But with both Harvey and me to look after, I have little left of me to give her. I just want to laugh again. I just want the heaviness in my chest to disappear.

"I know. Of course. Just don't be a stranger," she says, reaching out and grabbing my hand. She gives it a squeeze. I appreciate the gesture.

"We won't. But we do need to go." My family jet is waiting at the airport, my driver and town car parked outside, packed with our things, ready and waiting for us. I just need to get the box of books that are at my feet and then Harvey and myself out of this house.

"Well, call me when you land," she says, and I nod.

"Bye, Harvey." She looks at her only nephew and he gives her a wave, now totally engrossed in a book about planes from my brother, Huxley, and his wife, whom I know he is also excited to spend more time with.

"Bye, Melody," I say, walking to the door and holding it open for her. As soon as she leaves, my shoulders lower, my stress levels settle, and Harvey comes back to my side.

"Have we got everything?" I ask him, my smile now growing. Being a single dad has been one of the hardest yet most rewarding parts of my life, and I can't wait to spend more quality time with Harvey.

"Yes! I can't wait to see Grandma!" Harvey says excitedly.

"Oh, she can't wait to see you either, buddy," I tell him, ruffling his hair. LA stifles him. It stifles both of us. The city where I have spent my entire medical career feels almost claustrophobic. It has for me for years.

Like she can hear us, my cell rings, and I see my mom's name light up the screen.

"Hey, Grandma," I say, loud enough for Harvey to hear, and he giggles.

"Just checking in. Have you left yet?" she asks, trying to contain her excitement.

"Left? God, woman, how many times do you need to call him!" I hear my dad tell her in the background, and the fact that he is also close to the phone is enough to tell me that they are both ready for our arrival.

"Just about. We are locking up the door now." I grab my keys and take another quick look around.

"Okay, I have a pot roast on. It will be ready for you both when you arrive," she says, and my mouth waters. Mom's pot roasts are the best thing I have ever eaten.

"Sounds great, Mom. We will see you in a few hours," I tell her, smiling at my son, who is just as excited as his grandparents.

"Love you both. Safe travels," she says, and I hang up and look at Harvey.

"Can we go now?" he asks, hopping in place, and I take a deep breath. I am ready. We are ready.

"I'll get the box." I grab the box of his books, and his wide grin is instant as he starts to dance around again. Together, we lock up, saying goodbye to the house I called home for almost the past decade, and we pile into our town car, our driver waiting patiently.

"Will we have a driver in Whispers, Dad?" Harvey asks as we pull away from the curb, and I chuckle.

"Yes. Two of them. They are called Grandma and Grandpa." I laugh, knowing that there's no way they are going to let Harvey out of their sight for a while.

As I look out the window, I know that as this chapter of my life closes, I'm hopeful for the next one.

God knows this one has been hard enough.

3

LACY

"Mom, I'm home," I yell out as I walk into the house. I try not to notice the screen door frame starting to crumble at the bottom due to water damage or old age—which one, I can't be sure anymore. Instead, my stress peaked the minute I pulled up and saw a strange truck out front. It's new, one of the latest models, polished to a high shine, but it's unfamiliar, so my body is already in fight-or-flight mode.

"In here," she says, and I take a breath. She sounds okay, but I quickly look around the kitchen to ensure everything looks as it should. The house is clean, kitchen tidy. I drop my bag onto the kitchen counter and walk swiftly into the living room before I come to an abrupt stop as my heart stutters. Dr. Hudson Hamilton is in my living room, sharing a coffee with my mother.

"Hey," I choke out, startled, my eyes widening as my throat immediately dries up at the unexpected sight.

"Hi, Lacy. Good to see you," he says, jumping up from

the sofa where he was sitting to greet me. It's been months since I last saw him, and I wish I could say I almost forgot what he looked like, but that would be a lie. His face is one I remember vividly. Seeing him brings the memories back to me full force as I take a deep breath to try to calm my heart that is now thumping madly, reminding me that I am, in fact, a red-blooded woman.

He looks good. In a suit that matches his professionalism, the jacket filled out, covering his broad shoulders. His shoes are high shine and his watch glistens on his wrist. A Rolex, it's hard to miss. He's distinguished, expensive, and against our ratty old sofa, totally out of place. My stomach flip-flops, before I look down at myself. Sure, I have my work clothes on, but my hair is a mess, and I was running late this morning so my makeup is not at all on point.

Looking back at him, my eyes don't move from his as memories flash through my mind so rapidly I can't grasp them. A few months ago, he was my savior. I don't remember a lot from that night, but I do remember him seeing me tied up in that shed, untying the ropes that held me, picking me up, and running us away from danger. I had never been more grateful to see someone before in my life, and my grip on him was tight. I never wanted him to let me go. I also remember him taking care of me in the hospital, until one morning, he wasn't there anymore. Now as I stare at him standing in my living room, I clear my throat, trying to find words.

"Is everything alright?" I ask, looking at my mom with a frown. I have no idea why he is here, but he has his doctor's bag at his feet, so my eyes do a quick assessment of her to ensure she is okay.

"Everything is fine, honey. Hudson just came to do a house call and to tell us he is back," Mom explains, her smile wide as she glances between Hudson and me almost expectantly.

"For good," Hudson says quickly, and my gaze darts back to him to see he's watching me. I feel my cheeks heat under his attention. A house call is unusual here in Whispers unless it's an emergency. The only time a doctor has been here is when Mom is too sick to go to them, and clearly that's not the case today.

"Great." I mentally scold myself for my lack of vocabulary right now. My smile is forced from the surprise that filters around my body, because I wasn't expecting to see him in my home, on my sofa, having a cup of coffee with my mom.

"Honey, we were just finishing up. Why don't you walk Hudson out," Mom says, and I spread my smile wider for her and push through these feelings of shock taking over me. Hudson looks too good. Better than good. Tall. Dark. Handsome. I shake my head because these thoughts suddenly resurfacing are ridiculous, and I have absolutely no time or reason to start entertaining them. But if I was a normal young woman, without all my worries and responsibilities, then maybe I could daydream.

"Sure, Mom." I subtly wipe my palms on my pants because they are sweaty. The lethargy I felt only five minutes ago after a long day at work while mentally preparing for a long night at home has been replaced by anxious energy. I feel fidgety and need to do something with my hands. I lean over to grab his bag to carry it for him, at the same time he does, and our hands collide. My body jolts on impact, humming like I have been electrocuted.

"Sorry," I rush out, pulling back immediately. As I do, I gasp in some air and smell his woodsy aroma. The familiarity of his cologne quickly encases me, making me almost stumble as it both soothes me and feels like a protective shield.

"It's okay," he murmurs, his voice almost like a tonic to my soul as he watches me closely. His gaze burns into me and he steps forward a little as if he is going to take my hand before pausing. I look to my mom who is in prime position, watching it all unravel, and I shake my head a little, like it will get my brain back into focus mode.

I've never had a man in this house before and neither has mom. A product of a one-night stand, I've never had a father figure, and it's always been just Mom and me. My therapist says that's why I take on so much. Because now that Mom is sick, I don't feel that I have anyone else I can rely on, so I do everything myself. My trust issues have only amplified since the fire in the shed, one started by the very person I thought was a friend.

With that thought, I straighten my spine and turn on my heel to create some space and pace out the door toward his truck. I can handle this. It's just the new town doctor. He isn't here to see me. He isn't anyone I need to concern myself with. He is a billionaire, a dad, albeit a very good-looking, panty-dropping dapper man, but one who isn't for a small-town girl like me.

It's only when I'm outside that I finally pull in a breath of fresh air. Seeing him again after all this time brings that night back to the surface. The night when I thought I was going to die, only to be saved by him. The way he grabbed me and held me tight. How I buried my head in his chest, the smell of his cologne. The way he spoke to me, promised me that he would always protect me. All that, coupled with the fact that he is just as good-looking as I remember, has me on edge. I try to remember the techniques my therapist taught me. The breathing that helps relax my mind when I feel panicked or flustered. Usually only reserved for when I have night-mares. *Breathe in two, three, four and out two, three, four.*

I hear him say goodbye to Mom inside, and I open my eyes as I hear the screen door of my house and his steps on the gravel behind me.

"So... how have you be—"

"Fine," I cut him off, folding my arms across my chest as if they can protect me from getting too close with him, because falling into his embrace is feeling all too appetiz-ing. I roll my head on my shoulders as the familiarity of his eyes makes me nervous, his gaze almost piercing. He saw me at my weakest that night, my most vulnerable, and his arms were a safe place for me. Now, as he stands right in front of me, I just want to dive back in and have him hold me tight and never let me go.

"You know, I've thought about you a lot." His voice is a low rumble that sizzles on my skin as he takes a step towards me. He's close, well within my reach, and I tense my fingers on my arms, ensuring they remain there, to the point I almost bruise my skin. The need to hug him, touch him, feel him is more intense than what I could have prepared for. I seal my lips tight, keeping the words *I think about you too* from coming out. Instead, I take a small step, toward him or to the side, I'm not sure where, but as I do, I trip on the gravel underfoot.

"Whoa," I exhale, my arms flinging out to my sides to try and regain balance, just as he moves quickly, his hands coming to my waist to grab me so I don't fall. Instinct has me putting my hands on his arms, holding on to him. He steadies us, the two of us now standing so close I can almost feel his breath on my cheek. Memories swirl, familiarity sinking into my bones. My heart is thudding out of my chest, and I can barely breathe as I look up at him.

"You never responded to my messages?" he asks softly, not accusing and not angry, and I feel slightly guilty.

"I've been busy." I could tell him that I think about him all the time. That I have nightmares about that night and the only thing that soothes me is looking at those messages. But he doesn't need to know all that.

"Too busy to text?" he asks, raising his eyebrow in question, knowing full well that I have time to text him back.

"There's been a lot going on," I say, only half fibbing.

His gaze on me is intense, like he is trying to see through me and my bullshit, and it's working. I'm not sure if it was the near-death experience we had together, but it's like we're doing life on the same frequency. I feel his thumb move a little along my side, caressing me tenderly, the movement so small it's hard to feel. But I do feel it and my body starts to soften against his of its own accord. I have no idea what's happening, but I like it.

"Do I need to check your phone? Maybe teach you how to send a text message?" His lips quirk, breaking this tension we feel, and I roll my eyes and smile. He's letting me off easy, injecting a little humor, and I'm thankful.

"Hudson…" I say, shaking my head, needing his attention off me. I'm so tired; I'm surprised he is here, happy, confused, and my inner turmoil rages, yet all the while his thumb continues to run up and down, almost in rhythm with my heartbeat, keeping me grounded.

"You alright?" he asks genuinely and full of concern, and I take a deep breath, trying to steel myself. He lifts his hand, his fingers tenderly touching my cheek. I hold my breath as we stare at each other for a beat. I could get lost in his eyes, his hands so gentle, so tender. Somewhere in the distance, a cow bleats, and I come back to myself.

"I'm fine." I clear my throat and take a step back from him, needing the space. He drops his hands slowly and looks at me, his brow furrowed like he can sense my inner turmoil. I'm not ready to talk, not about us, not about that night.

"So… are you doing well since…" he trails off, and my breath leaves me as I look back at him sharply. It isn't like I don't talk about it. But I'm not ready to talk about it with him.

"I'm fine." I say the same words so much it's beginning to grate on me.

"That's the third fine you have said since you got home," he quips as he rubs his chin. Assessing me, his eyes drag across my face, down my body, and back up again, like he needs to look me over to ensure that I am actually okay. I feel myself blushing as a small smile threatens to dance on his lips. I push my own lips together as the words "I'm fine" threaten to spill. *Again.* I watch his Adam's apple bob as he swallows.

"How is Mom doing?" I change the subject to something other than me. He gives me a soft smile and offers me the reprieve.

"She's good. Going to that specialist in Williamstown for her treatment these past few months is working well. All signs indicate that she's getting better and better every week," he says, nodding.

"Good. I've tried to keep on top of all her meds. Ensure she rests."

"Well, you're doing a great job. Make sure you call me if you ever need anything, you know, since you don't know how to text and all. I'm not too far away from you here. I'm living back at the family ranch." It makes sense he would live at his ranch. I haven't been there, but from what I hear, they have a massive property at the start of Billionaires Boulevard. Where the rolling green hills meet the edge of town and the large cedar trees offer privacy and protection from the elements.

"Sure will," I tell him, because I won't hesitate when it comes to Mom's health. He watches me a little before giving me a small smile.

"I need to go get Harvey."

I finally take a small breath before I smile, remembering his adorable little boy. I love kids, although given that I don't have a boyfriend and am unlikely to find one here in this small town, I figure maybe being a mom isn't in my future.

"Sure. Thanks… for … seeing Mom," I say awkwardly and internally cringe because for some reason I can't find my voice around this man. *Thanks for rescuing me. Thanks for holding me when I cried.*

He moves past me slowly, his arm brushing against me as his fingers grab mine that dangle at my sides. Giving them a small squeeze, he lets go and continues to make his way to his truck. I hold my breath so I don't breathe him in. But it's futile because I crave the scent just as much. I watch him jump into his truck, looking right at home here in Whispers despite his professional suit. He closes his door and then looks back at me through his open window.

"I'll see you around, Lacy," he says, still watching me carefully and curiously.

"Sure. Thanks again." I offer him a small smile and a wave as his engine starts and he slowly drives away. I sigh as his taillights move farther in the distance, feeling that familiar sense of emptiness settle back in my stomach before I turn and walk back inside. I have dishes to do, dinner to make, and I need to look at our budget. With medical bills and a new screen door, I may need to juggle some things.

Hudson Hamilton and his good looks and strong arms need to be pushed to the back of my mind.

He's not a priority. Not for a girl like me.

4

HUDSON

As Tanner's bar staff put the glasses of whiskey on our table, I suddenly miss the young brunette who was doing this before I left. Lacy is just as stunning as I remember, and she took my breath away when I saw her during the week. Now that she is in a new position at Whiteman's Whiskey, she doesn't tend the bar here anymore. Even so, I still search for her among the staff members and feel a pang of unease when I don't spot her in the uniform I came to know so well before. I wasn't sure what to expect when coming back after leaving a few months ago. But the force of which Lacy is now front and center in my mind has taken me by surprise.

I watched her for weeks when I was here. We had some playful banter, some flirtatious moments. But that night I helped her, it shifted something inside of me. Remembering the way Lacy clung to me when I grabbed her from the rope. The way her body shook, and I held her so tight, never wanting to let her go. Holding her hand, stroking her hair, and keeping her safe when she felt anything but. I may not have been able to save my wife all those years ago, but I saved Lacy that night. With everything becoming so much clearer after that, moving home, being closer to family, and giving Harvey the same upbringing I had all just felt right. And I wanted to see her again. So much so, that I went to her house under the guise of a house call to her mother this past week.

"Cheers to a good first week," Tanner says, knocking me from my thoughts as he lifts his glass, his son, Connor, and I following suit.

"Cheers," I murmur, taking a sip of his latest whiskey release, feeling the burn that is much needed.

"So how has it been?" Connor asks me, looking like a younger version of his father. We are close in age, having grown up together, along with my brother, Huxley. Tanner, being a young dad, joined our group in our adult years, and now we are all close.

"Settling in. Getting things organized. I have some new processes I want to implement, but the hospital is a well-oiled machine." The hospital is great. It's new, with renovations happening regularly, due to the two men sitting opposite me from Whiteman's Whiskey and their investment in the town. The staff are older, but reliable and good at their jobs. While this week has been quiet, I know in a small town, things can change at a moment's notice, so one whiskey will be my limit. Even though I'm not on call tonight, as the only doctor within twenty miles, things are always bound to happen.

"Good. How's Harvey liking it so far?" Tanner asks, and my smile is immediate.

"He's loving it," I tell them, thinking about his week at his new school. He has taken to Whispers like a duck to water.

"I knew he would. It's the best place for kids. How good was it growing up here?" Connor grins at me cheekily, and I laugh at his enthusiasm. He's right. Growing up here was great. Riding bikes, running around, camping, swimming in the mineral springs. A big outdoor lifestyle and one I want my son to experience.

"He loves school. His teacher, Annabelle, seems great, and the other kids have welcomed him immediately. Not to mention, Mom and Dad are spoiling him rotten. He's living his best life. The change in him already is noticeable." I roll the glass of whiskey in my hand, releasing a contented sigh.

It's nice to have my parents so involved in our lives now. They take care of him while I work, and it frees me up to focus on the hospital and build up the services we can offer. It's only been a week, but the more time I spend here, the more I feel like myself. High-profile city doctor has been my life for so long that it almost feels like I'm a bear coming out of hibernation or a snake shedding its skin.

The good news is that I know Tanner wants me to develop the hospital into something bigger and better for the town. More technology, more support, new programs. It's the ideal job for me and one I can't wait to dig right into. I no longer work for the money. The basic salary I receive will go straight back into local programs. I work to help people, look at new ways of implementing medical care, and get positive outcomes.

"Good. I'm glad. He will be riding his bike around town in no time," Tanner says, smiling like the king who moved his chess pieces and got it right, because that is exactly what he did. He got me out here months ago to spend some time in the hospital and back in the town to see how I would like it, knowing before I even did that it's what I would want.

"So where's Victoria tonight?" I ask about his girlfriend. They are never apart these days.

"Over there," he says, nodding behind my shoulder, and I turn to look, immediately spotting her blond hair over at a booth on the other side of the bar. I look to see who she's talking with, and my breath catches in my chest. She's with Lacy, the two of them in deep conversation. Lacy must sense me watching her because her stare flicks to the side and meets my gaze, and my heart thuds more powerfully. Her deep-brown eyes are intense, like they hold so much. Maybe because they do. We stay connected for a few seconds before she breaks our stare and gets back to her conversation. But I continue to watch. Her long dark hair is down and around her shoulders, her makeup light, and under the bar lights, she looks like an angel. She's beautiful. I thought it months ago, and I still think it now.

"Are you staring at my woman or my staff member?" Tanner growls.

"How are they?" I ask Tanner seriously, ignoring his question. I haven't really spoken to anyone from that night, apart from Tanner, and even then, it's factual and to the point, given how busy we've been.

"Good. Victoria is doing great, actually. Still has

moments, but she's going to therapy. We both are." He nods, and my eyebrows shoot up. I didn't expect a man like Tanner to go to therapy. "I got in with a therapist from Williamstown; we all needed it."

"Good. And Lacy?" I ask him. As her boss, I'm sure Tanner knows.

"She seems okay. Time heals many wounds. Therapy is doing her good as well, but she has a lot on her plate with her mom and all," Tanner replies, watching me carefully. On her medical file, Lacy's mom Veronica lists Lacy as her caretaker. That in itself is a big role, but she is also working full-time for Tanner, which I know would take a lot of effort.

I hear a loud laugh and look back across the room. Both Victoria and Lacy are in hysterics, laughing at something. It's good to see them laughing and the way her face brightens, it almost makes me stand and walk over, wanting to just be in her presence. My smile is genuine and quick to my lips, as is everyone else's in this bar.

"It's good to see them both laughing," I comment, enjoying seeing Lacy smile again and drinking her in. She seems relaxed with Victoria, the two of them obviously close. My stomach drops as I think about how I found her all those months ago, tied to the rafters of the shed at Marie's Place. I panicked the minute I found her. Sure, I've worked in emergency departments at some of the busiest hospitals, but by the time patients get to me, they are removed from danger and need healing. That night, it was up to me to save her, before I could even assess her injuries. It was an entirely different feeling; the urge to get to her overtook all sensibilities, and when I got her, I struggled to let her go.

"It's been a few months now. There is still a lot they are working through, but they have had each other," Connor adds, the three of us men now watching them with admiration. My eyes don't leave Lacy. The smile on her face takes me back to when I was here months ago, seeing the joy on her face, her happiness, as she worked behind the bar. She was pure light and laughter, and while I've dated other women since my wife's death, talking and flirting with Lacy was the first time it actually felt right.

Tanner clears his throat, and I turn back to him, seeing both him and Connor staring at me.

"What?" I ask, brow furrowing.

"What's going on with you and Lacy?" Connor asks.

"Nothing," I tell him, then take another sip of liquor.

"You were watching her closely before you took off back to the city months ago, and now you are back and watching her just as closely," Tanner says, his eyes drilling into mine, not missing a thing.

"I have no idea what you're talking about." Removing my gaze from his, I'm not able to look him in the eye because, as usual, he's right.

"Bullshit," Connor calls me out.

"There's nothing going on," I say again, running my hand through my hair.

"But you want there to be." Tanner sits back in his seat, watching me like a hawk.

"She is too young for me," I state, not denying it, but trying to push them off the topic, and he huffs. It's true, though, and something I have thought about. Keeping her at arm's length is the sensible thing to do.

"Not really," he murmurs. "Victoria is about twenty years my junior." He disproves my point instantly. I'm in my late thirties, and I know Lacy is mid-twenties, at best. So there are at least fifteen years between us.

"I have a kid." Harvey is my everything, and for anyone who comes into my life, they need to get along with my son and actually want children in their life. Otherwise, I can't commit.

"So do I," Tanner says, side-eyeing his adult son, and I roll my eyes.

"Not the same." I take another sip. Clearly, Connor is an adult, and even older than Victoria.

"What? I love my new mom!" Connor jests, laughing, and Tanner smacks him in the arm.

"Seriously. None of that can hold you back. I thought something might have happened before you left last time," Tanner says in question, eyeing me over the rim of his glass as he takes a sip.

"You did leave pretty quickly," Connor adds. It's on the tip of my tongue to tell him that I had to. I had to leave so I could come back quicker. I had to leave because seeing Lacy in that hospital bed brought back searing emotions from seeing my late wife in a similar position, and it hit me then how short life really is. But I *saved* Lacy, and she gripped on to me like she never wanted to let me go as I did the same to her. I can't explain it. Not really. The feelings between us were intense, even though it was merely one night and too much for me to fully process. Leaving and getting things sorted to come back gave me the time to think through things, it made things clearer, and in the end, coming back here to Whispers was what I really wanted to do.

"Nothing happened. We turned up, I pulled her from the ropes, traveled with her to the hospital, and took care of her medical needs, just like any doctor would," I say honestly.

"I know. I'm not saying you did anything unprofessional," Tanner says.

"It was an emotional night," I tell him, shrugging, and he just nods, knowing exactly what I mean. "And now I need to focus on the hospital and my son." Taking in a deep breath, I square my shoulders. But as we sit here, I hear another laugh from across the room, and I don't need to look to know who it came from.

It feels good to be back.

5

——————

LACY

I squeeze my eyes shut, the pain in my head searing.

"Help!" I try to scream, but my head feels like it's in a tornado. I gulp in air, the fright in my body paralyzing.

"Help!" I scream again, the skin on my legs burning, my body full of pain.

"Help!" The familiar smell of dirt, animals, and gasoline infiltrates my nostrils.

Nausea swirls in my stomach and makes me light-headed, as my hands are yanked over my head. The pain in my wrists is instant, and I blink hard a few times, my vision blurry.

"Somebody! Please!" I yell, but my voice sounds muffled. I'm confined, constricted. I can't move, my arms aching from being tied together. Fear crawls up my chest, my heart races, and sheer panic starts to take over. I thrash around, but I can't get free.

"Help me! Somebody, help me!" My shoulders feel

like they are going to rip from my body, my wrists numb like they aren't even connected to me anymore.

"Help me!" I scream and sit up with a start. My eyes open wide, my panting breath labored, and I look around my bedroom in fear, clutching the sheets to my chest.

Another nightmare. *Just a nightmare.* My heart is beating out of my chest, the vibrations making me tremble. I rub my eyes, willing the fear to dissipate, grateful for the small lamp I left on last night, bringing the reality of life to my eyes immediately.

I'm in bed. I'm safe.

I try to unfurl the sheets tangled around my body, my skin hot, slick with sweat as my head starts to thump, the nightly headache now approaching.

Throwing the sheets off, I turn and sit on the edge of the bed, placing my feet flat on the floor. Grounding. That's what my therapist calls it. I look around the room and voice three things I can see.

"Pillows. Mirror," I say before I turn to look out the window, taking in the sparkles that decorate the sky. "The stars."

I take a deep breath in and verbalize the three things I can smell.

"Shampoo." I take in another breath, my now damp with sweat hair intensifying the wash I gave it earlier. "My perfume... and the half-empty herbal tea." I look at the cup on my bedside. Half-empty with chamomile tea I made myself, thinking it might help me sleep.

News flash. It didn't.

I grab my cell. It's 4:33 a.m. Too early to get up. Too

late to go back to sleep. So I pull on a robe and walk out of my room, needing some fresh cool country air.

Opening my bedroom door tentatively, I tiptoe past Mom's bedroom, the creaks of the floor sounding too loud in the quiet house. I quicken my pace down the hall to the screen door and walk outside.

The cool air hits me instantly, and I take in another deep breath, my body still convulsing involuntarily at the fear that consumed me only moments ago. I sit on the Adirondack chair on the porch and look up. The stars are beautiful tonight. Inhaling and exhaling deep breaths, I count them out slowly until my heart settles, my head is clear, and I feel normal. Whatever normal is.

I look at my cell and bring up the messages, searching for the ones that I need to see. Scrolling down, I eventually find it. *Hudson.* It's been months since the last one, but I kept it. I kept them all.

Just seeing his name makes me feel better, and I wonder why my nightmares never resolve themselves with what happened in reality. With him rushing in and rescuing me. With him grabbing on to me and freeing me from the ropes. With him telling me that he's got me and that he will never let me go.

Instead, they relay the dark parts. Where I'm confined, head throbbing, and smell gasoline, in complete terror and fear for my life. They always skip the rescue.

I click on the text and read it. It's a benign message, asking how I've been. I sigh. Time has now passed. The town has moved on, life kept going, and me?

I now suffer in silence.

I sit with Victoria at the distillery, the two of us just finishing a meeting about our new spa interiors she put together. She has such a great eye for interiors, and even though the build isn't complete, her plans for the interior are amazing, and we have pulled together a strategy for how to launch and what media we need.

"How's your mom doing?" she asks me as we grab a coffee from the distillery restaurant during our five-minute break. It's late afternoon and midweek so no one is around, just the two of us and a few other waitstaff preparing the room for the dinner rush. I love it here, the smell of whiskey, the smiles from our visitors. I'm not a big drinker, but I can appreciate a whiskey.

"She's doing well. She has finished her treatments for a while. More testing will follow in the coming weeks, but at this stage, she is stable," I say, remembering all the appointments and treatment plans we have and I try not to get too excited as my best friend beams at me. I stifle the yawn that threatens. Lack of sleep, coupled with too much on my mind, has me feeling dead on my feet.

"Well, would you look at that," she says, looking out the large windows to the parking lot. I follow her gaze and spot Tanner leaning against his truck. Victoria's face literally blooms whenever she sees him. It's good to see and a pang of jealousy hits me that I don't have the same thing. I grab my cup before my eyes dart to who Tanner is with, and when I see our new doctor, my heart stutters. I watch them for a beat, taking in his smile that has my own lips curling.

"Sugar?" I ask Victoria as I stir a little sweetener into my hot drink, avoiding looking at the men while I try to tame the jitters that now flick around my body just from seeing him.

"I'm so happy Hudson came back," Victoria says absentmindedly, and my eyes betray me to look back out the window. Hudson is in his signature suit, hair swept back, his handsome features highlighted even more in the afternoon sun that shines down on his frame. As he stands tall, confident, in control, I look down his body, wondering what it would feel like under that distinguished suit.

"Yeah, the town needs a good doctor." I take a sip of my coffee, my eyes remaining glued to the man standing outside. My gaze only moves when the steam from my drink hits my nose and fogs up my glasses, the ones I wear thanks to the increasing dizzy spells I have been getting every time I look at my computer screen.

"That we do," she says slowly, looking at me, but I get us moving, walking back to my office. I need the space to take a deep breath and roll my shoulders, because just seeing Hudson makes me nervous. As we walk, my cell vibrates, and I look at it quickly, waiting on an email I don't want to miss. But my stomach sinks immediately.

> Summer School Sessions are open for enrollment. I believe this would be a perfect opportunity for you to enhance your online learning on campus. I'm taking a special intensive class that I would love to see you participate in...

I don't read the rest of the very long-winded message

before I delete it and block it instantly. My skin crawls and I take another sip of my coffee to dampen the nausea that creeps up my throat.

"Have you two talked yet?" Victoria asks, and I blink a few times, thinking about what we were talking about as she takes a seat on the small sofa in my office. I join her, slumping in the armchair, needing all the caffeine today.

"He was around to see Mom the other day," I tell her as I try to stifle another yawn.

"No, I mean, really talked. About the fire. About him rescuing you and then leaving town immediately after. The therapist said it was good to talk about it."

"No. There isn't anything to say. He rescued me. He treated me as a medical professional would…" I start to tell her before she interjects.

"A medical professional doesn't sleep at your bedside all night, holding your hand," she adds, and my eyes flick to her in warning. I told her that in complete confidence. "Don't worry, your secret's safe with me."

"It was a traumatic night, with a lot of emotions for everyone. He's a doctor, he helped you, he helped Tanner, and he helped me. The rest is just nothing," I tell her, sick of thinking about that night. Thinking about the small glances we took of each other in the bar the weeks prior, the small smiles we shared. It was the closest I've come to being flirty since college. The closest I've come to having a man take some sort of interest in me in a long time. It felt nice. But we aren't anything. We can't be. He's just a new face in town, and I have too much to do to even consider getting to know him better.

"You two really should talk. Maybe go out?" Victoria

presses. "The way he was looking at you at the bar last week, I would say that he is keen on you."

"I think you need my glasses because you're seeing things. A guy like Hudson Hamilton wouldn't be interested in a girl like me." Waving my hand in the air, I try to act disinterested, even though the idea of it all has my pulse racing.

"Ahh, but are you interested in a guy like him?" she teases as she sips her coffee, already knowing that he's caught my eye. She leaves a bright-pink lipstick mark on the cup, her signature look.

"There is at least a fifteen-year age gap." I roll my eyes.

"So? Tanner and I are twenty years apart..." She smirks, like she has a checkmate on me.

"I'm fresh out of college, I have a sick mom to look after, I'm trying to build my career..." *I have a stalker problem*, I think to myself as I look back at my cell and thank the stars I don't have another message. "I don't have a lot to offer a man like Hudson, and I sure as hell don't have the time to play around."

Plus, history tells me that older men aren't really an area I should be exploring.

"You're being ridiculous. You're amazing, caring for your mom. You just got a promotion with the best whiskey distillery in the country. You are an extreme professional. This strategy we worked on this morning is out of this world, and I can't believe you already know all these media personalities and journalists. You're so beautiful, I can hardly stand it, and every time I look at you, I want to puke because I need your long thick hair more than I need to breathe sometimes."

"Oh, stop." I pretend to scold her as I get up and move around my office. I feel fidgety or nervous, like I need to keep busy. It always happens to me when the topic is on me or something I have done. But I hear her words, and I know she is right. I'm smart, capable, and resilient. "He's a widower. Probably still in love with his late wife. Besides, I went to sleep with him by my side, holding my hand, and when I woke up, he was gone. He saw me at my most vulnerable, then left. I'm kind of embarrassed. I was a mess. Shit, I still am a mess," I say, feeling my cheeks heat and rubbing my temples. I can be honest with her, and while I don't tell her everything, she knows more than most.

"Are you still having nightmares?" she asks quietly, and I stop. Swallowing, I look at her before I sit again.

"Yeah." I sigh. "Are you?"

"Sometimes," she says, and I nod in understanding. I know she does, but she has Tanner to curl up with, to soothe her night terrors. I just grip the cold sheets and try to breathe through the fear, feeling like a child who can't get her shit together. Another reason Hudson can't come close... I'm too damaged.

"Are they getting better?" I ask, feeling hopeful.

"Less and less, thank God," she says with a small smile of encouragement.

"Good." I'm looking forward to the day when mine start to ease.

"I think going back to Marie's Place helps." Lifting her eyebrows, she looks at me accusingly.

"I've been back. I drive past there every day to come to work," I tell her, although she is right. I have only been back a few times, and each time, I feel better. Maybe I need to go back again. Walk around the new shed, have a coffee in the new kitchen. Just be still in my thoughts.

"Yes, but you know as well as I do that sometimes the best therapy is facing demons head-on. I go to Marie's Place all the time. At first, it was hard, but now I refuse to let that woman take away the one place that I truly made mine. I put my heart and soul into that place; I'll be damned if I'm not going to enjoy it now." Hell, if Victoria can do it, I sure can.

"Fine. I will try and go some more."

"Maybe have your next therapy session there. That helped me," she offers, and I nod. I might take her up on that.

"Well, should we talk about the spa?" Sitting forward, she grabs her laptop, and I grin. We both can't wait for the day when a health spa is installed here at the distillery.

It's something the two of us will make very good use of.

6

HUDSON

With my phone stuck to my ear, I walk down the street, my smile wide as I watch my son skipping ahead of me.

"We just miss him all the time," Melody says, her voice pitching. I smile as Bob from the hardware store passes by swiftly. I offer him a small wave, to which he responds with the standard male greeting of a head nod, walking around us, and heading inside the nearby diner.

"It's only been a few weeks, Melody," I tell her, knowing it won't ease her melancholy. But we left the city merely weeks ago, and I've barely had time to get myself organized and Harvey in school and she is already calling. She has called me a few times, and each time, I've been unable to answer, busy with patients or Harvey. But today, as I walk down the main street of Whispers, I thought it would be a good time to answer.

"I know, I still can't believe you're gone. Especially so far away in Whispers." She huffs. My in-laws generally haven't poked their heads into mine and Harvey's business since Amanda died. But as soon as I told them we were moving, they weren't pleased. But I know Melody loves him, so I do expect her to have an adjustment period. He is the closest thing she has left of her sister.

"Harvey loves it." I come to a pause on the sidewalk, seeing him stop at the window of Tony's Toy World, the small toy store we have in town. He peers inside, his eyes wide. When he was born, I missed so many firsts. His first step was seen by our nanny. His first tooth was also something she highlighted to me. I was so busy trying to save his mother and then pushing through when she died, and before I knew it, he was already an energetic toddler.

"I'm glad, I really am. I just miss him." Melody sighs. She visited Whispers once, when I flew her and her sister out to see the ranch and the town. The two of them hated it. It was too quiet, too boring, too dirty, and the horses stunk. They grew up in the city, with money and prestige, and they had no appreciation for the small town at all, but I know the country lifestyle isn't for everyone.

I should tell Harvey to come to the phone to speak with her, but I think he would prefer to keep wandering down the street, discovering all the new things. And the bit of distance he has from the city now is doing him good. Mom and Dad have been helping me out with him a lot, and it's such a relief. The saying that it takes a village to raise a child is true, and while the nannies I had in the city were great, the fact that my parents get to dote on and look after him after school while I work is amazing for everyone.

"You know, I can see him outside near the horses, but I can't get his attention. How about I call you next weekend. He can chat with you then," I suggest, pretending we are at home on the ranch, instead of me watching my son laugh and smile in town, pointing to a toy he has found in the window display. Seeing him with so much glee on his face, I feel regret for waiting this long to move back. But coming back home here to Whispers, I now understand that this is exactly what we both needed.

"Ahhh, those smelly horses. Don't let him get too close," she says with distaste, and I sigh. I look across the street and notice the old florist shop now empty, newspapers stuck in the windows, and I pause my stroll to look at it. I haven't heard what is happening with it, but I'm not surprised it's closed now. No one needs that reminder.

"Alright, speak later," I say, and she says a quick goodbye before the call ends. As a doctor in the city, Melody is just as busy as I was, and I know she has a million other things to do.

"Hey, Dad, look at this!" Harvey yells, just as I reach where he is standing. He pokes his finger to the window. I peer inside and see a small kids' paradise. Sure, I've taken him to toy stores before, but this quaint little store is so colorful and has so many old-school toys, even I want to go in. As I look to where he is pointing, I smile.

"A model airplane..." I murmur, wondering if he is a bit young for such a thing.

"I love it..." he whispers in awe, and I look at him, both hands on the glass, his palms flat, his nose squashed against the window, his eyes staring at the box.

"You love planes, don't you, buddy?"

"I want to fly one myself one day." He pulls back to look at me, his grin bright, highlighting the small gap from where he lost his tooth this week. His first. One first I didn't miss.

"Well, maybe you can fly our jet. Be our own personal pilot?" I say, smiling.

"Really?" he says excitedly, his eyes widening in disbelief like I just gave him the world.

"Sure, why not." I shrug and laugh. Huxley and I share a jet. He lives on the East Coast and regularly visits Whispers, whereas I was on the West Coast. So we purchased a private jet together to ensure we could get where we needed to go. Whispers' airport is small, yet full of jets, just like ours; such is the lifestyle Whispers brings these days.

"Can I start lessons today?" he asks me, his eyes sparkling, obviously ready to go.

"Not today, buddy. I think you need to be a little older before you can start, but let's talk to Uncle Huxe about it. I'm sure he won't mind when you are older," I tell him, ruffling his hair. I love my son and would do anything for him. I think about maybe taking him to an air museum or something, so he can see other planes up close. It might be a nice trip to take together.

Whispers' town center is busy on a Saturday, people milling around, in and out of shops. I worked this morning and then wanted to spend the afternoon with Harvey, exploring some more. As I look around at the clean sidewalks, the graffiti-free shop fronts, the friendly greetings of people walking by, and the flowers blooming in the garden beds, I drink it all in like I have been thirsty for it for years.

There's a low hum about the place, no one rushing

and pushing; the air is clean and the sky is clear. I feel relaxed until I spot someone running across the street and my breath gets caught in my chest. While Harvey is preoccupied, I take a moment to look at her. She seems to know everyone; each person she passes gets her bright smile or a hello, taking great joy in seeing her. Her hair is down, blowing a little in the small breeze we have today, and she's wearing jeans and a green sweater that flatter her beautiful curves.

"Let's walk down a bit farther, buddy," I suggest to Harvey, and we step away from the window and walk down the sidewalk.

"Lacy!" Harvey suddenly yells excitedly, spotting her and running in her direction. My steps falter in surprise as I see Lacy's head shoot up, looking right at us, a smile immediately coming to her face as she watches my son sprint toward her.

"Hey, Harvey!" she says, her smile widening as her arms do the same, and I watch, confused, as my son runs straight into her arms for a hug.

"Ahh, you two know each other?" I ask as I step toward them both as they pull apart.

"Oh, we go way back, don't we, champ?" Lacy says, winking at him, and I smile at her candor. My body feels light; just seeing her makes me feel completely different. I feel fresh, new, energized, and like a fucking schoolboy again, crushing on the cute girl in town.

"Lacy taught me how to make paper airplanes," Harvey says, and my head tilts in question.

"You both came into the distillery once, and when you were busy with Tanner, I spent time with Harvey,"

Lacy explains. "Oh, and your mom brought him over a few times when she came to see my mom last time you were home." I nod. His love of airplanes is now starting to make a little more sense, since it was here where he picked up the new fascination.

"Old friends, then?" I say, smiling.

"Something like that." She laughs a little, her cheeks tinting a soft pink, making her even more breathtaking. In the afternoon sun, her skin glows, a natural beauty. *That's because she is fifteen years your junior, and you were dating before she was even born, asshole.*

"What are you up to today, Harvey?" she asks my son, giving him all her attention, leaving me bereft.

"I just found a model airplane in the toy store," he says, his words moving so fast they tumble out of him.

"I saw that last week, the red one? Your favorite color, right?" Lacy asks, and my eyebrows rise. She sure seems to know Harvey well, and my chest warms as I watch the two of them interact.

"Yes, that's the one. And Dad said I can fly his jet later," he says excitedly, and Lacy looks at me, eyes wide.

"Wow, really?" she says, looking between us.

"Maybe in another ten or so years, buddy. What are you up to?" I ask her, keen to know how she spends her free time.

"I'm just heading into the diner," Lacy says, just as the diner door swings open with others coming out and going in.

"Dad, can we go to the diner with Lacy? Pleeeaaasssee!" Harvey asks, looking up at me with his big brown eyes.

I flick my gaze to Lacy, who looks taken aback. "I don't think Lacy would want us tagging along, buddy."

"I don't mind," she says quickly, and my eyes rest on hers to ensure she's okay with it. Her face is flawless and a little flushed. Her big brown eyes widen, the color of them brought out more by the green of her sweater. She wears minimal makeup and minimal jewelry, like none of the heavily made-up women in the city, yet more breathtakingly beautiful than all of them combined. She is one of the most attractive women I have ever met.

"See, Dad, she said we can. Pleeeaaassseee?" my son begs, grabbing on to my sleeve and tugging, jolting me from my stare.

"You're free to join me… I mean, if you're not busy…" She sounds hesitant, but I'm not going to miss this opportunity. I want to get to know her more. I want to spend time with her.

"No, not busy. We would love to," I tell her, and her eyes sparkle, taking me back to those few flirty nights we shared at the bar many months ago. I'm not sure if it's the way the sunlight hits her face or if it's the fact that she's happy to spend time with us. But seeing her smile makes my heart feel like it's bouncing in my chest.

"Yippee!" Harvey yells from where he stands between us before grabbing Lacy's hand, and the three of us walk into the diner, Harvey pulling us both along, our afternoon now sorted.

7

———

LACY

As I step into the diner, I feel my cheeks heat. Everyone's eyes are on us, and as usual on a Saturday afternoon, it's a full house. Hudson looks perfect, and I can barely string two words together with fear that my thudding heart will sound louder than my voice and give me away. I'm glad that my small-town manners came out of my mouth before I could really think about this situation. I'm happy for them to join me, but sitting and sharing afternoon tea with Hudson is going to be difficult, given that I still think about the way he held me that night and what it felt like to have his hands on my body.

"Why, hello...?" Rochelle coos, looking between us all. I try to pull in air and falter at the now all-too-familiar masculine scent that runs up my nose, making me swallow quickly.

My mother has visitors every Saturday afternoon. In fact, I left her with Hudson's mom, who was making them both a coffee to have with some cookies she baked earlier. Our Saturday routine is consistent; she has a steady roll of visitors, and I get out to have a break, the weekly treat of a sundae at the diner something I have been doing since I was a teen.

"Hey, Rochelle," I say quickly, my breathing not yet regulated as a few nerves still tap dance on my lungs. I wasn't planning on having guests with me today. I usually prefer the alone time, but with Harvey looking at me with his wide smile, and Hudson's sexy-as-sin grin making my cheeks heat under his gaze, my mouth moved before my brain caught up.

I look around and see the usual suspects. Bob from the hardware store is sitting up at the counter, and next to him, Peter, who drives our taxis. Nikki, the new young girl in town, is behind the counter, pouring them a fresh cup of coffee. I smile at her. She keeps to herself, so I know she doesn't have a lot of friends yet, but she's always nice to chat with.

Over at one of the booths, I see some girls I went to high school with, the ones who never left for college but instead wound up young and pregnant and with a chip on their shoulder larger than the size of the distillery. I see them watching us, my eyes settling on Jolene, the leader of the pack, who always takes issue with me, ever since I beat her at a science project in eighth grade.

And then, as we got older, a boy she liked didn't like her back and liked me instead. I think that was the catalyst for her ill feelings toward me. She made the last few years of high school hell. It was hell at home and hell at school, so there was no escape for me at that time. Now that we are both adults, you would think that the chip on her shoulder would dissipate, but unfortunately, they haven't grown up, and I grew up too quickly. Almost a perfect bullying storm. I take a deep breath and let it out slowly, wondering how someone can hold a grudge for as long as she has.

Now nothing about the way she's staring is covert as her eyes bore into mine before they flick to Hudson and then back to me again. Throughout the week, I can forget all about her and her friends, the constant bullying in school still scaring me today. But every Saturday, I see them here. It's almost like they come here just to pick on me for their entertainment.

Near the window, our town lawyer, Jerry, is having a late lunch with his wife, Bernadette, the two of them, along with everyone else, eyeing us carefully. I can't escape their stares because I stand here with a little hand clenching my own, keeping me grounded.

"We're here with Lacy!" Harvey says, loud and proud, and Rochelle looks down at him and beams. It's hard not to; he's a cute kid and fun to be around. I hear Jolene snort from where she sits.

"Well, little Lacy has a little friend," she murmurs, just loud enough for me to hear, but I ignore her. She says these little quips to get under my skin, and I try to let them roll off me without penetrating, but I would be lying if I said that I was successful in that endeavor every time.

"Take a seat, and I'll be right with you," Rochelle tells

us, and Harvey continues to pull both me and Hudson along to a booth. As I walk past Rochelle, she wiggles her eyebrows and gives me a wink, and I internally groan. I know the gossip mill will be in overdrive with this tidbit for the next week. Yet another thing I just don't need or have time for.

"After you," Hudson says, his voice smooth and deep, running down my body like a warm liquid as we come to the booth. He and Harvey stand, waiting for me to sit first, like two peas in a pod. I'm not used to this kind of chivalry. It's nice. Makes me feel special. I look at them and it isn't until now that I notice they are dressed similarly. Tan slacks, navy sweaters. Harvey is almost like Hudson's mini me.

"So, your parents must be ecstatic to have you both home," I say as I sit, thinking about how excited his mom, Susan, has been.

"Ecstatic is an understatement. It's almost like they have a new lease on life," Hudson says, laughing, and I smile. He's so handsome when he smiles, and it's contagious.

"Your mom has been talking about Harvey nonstop since you were here last," I tell him, hearing Susan's voice in my head, her constant chatter with Mom in the living room always floating down to me in my room whenever she comes over.

"I had no idea our parents were such close friends before moving back," Hudson says, and I nod.

"Our moms went to school together. Known each other all their lives. I guess we may have crossed paths when we were kids, but I don't remember you much from that time," I say honestly.

"I was probably already away at college when you were little," he says, swallowing, and the topic of our age difference rears its head. He doesn't exactly look old. He's in shape. Broad shoulders, a thick head of hair. He may be graying slightly on the sides, but he looks strong, dependable, safe.

"Probably. So Harvey, how is school?" I ask, trying to move the conversation on as Harvey slides around on the slippery vinyl booth seat next to his father.

"I love it!" he says with so much enthusiasm, a smile comes to my face immediately.

"Really? That's great. Who's your teacher?" I ask, but of course, like everything else around this town, I already know. I don't miss the way Hudson is watching him, pride and deep love etched onto his face.

"Miss Annabelle," he says before perusing the menu.

"Is she good?" Hudson asks me, clearly wanting the local intel, his eyes intense.

"Yeah. I mean, she has been in town for most of her life, I think. She does the goat milk soap business with Victoria, and her son, Kevin, helps out Tanner and Victoria at..." My throat restricts, and I need to swallow again before I can talk. "...at Marie's Place."

I see his face visibly soften. He watches me, his eyes warm. I wait to see the sympathy in them like everyone else gives me in this town, but I don't get it. Instead, his eyes hold something more akin to understanding and admiration, and I appreciate it.

"How is Marie's Place going?" he asks, and my eyes

flick to Harvey, who is busy trying to read the food specials on offer, but I dare say most likely looking at the images instead. "Have you been back?" he prods, and my eyes shoot back to meet his.

"It's fine. All new and renovated. They have a few visitors stay from time to time. I don't go there much, but I have been back. Faced my demons, you could say." After my conversation with Victoria during the week, I know I need to go back more often. It has obviously helped her, and at this point, I will try anything to help alleviate my nighttime terrors. Hudson's jaw tics, and he goes to say something else, but we get interrupted.

"So what will it be, folks?" Rochelle asks, stepping up to our table with a small notepad in hand.

"My usual. Thanks, Rochelle." I smile, and she nods, not even needing to write my choice down.

"Your usual?" Hudson asks, his eyebrow lifted in question, a small smile dancing on his face.

"Oh, Lacy here comes in every Saturday afternoon at this time like clockwork. Has for years," Rochelle says with a chuckle. I feel my cheeks get even hotter, and I want to slide underneath the table and let the floor open up and take me.

"What do you order?" Hudson asks, sitting back, looking at me with intrigue. Shoulders sitting high, his hands clasp together on the table in front of him, a smirk quirking his lips. Might as well get this over with. It's not like it matters anyway. He's just the town doctor, no big deal.

"The special sundae," I tell him, waiting to see a look of horror on his face that I'm ordering a child's meal, a sundae no less. Now with him sitting opposite me in this booth, I wonder what got into me that I offered for them to join me today. I see a lot of Tanner's rich friends come into the distillery. I talk to all of them. Even Hudson's brother, Huxley, is a friend and we have friendly banter, but I never feel this nervous around them. Hudson has my insides so coiled, I wonder if the ice cream in my stomach will curdle once I start eating.

"Sundae?" he questions, but the look I was expecting from Hudson doesn't come. Instead, his eyebrows rise a little more in surprise before his mouth twitches.

"It's delicious," I murmur my defense.

"Hmmmm. A special sundae for a special woman... Sounds like a good choice," he says, grinning, his flirty nature coming back as he watches me, and my heart rate escalates. I look over his shoulder at the defibrillator on the wall, glad that I'm sitting near a doctor, and he will know exactly how to work it if I have a heart attack.

"I also have a fantastic chocolate brownie with ice cream and chocolate syrup." Rochelle looks at Harvey, who smiles cheekily, like he is getting the inside information.

"He will get the brownie," Hudson answers for him, and Rochelle nods.

"What about you, Doc?" she asks, and he looks back at me, then to Harvey before replying.

"Maybe bring an extra spoon. I don't think Harvey will be able to finish it on his own."

"Good to see you out and about, Doc," she says to him as she surveys the three of us at the booth. "And good to see you with company, Lacy," she adds, and I want to groan in equal parts extreme embarrassment and annoyance, but then I would really come across like a sulky teenager.

"We are glad to be here. It's nice to be back in town," he tells her, and I ignore her comment and breathe a sigh of relief when she leaves, called to help out the back.

"So things are going well, then? At the hospital?" I ask him.

"So far. There is a lot I want to do with it," he admits, his eyes locking on mine.

"Well, I'm sure you're the perfect person for the job," I say, still a little jittery. It feels like a first date, with the butterflies swirling in my stomach, but it obviously isn't. His son is right next to us, and pretty much the whole town is in here, stealing not-so-subtle glances.

"How's the distillery going? Tanner working you hard, I bet?" he asks me, and my body stiffens at having the attention back on me. I take a deep breath and look at the man sitting across from me, barely resisting checking him out all over again.

"It's great. I'm currently working with Connor on a new release," I tell him proudly. I do love my job. I'm building strategies, working with the owners. I hit the jackpot with working at Whiteman's, and I'm not going to take it for granted.

"I think they mentioned that the other night at the bar. Tell me about it," he prompts, just as Rochelle pops back over and fills two coffee cups and slides a juice to Harvey.

"On the house." She winks to the little boy, who grabs

the straw and sucks like his life depends on it, and Rochelle lets out a small chuckle as she leaves again.

"It came as a surprise. We had an accident in the barrel room, lost a lot of product, and weren't sure what to do with the small amount we had left. I suggested to Tanner that we make it a small, exclusive batch." I shrug, like my idea was no big deal, but in reality, it was not only the catalyst for me getting a promotion, but the label itself is now highly sought after by the wealthy around the country. "Together, Connor and I came up with the name, Whiteman's Next Door, the whiskey you enjoy with your neighbor," I tell him, and he laughs, catching on that next door to the distillery is Marie's Place, where Tanner's now girlfriend Victoria was living at the time.

"Very clever. So you are managing that brand now? That's a big responsibility." His attention is fully on me, and he seems interested in every word that drops from my mouth as he sits back and enjoys his coffee, his eyes not leaving mine.

"Yeah. With Connor," I add quickly. While I came up with the idea and Tanner put me in charge, I'm learning a lot from Connor and taking it all in like a sponge, wanting to remember everything and not make any mistakes.

"I'll need to get my hands on a bottle, add it to my whiskey collection. I guess you are also organizing this event Tanner has planned?" His eyebrow quirks with curiosity, and there goes my stomach flipping again for no damn reason because he makes me nervous, he makes me flirt, he makes me feel things that I haven't felt before.

"Yeah. Are you looking forward to it? It should be

fun." I sit back and take a sip of coffee, thinking through the long list of to-dos I must tick off before the welcome party for Hudson that Tanner is having at the distillery. I want to make it perfect. I want it to be special for him.

"If you're organizing it, I'm sure it will be great. I mean, it will be a good way to meet everyone from town again. Some of Tanner's other network is coming, plus Huxley will be there."

I nod, having seen all the names on the guest list already.

"Hopefully, I'll have the distillery sparkling for you," I tell him, smiling.

"If you are there, it will be radiant." His lowered voice turns a little gravelly, and I forget to breathe. We stare at each other for a beat. His smile is small as he watches me, and I lick my lips. I don't miss the way his eyes catch the movement. Something about that has me relaxing in the weirdest way.

"You think too highly of me, Dr. Hamilton," I tease, feeling my feminine energy come through. My body relaxes a little, and I begin to feel like I'm the young woman flirting with him from before the incident happened.

"Hmmm. I think a lot of things about you, Lacy," he says, and his eyes are pure fire as they stare into mine. I swallow roughly before clearing my throat. *Is it getting hot in here?*

"So you have a whiskey collection?" I ask, getting us back on track. Our flirty banter feels too good and with little ears nearby, I need to be careful.

"Mostly Whiteman's, but I have a few exclusives from

Japan, of course some Scottish, and a few boutique ones from Australia that I picked up when I visited a few years ago."

Suddenly, that familiar feeling of insignificance barrels back into me. Of course this man is worldly and has traveled all around the globe. Of course he has a whiskey collection that's probably worth more than my house. I was lucky enough to go to college on a scholarship and survived by working two part-time jobs, plus a third casual cash-in-hand weekend job in promotions, and almost every cent I've ever had has served the purpose of survival. No overseas trips to sightsee or a whiskey collection or a shiny Rolex, like the one on Hudson's wrist.

"Australian whiskeys are pretty special. I tasted a few at an event in New York that Connor and I went to a month or so ago," I say, remembering the week-long trip I had. It was great for my career and networking, but I had anxiety every day for leaving Mom that long. Thank God for her friends and our neighbors.

"You like whiskey?" he asks, surprised.

"It's a bit hard not to when you work at a distillery. It's growing on me. I like single malts," I add, and he nods in appreciation.

"I spent some time in Scotland, traveled the highlands and tried some of their famous whiskey for a few weeks. I highly recommend that if you are interested in learning how they go about making their batches."

"Hmm, sounds like a dream trip." I wonder if I could do it as part of a work research trip or something.

"So aside from New York, have you traveled much?" he asks, basically reading my mind, and I sigh.

"No. I would like to, but life just doesn't offer that to me at the moment," I say honestly. I'm not going to try to be someone I'm not. Traveling is absolutely out of the question for me and will be for a long time, even though I yearn to see something different.

"Where would you like to go? What is the first place you would visit?" he asks, sitting forward, looking interested and not at all dismissive as I assumed he might be.

"Rovaniemi," I tell him, my mind already wandering.

"Rovaniemi?" he asks, frowning. "Where's that?"

"Finland. Arctic Circle. It looks like such a magical place."

He looks stumped, clearly not familiar with it.

"It's supposed to be one of the best places to stargaze in the world. They have these glass igloos that you can stay in, so you are surrounded by snow, but you are warm in bed, just falling asleep under the stars," I say, sitting forward, resting my hands near his on the table, my voice turning whimsical as I dream about it in my head.

"An igloo?" Harvey pipes up, and I nod, giving him a wide smile.

"Plus, it's where Santa's village is, and I would really like to see that," I tell him excitedly, and his mouth drops open.

"That would be so cool..." he says in awe, making me smile.

"Very cool." Even though I'm an adult, Christmas is my favorite holiday.

"Sounds like fun. So you like astronomy?" Hudson's

handsome features make me breathless, and my mouth moves before my mind catches on. I like this. Our conversation is light, nothing too deep, while still getting to know each other.

"I just like stargazing. There's something settling about it. I like looking up and seeing the different stars in the night sky."

"So you like the stars?" he says, smiling, looking content. Like he is happy with what he is uncovering about me.

"I wish on one every night," I whisper to him, our gazes locked for another moment. My chest feels like it is pulling me to him and I sense the same feelings from him as his eyes look deep into my soul. Our hands are near each other's on the table and I feel his touch and look down quickly, seeing his finger tap mine before it curls around it, like a little secret finger hold. I take in a deep breath and look back at him before Rochelle comes back.

"Here we are. One chocolate brownie, and your usual, Lacy darlin'," she says, sliding the dishes on the table and I pull my hand back, away from Hudson and to make room for the dishes. "And an extra spoon for the doc." She passes a spoon to Hudson, whose eyes are wide, looking between the sundae and brownie. Both portions are huge.

"Thanks, Rochelle," I tell her, and she smiles.

"Always a pleasure for you, honey." When she gives my shoulders a squeeze, my heart drops again at the sympathetic look she gives me before she leaves us to it. *Everything felt normal, if just for a few minutes.*

"This is yum…" Harvey is barely audible over his full mouth, chocolate sauce already dripping from his lips.

"That does look yummy," I tell him, chuckling, and he nods, clearly enjoying it.

I look at my sundae. Ice cream, chocolate syrup, cream, nuts, and sprinkles, with a big red cherry on top. Nothing could be more delicious.

"Do you want to try?" I say to Hudson, who is eyeing it like he wants to devour it all himself.

"I can't say no to that offer." He laughs, and I smile as I push the dish toward him to taste test. As he does, I grab the cherry from the top, my favorite part, popping it in my mouth and enjoying the sweetness before twirling the stem and making a knot with my tongue. Yet another thing I do. Every Saturday. Alone at this diner. It's always the first thing I do before I dig in. As I take the stem out of my mouth and place it on my napkin, the knot perfectly tied in the middle, I look back at Hudson, whose lips are parted, watching me, his spoon halfway from my dish and his mouth.

"Ahh, you okay?" I ask, confused, as I take a spoonful of ice cream, and he clears his throat.

"Yeah, just… you like cherries, huh?" he asks, eating his spoonful quickly.

"Oh, yeah… College trick," I tell him, my cherry habit happening so automatically that I totally forgot about how it might look to someone witnessing it. I take a spoonful of ice cream to cool down my flush.

"Can I try?" Harvey asks, his spoon already digging into my ice cream.

"Delicious, right?" I ask him, seeing him nod in approval.

"Here, try mine!" Harvey says, pushing his chocolate brownie toward me.

I take a spoonful and bring it to my mouth, the warm chocolate cake hitting my tongue, and I hum in approval as I close my eyes and savor it.

"Mmmmmmm... So good," I murmur, opening my eyes, again seeing Hudson watching me, his eyes barely blinking.

"You, ahhh... you've got a bit of syrup," he says, rubbing his lip.

"Ohhh." I grab a napkin, my cheeks heating all over again.

"No, just here..." His eyes are hooked on my face as he points to a spot on his lower lip. I swipe my finger across my lower lip, following his instructions, and feel the syrup gathering on my finger before sucking it from my skin. He swallows as his eyes watch the movement, his stare almost burning into me, pupils dilating as my heart beats out of my chest.

"Thanks," I whisper, not confident in my own breath as his stare continues to heat my insides.

"Anytime," he murmurs. With his eyes on me, a silent feeling bounces around us, both overwhelming and intense.

"How about we try them together? They are both good, but things are always better together," Harvey says, startling us from our intense gaze as he scoops up a little brownie, then dunks it in my ice cream, his spoon now full of both before he shoves it in his mouth. I watch him devour the sweet treat as I wonder what the hell just happened. The sizzling tension between Hudson and me is something I haven't experienced before. I take a deep breath in and count it out in my mind. It doesn't take long for my nerves to settle as Hudson and Harvey both smile and laugh, and we all eat up our treats, chatting some more and enjoying the afternoon together. It's the best Saturday sundae I've had in forever.

8

HUDSON

I stand with Connor, surveying the room. Tanner has put on a welcome party for me, with some people from the town, his whiskey flowing, and his distillery lit up with flowers, fairy lights, and a blues band playing soulful tunes in the corner.

"Good turnout," Connor says to me as we look at everyone. I've worked the room, talking to more people tonight than I have in a long time. I've caught up with some old friends, met new ones. Everyone is welcoming and happy to have me in town as their new medical professional. Tanner and Connor also have a few of their whiskey contacts here, always trying to mix a bit of business with pleasure when they can.

Throughout it all, though, my gaze hasn't wandered too far from the brunette in the red dress across the room. Lacy looks stunning, breathtaking, really, and my heart clenches just like when I spotted her in town outside the diner last weekend. I wasn't sure if it was the right thing to do when Harvey invited us along to her afternoon tea for one at the diner, but the minute she sat opposite me and I got to learn more about her, see her smile and laugh, then watch as she curled that fucking cherry stem with her tongue, I was glad we did.

Tonight, everyone in the room seems to know her and want her attention. She has been working the room too, as well as running around, organizing everyone and everything. She does it so effortlessly and with grace, yet she hasn't had a break at all, and from what I've seen, she hasn't even had anything to eat. I know because I've been watching her all night. She gives everyone time, speaking, smiling, and as I look at her, I admire her outfit, the dress fitting too well, her hair curled just right and shining, her brown eyes drawing me in.

"She went to an Ivy League, you know. Top of her class," Tanner says, stepping up beside me. He's obviously proud that he managed to not only hire an intelligent, highly skilled person for his team, but also that she's local and from the same small town he has called home all his years.

"Who?" I ask him, playing dumb, my eyes not wavering from the vision in red across the room.

"Lacy. The woman you haven't stopped looking at all night," he says, and Connor huffs a laugh, coughing to hide his amusement. I look at Lacy again, knowing that she would hate people talking about her like this. It's something I've noticed about her. Her excellent ability to move the topic off herself, hating people worrying or focusing on her so much.

I scoff at him. "She's too young," I say, having already had this conversation with him. The age gap is my default, even though the issue is less of an impediment for me by the day.

"That's why you had a date with her at the diner on Saturday, was it? Because she is too young to date?" Connor says, calling me out on my bullshit, and I look at him, my eyes narrowing.

"It wasn't a date." I don't need to explain anything to him. It felt a little like it, though. Like we were edging into each other's lives, and I thoroughly enjoyed it.

"Hmmm... Rochelle said you two were pretty cozy. Talked all afternoon. She said you had her smiling like she hasn't smiled for a while," Connor continues, and I wonder if that is true. I like the fact that we had a good time together. I know I was on cloud nine for the rest of the day and night.

"It was just a friendly catch-up. Nothing more." My voice makes it clear, but my mind and body yearn for something else entirely. We had fun. She was easy to talk to once the slight nervousness went away. Harvey loves her; they already have a rapport, and it seems like Lacy loves him just as much. It may have been just dessert on a Saturday afternoon, but when she twisted that cherry stem in her mouth, I was thinking things I really shouldn't have been at the diner, in broad daylight, with my son around.

"I think I have well and truly broken the age gap record. Don't wait as long as I did. You miss out on too much," Tanner says, taking a sip of whiskey as Connor stands by, watching us both. I think about Tanner's words. He's right. I know how quickly life can change. But Lacy is young. Sure, she's smart and independent. More grown-up than other women her age. But I'm still not sure me swooping in, being fifteen years her senior, is the right move. But I want to. God, I want to.

"Hi, gents." Sawyer steps up to our group, and I shake his hand.

"Good to see you. Sutton says hi, by the way," I tell him about his brother.

"Did you see that asshole on social media today? The gossip pages have photos of him on some yacht in the South of France with a new leading lady. Lucky asshole," he murmurs.

"He just finished a movie, right?" Connor asks, brow furrowed.

"Some action film. It comes out next year, I think," Sawyer says.

"Does he ever introduce you to any of these ladies?" Connor asks, wanting the inside scoop. But to be truthful, there are so many ladies Sutton mingles with, it's hard to keep up.

"No. Says he will never introduce anyone to a girl until it is *the* girl." Sawyer shakes his head at his brother's antics.

"So, Sawyer, when are you moving here? Poor Jerry over there is almost at retirement age," I ask, spotting the town lawyer sitting at a table with some others, looking weary, his retirement almost here. Now that I'm in place, Tanner is going to be moving more chess pieces to get Sawyer here to Whispers, I'm sure of it.

"Not likely. Do I look like I belong in a small town? Born and raised in the city, no other place for me," he says smugly, running his hand down his tie, and my eyes flick to Tanner with a knowing grin on his face. Sawyer is growing his business tenfold, with a very successful law firm in New York and another on the West Coast as well, which is exactly why Tanner wants him here. Poor Sawyer doesn't even know what is about to hit him.

"This release is smooth, Tanner." My brother Huxley appears, having arrived today with his wife.

"It's Next Door, the one Lacy and I are working on," Connor tells him, and I feel a pang of jealousy that my best friend gets to work with Lacy and see her daily. I look at him watching the room. My eyes follow his line of sight, and when I see him staring at Lacy and a few others, my shoulders tense. He hasn't said anything, but I wonder if he has his eyes on Lacy too. It makes sense; they seem close, and they work together every day. I swallow the jealousy that rises, hoping I'm wrong.

"She's a smart girl, Lacy. Good hire, Tanner," Huxley says, and my eyebrows rise, my jealousy spiking even more.

"You know her?" I ask him abruptly, which gets his attention.

"Known her for a while... I see her every time I come past the distillery." He looks at me curiously, eyebrow quirked.

"Where is Mrs. Hamilton?" I snip at Huxley accusingly, ensuring his eyes are still firmly on his wife and not Lacy. My brother glances over my shoulder at something and then back at me.

"Over there, looking as ravishing as always." He nods over my shoulder, and I turn to see my sister-in-law talking with Lacy and Victoria, the three of them animated and laughing. The conversation around me moves on to other topics as my brother leans in toward me a little.

"Everything alright? You seem a bit uptight tonight," Huxley whispers.

"I'm fine. It's a great night," I say, lifting my whiskey glass to my lips.

"Wouldn't have anything to do with the lady in red who has this whole room captivated?" he murmurs, and I want to punch him in the face. But he's right. My best friend Connor even continues to glance her way before he walks off to talk with some people. But it isn't just her good looks, it's her energy. The way she talks to everyone and gives them her full attention. The way she's so graceful, polite, her small-town manners not leaving her when she went away to college, and I know that's something many people around here appreciate. She gives a lot of herself, to her work, this town, the people.

"Have no idea what you're talking about," I mumble, then toss the rest of my whiskey back as my brother cackles beside me.

"Asshole," I grumble.

"Yeah, but you love me." He smirks.

"Someone has to," I tease, loving our brotherly banter and grateful that I can see him more now that I live here and he spends much of his time here now too.

"My wife loves me very much," he quips.

"I always thought she was intelligent... but now I'm having my doubts."

"Well, at least I went for what I wanted. Be careful, brother. You wait too long on someone as good as Lacy, and you might miss out." He nods over my shoulder again before he walks away. I look back to where the girls were and still see Lacy, but the other girls have gone, and she's talking to Connor. The two of them laugh, Connor standing way too close to her, and I make up my mind then and there. I'm going to ask her out. Because even though he's my best friend, there's no way Connor is going to get the girl.

9

———

LACY

I have a rare opportunity of being alone, so I walk to the side of the room, needing to get some air in the distillery garden. I push through the door and step down the path, my cheeks hurting from smiling so much and my head starting to thump from that familiar headache.

I have been running around all night, trying to be the perfect hostess, ensuring everything is happening on schedule. Making sure the band turned up, our catering is ready, and that we have enough bottles of whiskey to suit the crowd. I've talked to so many people that my throat is a little sore, not having time to grab a drink. Then, just as I was going to sneak away for a moment, Connor came up to me, panicking. He forgot to put on deodorant and then stepped closer to me, wanting me to check if he smelled because he saw some hot girl on the other side of the room he wanted to chat with. I don't have any siblings, but Connor is what I imagine an older brother to be like, totally annoying and completely self-absorbed.

Now as I take a big breath of fresh cool air, I stand among the lavender in the garden. Exhaustion nips at my shoulders, and I long to take off my heels. It's nice to get dressed up, as it doesn't happen often, but my fluffy socks and a warm cup of tea at home beckon me. At least it's peaceful in the garden. I enjoy the quiet and look up at the night sky. It always comforts me. I love seeing it clear of clouds and bright with stars.

"Hey." A voice startles me, and I jump a little, looking around. *Hudson.*

"Hey. Shouldn't you be inside? This is your welcome party, after all," I ask, smiling as I feel butterflies fluttering in my stomach as he looks right at me as he walks down the garden path. He was warmly welcomed tonight. Tanner is obviously proud and happy to have him home, and the two of them worked the room all night. Talking, mingling, smiling, owning the space like only billionaires can, with people staring at them, all jostling to speak to them. He steps up beside me, so close our arms brush, and I take in another breath, my shoulders lowering as my body temperature rises at his proximity.

"I needed a minute. All the formalities are done, so I thought I would just take a break. You?" he asks.

"Same. I just needed a bit of air. It's been a busy night," I tell him honestly. He looks so good. He's wearing a sharp suit, obviously expensive from the way it sits on his frame like it was made just for him. His shirt is white and crisp, and his tie is red, the color almost matching my dress. The strapless gown now helps me cool off outside, but I shiver as a slight breeze ghosts across my bare shoulders.

"Here," he says, shrugging off his suit jacket.

"Oh, it's fine. I'm okay," I say quickly, not able to help another shiver that runs through my body.

"Take it, Lacy. You're cold. It's just a jacket." He smiles as he places it around my shoulders. His movement is careful and considered, so I don't miss the way his fingers trail on my bare shoulders, my skin prickling at his touch, the feeling traveling down my body as I struggle to breathe. I try to pull myself together. It's been a long time since I had a man touch me and I wanted him to. Even longer since they touched my bare skin.

"Thank you," I say, succumbing to his kind gesture. I don't usually like to take people's help. I prefer to look after myself, but I guess it's just a jacket. I stand quietly for a moment, not confident in my ability to talk right now. We had a nice afternoon at the diner, but we had Harvey there as a buffer. My dating history is sparse and all from college since our small-town high school didn't have a lot of options. Not that college was full of potential boyfriends for me either. I shiver again just thinking about that time.

The few college boys I dated were extremely under-whelming in all aspects. I lost my virginity in my dormitory during my sophomore year. The guy I was seeing took me on a few dates, and I liked him, but after a few weeks together, he moved on. There was another boy who showered me with affection and swept me off my feet, but again, after we had sex, he seemed to cool off on the idea of being with me. By the time I hit my senior year, between work and study, my time at college was different than most kids. Parties and boyfriends were not something I indulged in because, when I wasn't studying, I was working to pay my way and helping to support Mom. Then everything happened, and I couldn't get away from college fast enough.

I grab the lapels of Hudson's jacket, pulling them around me as a small breeze flows through, appreciating the warmth it now provides as I'm enveloped by his scent.

"The stars look nice and bright tonight." He looks up at the midnight-blue sky. I lift my gaze upward and take in the evening.

"That one there..." I point to a bright star in the sky. "It's called Sirius, also known as the Dog Star. It's the brightest star in the night sky," I tell him.

"It sparkles bright. What about that one?" he asks, pointing upward, and I smile at his interest.

"I think that one is called Canopus. It's actually a giant star, ten times as big as the sun. It's much farther away than Sirius, but exactly how far away remains a mystery." I love the stars. It's always so peaceful to take them in. Life almost stops at night when I stare up at the sky.

"What about that one?" He points again, testing me now, his body and mine joined at the side. Warmth runs down my arm as it brushes against his.

"That is the Coma Star Cluster. It doesn't look like it, but it's a group of fifty or so stars," I say, enjoying myself. I don't get to take time out like this very often. Sure, I catch up with Victoria when I can, but that's different. Usually, our conversation is about work or the town.

"You know so much about astronomy. Did you take a class in college or something?" he asks, sounding intrigued.

"No. I just spend a lot of time looking up." I suddenly feel a little silly about it all.

"You can't really see too many stars in the city. I forgot how beautiful it was here," he says quietly, and I look over at him, catching him staring at me. My heart thuds harder before I swallow and pull myself together.

"So did you have a nice night tonight?" I ask him, steering the conversation back to him.

"It was great. Thank you. I know you and Victoria organized it all. I appreciate it."

I give him a small smile. Sure, I helped organize it, but that is my job.

"What about you? Did you have time to relax? Enjoy the evening?" He turns his body to face me as he pockets his hands in his trousers, looking at me intensely like my answer matters to him.

"It was great. It's always nice to get together like this. But..."

"But what?" he prompts me to continue, frowning.

"But Rochelle forgot to drop off my favorite chocolate cookies that I had ordered for the dessert table, and now I'm craving them," I say with a broad smile, even though I feel a little lightheaded. My stomach is empty, as I didn't have time to eat today at all with all the preparations for tonight taking priority. I'm so hungry I could eat for days.

"Hmmm... I'm starting to think you have a bit of a sweet tooth?" he says cheekily.

"Guilty as charged. Life is too short not to enjoy all

the things that bring us joy," I tell him, knowing he understands.

He watches me for a moment, a look of awe on his face. "You are such a breath of fresh air, you know that?"

"Is that a good or a bad thing?" I ask, laughing, hoping for the former.

"Good. Definitely good," he says, stepping back to my side, and we continue looking up. "What's that one?" He points upward.

"That's Betelgeuse, it has a red color to it." I don't know what it is about Hudson, but I feel nervous every time he's around me. I don't have that with any of my bosses, other friends, or any previous doctors that we have seen. Although none of them have his looks, his confidence, or his openness.

"Like the movie?" Hudson asks, and I turn to look at him and freeze. I didn't realize how close we were. We're mere inches apart, his body now giving me more warmth than his jacket does. My heart rate spikes, my throat becoming drier.

"Movie?" I ask, breathless and confused. He's looking down at me, and I can feel his warm breath hit my skin. His eyes gaze into mine, and I swear my heart thuds so hard he can hear it.

"Like *Beetlejuice*? The movie with the guy in the black-and-white striped suit? You know, say his name three times and he appears?"

I frown, having no idea what he is talking about, my brain suddenly misfiring and not connecting because I'm caught up in his eyes, his warmth, his scent.

"Are you telling me you have never seen *Beetlejuice*?"

His words are low, like a hum, almost teasing me as his eyes trace over my face, taking in every inch. His eyebrows rise a little, and his lips turn up into a small smirk. He's enjoying himself, and I realize that I am too.

"Never. I have no idea what you are talking about." I shake my head, smiling.

"Shit, I'm older that I thought," he murmurs, and I laugh.

"You're not that old... maybe a little gray..." I tease. He has a small sprinkle of gray at his temple; otherwise, his hair is as black as the sky tonight.

"Hopefully, wise as well... Maybe we should go sometime?" Hudson asks, and I clear my throat before I speak.

"Go?" I ask.

"Go out together. I can take you to the movies to see *Beetlejuice*. It's a classic." Is Hudson Hamilton, billionaire from the city, one of the country's leading doctors, asking me on a date?

"Like a date?" I ask and immediately regret it, but Hudson smiles so wide it's almost blinding.

"Yeah, Lacy, like a date," he confirms, and I feel his hand grab mine from where they dangle between us.

"Ohh..." I exhale, shaking my head, because the whole thing is ridiculous.

"I don't date." I know I need to say it, even though the words feel bitter on my tongue, and instant regret settles in my stomach. I want to go out with him. I really do.

"You don't date?" he questions slowly, his face puzzled, a small smile still on his lips as he tries to understand what I'm saying. I take a deep breath to bring me back to my senses. I need to wrap things up here and head home. I need to get a load of washing on, prepare Mom's meds for tomorrow, eat a little something before collapsing into bed.

"I can't date," I say again, my mouth shooting off entirely on its own as I take a step away from him. It's for the best. Nothing can happen. I shuffle a bit, wondering how he will take the rejection. Anxiety crawls up my spine, thinking about how another older man treated my denial. I want to go out with him; I know Hudson is different. The way we talk, the way we are together. It's all different.

"You can't date?" he clarifies, looking even more puzzled.

"No. I can't." I give him a small nod, glad he understands.

"Not date generally or not date me?" He tilts his head, his eyes locked on mine.

"Not date. Anyone. It isn't just you. I mean, you are..." I trail off as I wave my hand over his frame. "Well, you... and I am... busy," I tell him and he continues to watch me, his smile small, almost like he's trying to hold in laughter.

"So what if you had some time? Would you be open to a date then?"

I'm surprised about his perseverance. He isn't pushy, isn't violent. He's a bit coy, flirtatious, funny. *Yes* is on the tip of my tongue. If my life was different, if I didn't have to manage so much, then yes. That's what I want to say.

"But I don't," I say quickly, really needing to pull myself together. "Have time, I mean."

"I haven't dated in a long time, Lacy, but I can wait."

I think about his words. He is a widower, and I'm sure probably still madly in love with his late wife.

"Wait?" I ask, confused.

"Until you're... not busy." He smirks, and my eyebrow rises, a small smile toying at my lips.

"Unless you have some special magic potion that can free up my life..." I start to say, trying to figure out exactly what is happening and failing.

"Challenge accepted." He grins wider now before he lifts my hand to his lips and kisses the top of my knuckles, and I almost gasp. His lips are soft, the feeling of them tender on my skin, the buzz trickling around my body. It's almost as if time is standing still as I stare at him, and he stares at me.

"Hudson!"

We both startle at the sudden voice that breaks through our conversation. I take a deep breath and pull Hudson's jacket tighter, shaking my head, trying to get my thoughts in order.

Hudson clears his throat and runs his hand through his hair.

"Coming!" he shouts, sounding frustrated, and I take the seconds to compose myself. *Shit, Hudson Hamilton wants to date me.*

"I need to go. I swear my brother always knows where to find me," he says, smiling, starting to step away.

"Oh, your jacket." I move to pull it from my shoulders.

"Keep it. Stay warm. I will grab it from you tomorrow. Good night, Lacy." He gives me a wink before turning and walking back up the path, his strides long and strong.

"Good night," I say quietly. As I watch him retreat, I

wonder for the briefest moment what it would be like to be kissed by a man like Hudson. Would it be soft, slow, hard, or fast? Then I remember who he is and who I am and start to feel deflated. My shoulders sink, and my heart feels heavy. We can be friends. Acquaintances. Maybe even share a sundae at Rochelle's from time to time. But we can't date. We can't be anything. I don't have time. I can't go out and have a great time and leave Mom at home. What kind of daughter would do that? Leave their sick mother at home while she was getting wined and dined by a billionaire night after night.

I push my selfish feelings down and take a deep breath to lower my racing heart. As I stand in the peacefulness of the night, I look back up at the sky. I can't see it yet, but I look at where the Heart Nebula is usually positioned—the small galaxy that is in the shape of a heart. I have only ever seen it a couple of times, but as my own heart pounds, I search harder, needing to see it. I finally spot it and release a heavy breath. It's faint, but it's there.

A little like my own heart, I suppose.

I smell smoke. Gasoline fumes burn my nostrils. I wriggle around and try to move but feel trapped.

Help! I yell, but my voice sounds muffled, the material around my mouth tight.

I see Jasmine. I see the shed. I see Hudson. *Hudson.*

"Hudson!" I jolt upright, panting. My room is dark, the house quiet, my labored breathing the only noise.

"Shit," I say, scrubbing my face, my skin clammy. My

bedsheets are rumpled around my body. I look at my phone on the bedside table. Two a.m.

"Great," I mumble before I lie back down, my body involuntarily shivering, my hands tightly gripping on to the sheets as I try to take deep breaths. *One, two, three, four.* My eyes look toward the small armchair in my room where Hudson's jacket is draped neatly. I hesitate, but my body is jittery, and there's no way I'll be able to rest. So I jump up and grab it, taking it back to bed with me. Draping it over my torso, I bring it up to my neck and take in a deep breath.

The slow intake of air helps my pounding pulse, my muscles to stop twitching, and the tension to ease from my body. I close my eyes and see him. I see Hudson. But not from that night anymore. From tonight. His smile wide, looking handsome in his suit, his hand holding mine, and I calm myself and keep my eyes closed, thinking of him.

And for the first time in a long time, I don't open them again until morning.

10

———

HUDSON

I finish off an email to a doctor friend in the city and sort out my files for the day. It's early, but I left Harvey with Mom to drop at school while I came in to get a few things sorted. The stark white of my office looks sanitized but not overly welcoming and the coffee is doing little to get me going this morning.

"Good morning. Hope I'm not interrupting?" the sweetest voice I have ever heard says, and I look up, seeing a vision in my doorway, her mother by her side.

"Morning," I say, standing up from my desk. I'm unable to help the large grin that comes to my face at seeing Lacy standing before me.

"We were just heading to the pharmacy next door, and I wanted to drop off your suit jacket. I wasn't sure if you needed it for today." She takes a few steps into my office, my designer jacket looking freshly pressed in her hand. I don't need it. I have many suits—too many, probably. My wardrobe is full of them. So much so, my brother teases me about it, and Tanner takes great pleasure in telling me my wardrobe now needs to change since I'm back in Whispers. Suits don't really fit in with the lifestyle here.

"Thank you. That was quick," I say to her as we step toward each other. I move forward to grab the jacket hanging from her fingers, bumping her hand, enjoying the contact almost as much as I did standing with her last night, looking at the stars. She smiles at me, the light blush to her cheeks fucking adorable, and I can't move this stupid grin from my face.

I had a feeling she might turn down my offer of a date last night. I know it isn't because she doesn't want to. The chemistry between us is undeniable. But I understand her life is busy and stressful, so I plan to find a way to take her out. Give her some time to be just Lacy for a little while.

"Oh, Lacy doesn't like owing people things. She likes to make sure things are returned promptly." Her mother laughs, and at the sound of her mom's voice, Lacy drops my fingers like they burn her. I frown, but nod to her mom in understanding. I can see that about Lacy. Never wanting to ask for help, never wanting to take anything from people. Preferring to handle things herself. Hell, she didn't even want to take my jacket at first, even though she was shivering.

"Well, I'm glad to see you, both of you, actually, because I wanted to talk to you about something," I say to them, getting back into professional mode and gesturing for them to take a seat. They do, and I take the jacket to hang it on the back of my door, trying not to look at Lacy too much, which is hard because she's wearing black high heels and a black corporate dress that follows her curves a little too well. Her hair is down and her lips glossy; she is clearly on her way to work after this visit. She looks just how she did in my dreams last night, and my mouth suddenly dries.

"What's up?" Lacy asks, eyeing me inquisitively. She gets these little wrinkles near her eyes, not dissimilar to how she looked last night while staring at the stars, and I like her looking at me like this. Like she's seeing something deeper in me, listening intently and giving me all of her attention. It's new. Even my late wife didn't really look at me that way. Any female attention I've received since hasn't either. My status as a doctor and my bank balance are seemingly the key things women look at when they notice me. But not Lacy. I don't see that in her gaze at all. My eyes flick to her glossy lips, and I can't help but think of the way her tongue tangled that cherry stem at the diner last week. I clear my throat and shuffle some paperwork on my desk, trying to get my mind out of the gutter.

"I'm introducing a new initiative to Whispers to improve patient medical outcomes," I say, looking at them both as they eye me, wanting more information. This is something I have thought about for a while, and I would be lying if I said that Lacy and her mom were not the catalyst for this new program.

"Okay. What does that mean?" Lacy asks, sounding tentative, almost like she is ready and waiting for an onslaught of some sort. I give her a smile. I like that she's protective of her mother, but she's tense, too stressed, and I want to put her at ease.

"I'm thinking of introducing a visitation schedule,

where I can fly specialists into the hospital and have them see the people who need specialist treatment, so it's the doctor who travels, not the patient," I say, looking at her mom, who's nodding. This is a special program I want to develop, something I have been thinking about for a while. One I know Tanner will be very supportive of. Bringing more people to the town, offering the town residents more medical attention than they have ever had before.

"So how does it work exactly?" Lacy asks me, she and her mom now holding hands. I know they are close; they are all the other has. A program like this would alleviate Lacy's burden, reduce the need for so much travel to Williamstown, and get them immense insight and new treatment ideas from some of the country's best doctors. All right here in Whispers.

"In your example, I would fly in a cancer specialist who can not only look at your file and assess your condition from the test results we've done, but someone who can meet you, see you face-to-face, talk about your symptoms and lifestyle, and take a whole of person approach. Williamstown is great, but some of the things the researchers and doctors in the city can do and have access to is immeasurable, and I want to bring that to Whispers."

I watch Lacy, and I see her swallow. She's unsure but open to it, I think.

"It wouldn't just be a cancer specialist for the town to utilize, but I would start with that. I know your prognosis now, Veronica, is good, but I think another opinion on things is always helpful. I also hope to bring in trauma support, elderly care, and pediatrics. There's so much that small towns miss out on that I can bring here to really make a difference for the people of Whispers. I have a lot of contacts; I know most of the top specialists. They could give one week every few months and touch base, provide insights to both me and the patient, as well as bring others with them."

"It all sounds good to me. I'm happy to be a guinea pig," Veronica says, seemingly positive about the opportunity to be my case study, and Lacy looks at her sharply.

"Are you sure? I mean, I don't think our insurance will cover something like that." Lacy's frown is visible, but even when she's unhappy, she's beautiful.

"To be clear, you still need to approve everything. As I said, you are doing really well, Veronica, so you will not just be given new medication or treatment plans without thorough consultation or anything like that, and I will be here, still overseeing it. And because it's new, experimental, you could say, the cost will be covered. You don't need to worry about any of that," I tell her, adamant that if I have to pay for it personally, I will. Lacy looks at me, the pride she has showing through the stare she is giving me, not happy about taking something for free, but then she glances at her mom and her hardness melts.

"If Mom wants to do it, we can do it," she says quietly, and my chest thuds so hard I need to rub it. Lacy's mom has had so many medical interventions over the years. Clearly, she's happy to try anything to help her, and I know that's what has kept her with us all these years. But cancer is not curable, and while she has good days and bad ones, at some point, the bad ones are going to start outweighing the good. I want to ensure that we try absolutely everything.

"There is a doctor from LA who is a cancer specialist. She's who I'm thinking of for you. Full disclosure, she is my sister-in-law. Or my former sister-in-law," I say, taking a breath. Melody is brilliant at her profession.

"We are sorry for your loss," Lacy says quietly.

"Thank you. It was a few years ago now," I tell her, a silent look shared between us, hoping she understands my past is in my past.

"Sometimes it's hard to move on from such a loss, and we appreciate you being here in Whispers, helping us," Veronica says. Lacy remains tight-lipped. This conversation feels heavier than I was wanting, especially for this time of the morning.

"She had breast cancer. We didn't catch it early, and she chose to delay treatment. It was aggressive. It was a perfect storm and one we couldn't weather," I tell them honestly.

"Well, she lives on through little Harvey," Veronica says with a small smile, squeezing Lacy's hand.

"She does," I say, nodding and returning her smile. Lacy takes a deep breath, looking uncomfortable. I pause briefly, wanting to move on. "So from here, I will make a few calls, see what I can arrange. If all goes to plan, then hopefully we can have our first consultation with her next week remotely and then get her out here in a few weeks."

"Thanks, Doctor Hudson," Veronica says, sighing. "It's so good to have you here. Lacy, I just want to speak to Patti at reception. I'll meet you at the car," she tells her daughter, and Lacy and I stand in my office, watching her mom walk away.

I turn and look at Lacy. "Your mom is doing great."

"Yeah, she is a fighter," she says, a small smile on her face.

"Like her daughter."

Lacy huffs a laugh like I'm ridiculous.

"Are you sleeping okay?" I ask, because as beautiful as she is, she does seem a little weary at times.

"Yes. Great. Never better," she says all too quickly, and I frown.

"Are you feeling well?" I prod, taking in how she also looks a little pale.

"Of course." She hardly looks at me, and I can tell she's lying.

"You know if you need anything, help with your mom or—"

"I'm fine, Hudson. Really," she cuts me off, but I see the way her shoulders rise, tensing. She isn't happy.

"What do you do to relax?" I ask, trying a different tactic.

"Like last night, I go outside and look at the stars," she says, blowing out a breath like she is forcing herself to relax in my presence. My fingers twitch, wanting to reach out and grab her hand, but right now, here in my office, with her mother just out the front, I need to remain professional.

"And wish on one every night..." I say quietly, her words to me at the diner last week coming back.

"Yeah. It is usually so peaceful; it's calming looking at the stars."

My heart feels like it is stretching out of my chest to get to her.

"You know I still remember that night vividly," I tell her. What happened to her, to us, months ago, is still at the forefront of my mind, so I know it must be for her as well.

"You do?" she asks with a furrowed brow.

"I don't think I will ever forget seeing you in that shed, Lacy." Giving in, I reach out and grab her hands, our fingers merging together like magnets.

"Doctor Hamilton, I just need— Oh sorry, I thought you were finished," Patti, my receptionist, walks into my office, and Lacy jumps at her intrusion. Her hands drop mine, and I run a hand through my hair, trying to pull myself together.

"Hey, Patti, we are just finished. Perfect timing," Lacy says, a big smile plastered on her face, hiding her true feelings well.

"Thanks, Doctor, and thank you for the jacket."

I watch her leave, Patti moving along quickly behind her. Stepping to the door, I pull the jacket from the hook. I'm not sure why, but I feel the need to assess it, see if it smells like her. I run my hands over it and am about to hang it back, when my hand hits something hard in the pocket, and I pull it out. It's a pocket-sized book, *Stargazing for Beginners,* and I huff a laugh as I flick through it, seeing her pages tagged and annotated. It's one she has used a lot, if the creases on the cover are anything to go by, as well as her remarks and comments about some of the galaxies and such.

I smile, my body feeling like it's defrosting. With

thirty minutes left until my first appointment for the day, I take a seat at my desk and start reading. I want to be prepared for our next outing. I already know where Lacy goes to breathe, and under a night sky might be where she has some time. For me.

11

LACY

I have felt a little off all day. It could be the nightmares that woke me in the early hours, or the fact that I took Victoria's advice and booked a session with my therapist at Marie's Place which I had earlier today. I was also out of sorts last night at the party after Hudson and I shared a moment in the garden.

My focus for years has been solid. Get Mom well, help her through it all, and make money to run our household and pay her medical bills. But my usual steadfast approach to life has hit a bump in the road when Hudson whirled into town like a storm blowing in a fresh breeze.

This morning with my mom at his office, when he spoke about his wife, the feeling in my gut was a mix of sympathy for his loss, raw emotion because of my mother's health, and jealousy of a dead woman, which I immediately felt bad about. I knew, of course. Mom was always talking to Susan about it, whenever I was home from college, but at the time, I had little investment in the information.

I also feel off because he is clearly offering us medical support, which will be expensive, and I can't afford it. I don't like being in someone's debt.

I shake my head of the thoughts and look back at my emails. I'm waiting on an email from a supplier, so I'm trying to keep on top of them. I scroll to the top and see a new one sitting there, and my body stills.

Statistics Summer Camp is the subject line, and I swallow quickly as my pulse races. It's professional, the college logo on clear display as it is in all his correspondence, but I understand the tone. My old Professor has been contacting me relentlessly for months. My eyes skim the words. A summer term back at college to complete a statistics unit face-to-face. I huff my anger down because he knows I completed it remotely, but he still acts like he is in control, using phrases such as *direct personal tutoring* and *one-on-one personal assessments*. I feel sick and delete the message, like I have all the others. I never want to see him ever again. His contact has increased lately, and I'm not sure why. But with a myriad of other things going on in my life, my infatuated former professor is the least of my problems.

"A penny for your thoughts?" Connor asks, waltzing into my office through the open door.

"I was just wondering if your beard could get any longer," I murmur, teasing him, coming up with the lie quickly. We didn't get along at first. He didn't like the idea of working with someone new whom he had to train, but now we are almost like siblings, teasing each other and pushing each other professionally almost daily. We get along well, and I'm so grateful.

"What's wrong with it?" he asks, running his hand down his beard, looking affronted.

"Could do with a trim…" I murmur, sorting out my files. It doesn't; he looks fine, if the lumberjack look is one you go for.

"The ladies love it." He shrugs, plopping down in the small armchair on the other side of my desk.

"Which ones? The ones who see your shiny shoes, your expensive watch, and your fat bank account in the city?" I tease some more, knowing that Connor is a ladies' man and is always having dinner with a different woman in the city.

"Touché…" he admits in defeat, knowing that all the women he spends time with can smell his millions miles away. None of that matters to me.

"So what's up?" I ask him, leaning back in my chair, feeling exhausted.

"We need to go to the city," he tells me, and my eyebrow rises. Connor is often at our city office, but I have only ever been once.

"Really? When? Why?" I try to ignore the slight panic that tightens my chest. I love going to our city office, and spending time in New York is amazing. But I hate leaving my mother. When I left last time, I put together a roster of people who could come to see her and ensure she was looked after, and Susan stayed the night with her. It was fine, but a lot of work. Mom is much better and more capable now, but she is my responsibility, no one else's, and I hate asking for their help.

"We need to start researching spas, therapists, products, treatments... Or rather, you do," he says, looking less than pleased about it all.

"So you're telling me that you're going to pay me to fly in your private jet to New York, spend a week there, going to all the different luxury spas for treatments so I can come back and tell you which ones we need to incorporate here at the new spa we are building?" I ask, sitting forward, already liking this prospect.

"Perhaps take Victoria with you. Dad will hate to have her gone, but I'm sure she will love it."

"And why is it that you don't want to be pampered in mud and scrubbed from head to toe?" I tease, knowing that Connor is the last person you will ever catch at a spa. He's the definition of masculine.

"Sounds like a thing for women, not really my idea of relaxation," he grumbles.

"Oh, what is your idea of relaxation?" I ask, laughing.

"Corporate box at the Jets, with my whiskey in one hand and a beautiful blonde in the other." He smirks, and I roll my eyes. Typical.

"Hey, folks, sorry to interrupt." I look up and see Rochelle at my door.

"Hey, Rochelle," I greet her, and Connor and I both stand.

"Sorry, no one was at reception. I just need to deliver these," she says, and Connor takes the box from her.

"Oh, is it something for Dad?" he asks, looking at the box.

"No, it's for Lacy." Rochelle looks like the cat that got

the canary. My eyebrows rise, not expecting a delivery. I hadn't ordered any catering for us today.

"I need to run. Have fun, you two," She offers a small wave and a cheeky grin, walking back out the door.

"Here, there's a note." Connor passes the box to me, seemingly just as confused as I am.

I put the box on the desk and grab the note, opening it.

Lacy,

I didn't want you to miss out on the cookies you like so much. Also, did you know that there are over nine thousand stars visible to the naked eye in the entire night sky?

Hudson.

"Oh." My cheeks heat immediately, and I huff a small laugh. I'm in my head so much, I don't even see Connor looking at the note over my shoulder.

"Hudson, ayyy…" he jibes, and I fold the note back. Giving him a scowl, I open the lid and see twelve of Rochelle's chocolate cookies staring back at me, so fresh they are still warm.

"Yum, my favorite," Connor says as his hand dives in and grabs one quickly, taking a bite as he sits back down.

"Hey! Hands off my goods," I scold him as I grab one myself and sit down, my stomach doing flip-flops so fast I'm not sure I will be able to eat it.

"Sooooo, getting cookie deliveries from Hudson…" He and Hudson are best friends, and he looks at me now with a shit-eating grin on his face like he knows everything.

"He is just being nice because of Mom." I brush off his remark, needing time to process this gift. I mean, they are just cookies, but they are my *favorite* cookies. I told him about them just last night, and he remembered, ordered them, and had them delivered to me at work today. I swallow the gooey goodness, my head now whirling.

"How is your mom doing?" Connor asks, having already finished one cookie and diving in for another. I don't mind, they are delicious, and I can't eat all twelve by myself.

"Good. Great, actually. Hudson has plans for some fancy doctor to fly to Whispers to see her, just for another opinion and as a case study for a new program he wants to implement. His former sister-in-law or something?" I watch Connor closely, and his eyebrows rise in surprise.

"What?" I ask skeptically, waiting for the information.

"Well, you do know how hard it is to get fancy doctors to small towns. It isn't something those doctors do lightly. They hate to travel and are usually so busy at their own clinics, they can't spare the time. Hudson must be pulling some strings for you. Either that, or he wants his sister-in-law closer to him and Harvey. It makes sense; she was really close with his wife. The two of them looked almost identical, from what I remember," he says, finishing the second cookie in one bite.

I balk. The cookie is sitting heavy in my stomach. When Hudson mentioned it this morning, I thought it was a whole program, something he was implementing for the town and Mom being ill would be one of many people who benefitted. But what Connor says makes sense. Maybe he does want his sister-in-law closer. Maybe he misses his wife. Maybe he wants to go on a date with me just to get over her? But it has been a few years now, so it's hard to know.

I take a sip of water, needing the moisture, my throat now dry. It doesn't matter. He is just Mom's doctor. There can be no more daydreaming about what it would be like to date a man like Hudson. The stars, our friendly banter, his sexy-as-sin smile. It all needs to stop.

"When are we going to the city?" I ask, suddenly feeling the urge to get to New York on this research trip.

"Chat with your mom, let me know about your schedule, and we can lock it in then. I've gotta go. I've got a meeting with Sawyer," Connor says, jumping up and walking out of my office, but not before he grabs another handful of cookies, giving me an annoying smirk in the process.

12

———

HUDSON

I pull up to the distillery late in the day, seeing the parking lot almost empty. I'm meeting Tanner to go over some thoughts I have about the hospital and the new program. Something he's all on board with and he's keen to look at the financial implications to see where he can help.

I see his truck parked at the end of the lot in his usual spot, alongside Lacy's small hatchback. I didn't realize she would still be here so I'm smiling as I jump out of my truck and start walking inside.

"I just need to run next door to grab a few things. Go inside, Lacy is in her office," Tanner says as he runs down the office stairs toward me.

"No problem," I tell him, as he jogs to his truck and I race up the stairs, straight inside before he has even left the lot.

The office is quiet, the receptionist already gone for the day, and I make my way down the hall where I know Lacy's office is.

Seeing her office light on, like a moth to a flame, I stop at her open door. She hasn't seen me, so I watch her for a moment. Sitting behind the desk, looking over some paperwork, she has glasses on that I didn't realize she wears, giving her a sexy librarian kind of vibe that I instantly appreciate. She has a pen in one hand that she chews, her hair falling into her face a little, her brow furrowed in deep concentration.

"Working late?" I murmur and hear her gasp as her head shoots up in surprise.

"Hudson?"

"Sorry, didn't mean to startle you," I say, taking a few steps inside as she stands.

"No. It's fine," she says with a smile, closing the folder of documents and removing her glasses.

"I have a meeting with Tanner to talk about hospital funding," I tell her, putting my things down on her side table and pocketing my hands as I walk over to her.

"I was just finishing up for the day," she says, coming to the front of her desk. As she walks around, I get to admire her work outfit again. She looks just as fresh as she did this morning.

"So, did you eat all the cookies?" I ask, spotting the empty box nearby. She smiles a little, a soft-pink tint coloring her cheeks.

"Had to. They are Connor's favorites as well, so we had a fight over the box. Plus, Tanner stole a few this afternoon too. Thank you, it was a lovely gift." She shakes her head with a soft laugh, and I frown.

"Connor needs to get his own cookies," I grumble, obviously needing to talk to my best friend. The jealousy

I feel that he might like Lacy too, still swirls in my stomach.

"Yeah, but he offered me a good work project this afternoon, so I couldn't say no." Her smile is small but glowing.

"A new project?" I watch her carefully, trying to gauge her reaction, and I relax as I see her smile widening.

"I need to do some research on day spas. We are opening one up at the distillery, which I'm sure you know. Connor oversees that project, but he isn't really the pamper kind of guy."

"Connor is the last person you would catch at a spa." I almost bark a laugh. Connor is a man who's the epitome of masculine. Lacy giggles, and I feel like I almost puff out my chest at hearing her laugh at something I said.

"Which is why he's so eager to send me to New York for a week to trial a few research treatments and products. Victoria is coming as well to look at design and aesthetics," she says, and my eyebrows rise.

"Sounds like a great project and one I think you well deserve," I tell her, knowing that a break like that is not only good for business but will also be good for Lacy.

"Yeah," she says with a sigh, sitting on the edge of her desk. "It should be fun."

"So why are you looking worried?" I ask, stepping closer to her, seeing stress written all over her face.

"It's just hard to leave Mom for a week. That's all." As she rubs her face, I see her exhaustion.

"Have you ever thought about some caretaker support?" I ask her, and she looks at me, confused.

"Caretaker support?" she questions, and a bright idea comes to me.

"Someone who can come in, make some meals, visit your mom, do house chores, that kind of thing. That way, you can work knowing that everything at home is taken care of." I see her mind ticking over.

"I don't even know where to find someone. I don't think there is anyone here in Whispers."

"Leave it with me. Let me look into it for you," I say, wanting to do this for her.

"You don't have to..." Standing, she looks ready to deny she needs the help.

"As your mother's physician, it's something I would look into anyway. Having help at home while you are not there is not only beneficial to you but also for your mom." While the statement is correct, I know using her mom is the only way she might come around to the idea.

"Okay, maybe." She gives me a small nod of approval, and I smile before I notice her cradling her hand.

"What happened?" I ask, my frown deepening as I automatically walk closer to her.

"Oh, nothing. It's nothing." She tries to act casual, but I see her wince. I stand before her and grab her hand, lifting it into the light.

"What is that?" I ask, seeing a small piece of something stuck in the side of her finger.

"Just a thorn," she says, and I look up at her, surprised.

"Thorn?" I clarify as my hand cups hers carefully.

"I was out in the garden this morning... I just picked a few roses for my office... It was a small prick," she says, and I look to see the vase of fresh roses on her desk before I try to grab the thorn with my fingers for her. My tweezers from work would be extremely handy right now.

"This morning? This has been in your skin all day?" I question, seeing the skin around it is irritated. While I'm sure the pain is minimal, it would be extremely annoying.

"It's in my right hand, and my left hand isn't that coordinated to grab it out. I was just going to get Mom to try to remove it when I got home. It feels a bit stuck." She says, dropping her hand a little.

I look at her, and my lips thin. She doesn't even like asking anyone for help here at work. She is so stubborn.

"Give it to me," I tell her, putting my hand out to her, palm up, waiting for her to place her hand back in mine.

"It's fine," she says, shrugging it off, trying to minimize the issue.

"Give me your hand, Lacy," I say in a tone that is a little more demanding, and she huffs before she does exactly what I ask, lifting her hand and placing it softly in mine. I smile, liking that she does what I ask, and I take a closer look at it and then look back at her.

"I don't have tweezers, but sometimes teeth are better," I tell her quickly before I lift her hand to my mouth. My eyes meet hers as I hear a small gasp of surprise pass her lips. I move slowly and gently as I put my lips to her skin, and with my eyes firmly on hers. I used to do this all the time around the ranch when I was younger, and even more recently on Harvey. But none of those times did I get a hint of a sweet rose scent. It's familiar and not from the flowers in the room, but from her fragrance on the inside of her wrist.

Her eyes widen at the contact, her chest rising and falling, mouth agape as I rest my lips against her skin. I get the thorn in between my teeth and remove it, feeling her fingers from where I hold her palm resting against my jaw, her hand almost cupping my cheek. Lowering her hand, I pull the thorn from my teeth and place it on the edge of her desk.

We stand facing each other, me still holding her hand, and I hear her breathing. It's rapid and my eyes haven't left hers as tension wraps around us that has my heart pounding in my ears. She's fucking breathtaking. I swallow roughly, and my eyes flick to her lips, the gloss reflecting the overhead lights. My body moves on instinct.

I pull her by the hand toward me as I lean forward, sliding my other hand around her waist and sealing her body against mine, and before I realize what I'm doing, my lips are on hers.

I almost moan at the contact, her body molding straight into mine. Letting go of her hand, I run my palm up her arm to cup the back of her head, deepening the kiss, the feeling of relief at finally having her in my arms, along with the intense burn I have to take more from her, building in my chest and heating my skin.

As she kisses me back with just as much desperation, her hands rest on my arms, her breasts pressed against me, her body fitting perfectly with mine.

"Wait!" she says suddenly, pulling back. "Hudson, wait."

I stop immediately, although my hold remains, just

loosening, giving her some space. She's panting, and I blink a few times, feeling like I just woke from a dream.

"Hudson... I can't... I mean, we can't..." she starts to say, looking crestfallen. Swallowing audibly, her big eyes look up into mine, and I can see she wants me. But she's holding back.

I clear my throat. I overstepped. I need to go slower. To show her that she's safe with me.

"It's alright, Lacy. I've got you." I tell her the words I told her that night and will repeat to her until I know she believes them. I see her take a big breath, and my eyes trail to her reddened lips before meeting her eyes again.

"But I'm not sure I can let you," she whispers, and I know it's her internal struggle. Shit, no one can go through life like she has and not be fearful of giving up control and putting herself first.

"We'll move together. Slowly. I'll wait. We can do everything at your pace." My thumb rubs along her back slower, where I still hold her, trying to give her a bit of comfort and reassurance and give myself a little more time just to have her in my arms. She swallows again and nods.

"Maybe," she says, and I smile. It isn't a yes. But it isn't a no.

"I need to go meet Tanner and you should get home. It's dark out," I tell her as I step back, and Lacy drops her hands from my arms. I see her grip on to the desk behind her. Our eyes haven't left each other, and I take in a breath, my nostrils flaring to get as much oxygen in as possible, because I find it increasingly hard to breathe around this woman.

"Ahh... Thank you for the thorn..." she says hesitantly as she licks her lips. The air around me cools now that we are no longer standing together and helps me get my head back into the day.

"Drive safely." I grab my things and start to step backward, away from her and toward the door. The grin on my face is impossible to remove. Whether it's because I had my mouth on hers, the fact that I think she is warming up to me, or just that I got to see her again, I can't be sure, but she's smiling back at me and that makes me feel good.

"Next time, I will save you a cookie," she teases. "I mean, if there is a next time."

"There will be a next time, Lacy. I will make sure of it." I huff a laugh and leave her office, forcing myself out the door, almost dancing down the hall to meet Tanner.

13

HUDSON

"Dad, who taught you to catch?" Harvey asks me as we throw a ball in the yard, my parents nearby.

"Grandpa. Right here on this very lawn, actually," I say, throwing the ball to him, his glove catching it instantly. He has some innate skill with baseball, his coordination on point.

"So Grandpa taught you, and then you taught me!" he says, his smile bright. How the hell did I get so lucky to have such a great kid? I'm not looking forward to the teen years, but right here, right now, I feel like I have done something right.

"That's right. The Hamilton throw is something passed down through the years of time," I joke, smirking, enjoying this moment. This is what I wanted from Whispers. The quiet. The peace. The simple life of having space to throw a ball with my son, to have our bare feet in the grass, the late afternoon sun on our backs, and the fresh air in our lungs.

"Your throw is better than your father's!" my dad says, walking up to us, chuckling. That's something else I have noticed—how much my parents love having us near them, how much more life they seem to have now that Harvey runs around our property.

"Oh, stop. Both my boys could have played professionally," my mom says, winking at me, and I huff a laugh.

"Really?" Harvey says, his eyes widening at that prospect.

"Maybe." I shrug. "But being a doctor is way more fun." Even though he's young, Harvey shakes his head at me. The act is simple enough, but the fact that my father does the exact same movement at the exact same time has me pausing.

"Come on, Harvey, let's go down to the lake to find some tadpoles." My dad grabs the ball and throws it to me as Harvey chases him down the hill. I relax and walk back to the house to where my mom sits, watching us all.

"He runs so fast, he is likely to break a leg if he isn't careful," I murmur to her, watching Harvey speed down the hill with his grandfather.

"He's just like you were as a kid. It's nice to see you both settled in so well back here in Whispers. I assume you are happy with the move?" she asks softly.

"It's going great," I tell her, smiling. Everything is falling into place. I take a deep breath, loving the fresh air, and I hear my son's squealing laughter below, my heart inflating even more.

"Veronica told me today that you're getting her a

specialist from the city?" my mom prods, and I need to be careful because I can't discuss my patients with my mom.

"I was thinking Melody could help her out. Offer a second opinion," I explain, and my mom nods.

"It couldn't hurt. Veronica has been sick for a long time. She was sick before Lacy went to college. That poor girl has had to look after her mom twenty-four seven since she was a child. She never gets a break." My mom clicks her tongue, clearly not happy about the situation, which makes two of us.

"Actually, I wanted to talk to you about that..." I say, rubbing my chin. The late afternoon sun is starting to set, and there is little to no wind. Dusk in Whispers is my favorite time of day.

"Go on." She nudges my elbow.

"Well, I was hoping to take Lacy out, actually..." I say, not able to help the smile that comes to my face just thinking about her. "So I was wondering if you could visit her mom while I did that." I know Lacy will never leave her mom alone. I also now know her mom and my mom have been friends for years. I look from my son, who I see dancing down below, my father appearing to teach him how to skim rocks at the small pond, to my mom, and catch her watching me, a smile on her face.

"I was wondering how long it would take you," she says, and my eyebrows pinch.

"For what?" I ask, trying to gauge where she is going with this.

"To ask Lacy out. She is a catch, you know. Pretty, of course, mature for her age. She has a lot of responsibilities but handles them well. Resilient because, well, she has come through her own demons too. Not to mention, she's smart. Did you know she was top of her class at college?" my mom asks, and I smile at her because I did know that.

"Yes. But you need to wipe that smile from your face. It's just a date." I try to downplay it, seeing my mom getting excited that I am taking her best friend's daughter out.

"I know, but honey, it will be one of your first ones... you know... since Amanda," she says tentatively, looking at me with empathy. It isn't my first date since my wife died. I've been on a few, had many one-night stands, but this is the first date that I actually really want to go on.

"Amanda has been gone for years now, Mom." Running my hand through my hair, I wait for that feeling of heaviness in my stomach that usually comes when I speak about my late wife, but it doesn't feel as strong today. In fact, I haven't felt it much at all since I moved back.

"I know, but so have you," my mom says, and my eyes flick to meet hers. I sit with her words for a moment.

"I've been busy... Harvey..." I tell her my usual reasoning for not dating seriously, and her smile falters.

"You have drowned yourself in work and Harvey, but I'm glad to see you coming to life again," Mom says delicately.

"I didn't do it purposefully. I just..." I sigh, thinking about it all. This is the first real conversation we've had about it, and I'm not sure why I waited so long. It feels good to get some things out.

"Felt guilty," my mom finishes for me. I remain silent so she continues.

"You felt guilty because you didn't love her like you thought you should. You felt guilty because she was sick and you're a doctor and you couldn't save her. You felt guilty because she died and doesn't get to see her son grow up like you do." Like all moms, she knows exactly what's going on.

"Yeah…" I sigh with my confession. "I feel guilty."

"Amanda was wonderful. But I know that if you hadn't fallen pregnant with Harvey so quickly after you started dating, you wouldn't have married her." She's right. I wouldn't have. Amanda and I got along in many ways, but I knew she wasn't my forever, and deep down, I think Amanda felt the same.

"I had to do the right thing. She wanted to keep the baby, and I wasn't going to be an absent father. Then when she got sick, everything just snowballed," I say, finally feeling like I have come out the other side. That doesn't mean I don't still grieve, but I'm slowly letting go of the guilt as well.

"Amanda will always live on in Harvey, but now it's time for you. You need to start living again." I can see the look in her eyes. The one mixed with fear about me and excitement about what this could mean. It is a turning point; we both can feel it. "It's good to see you smiling again, son. And I hope you only get happier following your heart."

I nod, smiling to myself as my mom watches me with interest, before my cell rings in my hand, and I see Melody's name on my screen.

"Melody. How are you?" I ask, my voice straight into professional mode.

"Hi, Hudson. I have a message here that you called earlier. Is everything alright?" she asks, and I take a breath. I did call her this afternoon to chat with her about a visiting position at the hospital.

"Thanks for calling back, I know how busy you are," I tell her, because she is. Head of her specialty at the LA hospital where we both worked.

"Always have time for you. What's up? Harvey okay?" she asks, and my eyes flick down to my son again, playing with Dad still, my mom now walking toward them to give me some privacy.

"Yeah, fine, loving it. I wanted to speak to you about work," I broach the subject.

"Sure, what's up?" she asks, her voice higher pitched and laced with excitement.

"I wanted to introduce a visiting schedule for specialist doctors to come to Whispers for regular consults, to help the people of the region with their advanced medical needs. I have a cancer patient here who could really benefit from your expertise as a second opinion. Plus, I feel that since she's a family friend, I might be a bit too close to the situation, and I would appreciate you stepping in."

I was too involved in my late wife's care, and it took a toll. Now that I'm back, assisting my mom's best friend and consumed with thoughts about her daughter, I think it's smart to create some space with her medical care, while also ensuring she has the top care available. I wait for Melody's response. I did send her an email about it all, which I know she has read, so it isn't a total surprise. I hear her take a deep breath and sigh.

"I'm so busy, Hudson…" she starts to say, but I cut in.

"I know. But we both know you are the best at what you do. I would send my jet to pick you up. You can do day trips or stay here at the ranch overnight, see Harvey, and then fly back the next day. Whatever works," I tell her, hoping to remove some barriers and only feeling slightly bad that I dangled my son like a carrot. But if she does come, she'll want to see Harvey, I'm sure of it.

"Fine. I can fly in and out in one day. Send me an email of dates, and I will see what I can do," she says, and my smile is instant.

"Great. Thank you," I tell her, my gratitude heartfelt. Lacy's mom has had a lot of treatment over the years, her health ebbs and flows, but I know there are some new treatments being researched, and maybe she can benefit.

"Send me the file of your patient. I will take a look. I think I have half an hour tomorrow to do a video consult," she offers, and I swallow.

"I appreciate it. I will email your office now and see if we can lock it in," I tell her, needing to stand and pace. Excitement that I can get her here to at least look at the situation has me more energized than ever that this program will be of great benefit to the community, with this being just the beginning.

"Great. Gotta go," she says quickly before she ends the call, and I let out a deep breath. I heard the busy hospital in the background, the alarms, the chattering of the hectic life I left behind.

Now as I look down at the grass before me, I see my

son laughing and squealing in delight with his grandparents, and I'm even more grateful to have made the move. In the city, my role was less hands-on. Doing special research projects and advising. While still busy, it was a rare day for me to be in front of patients. But now, here in Whispers, my role has changed, being at the forefront again. I want to help. I want to have a positive impact, not just here in town and in the community, but with Lacy's mom.

I hope I can make it all work.

14

LACY

I see Mom crowding around the laptop, finishing up her online consultation with Melody. The amazing specialist from LA and Hudson's former sister-in-law. I joined quickly at the start to say hello, asking her a few questions about it all, before I left Mom to talk privately. She's stunning. Connor's words from earlier in the week ring in my mind, about how she looks identical to Hudson's late wife, and again the stab of jealousy in my gut rises. Like I conjured him, my cell vibrates with a text from Hudson.

> I enjoyed seeing you at the office the other night. Hopefully no more rose thorns have found their way into your hands?

My lips twitch as I look at the message. Just as I'm about to reply, I pause. I can't. I shouldn't entertain it. Instead, I push my cell to the end of the counter and start scrubbing the sink, the dishes from today already done, but the need to do something with my hands even greater.

"All done, dear," Mom hollers as she walks into the kitchen. She's looking so good lately. Becoming more independent. I like these days and weeks. The ones when she isn't tired or nauseous. It feels almost like how a normal family would be. Ones that aren't plagued by sickness. But I don't really know that reality.

"Great. How did it go?" I ask. We share everything, Mom and I, but it's her medical situation, and I need to be mindful that she gets the privacy she needs.

"It all sounds fine. She looked over my file and talked to Hudson. She seems to think that we're doing everything we can at the moment. She wanted to run some updated blood tests and things, which I will get sorted for her today or tomorrow," Mom says, and I nod, admiring how she can be poked and prodded so much. It would drive me mad.

"Okay..." I say cautiously. I don't want to get too excited.

"She's flying in to talk with us face-to-face, hopefully next week," Mom says, and I nod as I take in all the information. "Lacy, honey. Remission is great; it's what we have been striving for, but we know there's no cure..."

"I know." I nod as my eyes start to water, sniffling, trying to act like the mature adult I need to be, yet feeling like the young girl who doesn't want to lose her mom.

"We have known about this for a long time. I have lived well beyond what any doctor has ever said," she reiterates, and I hate this conversation. We have it regularly. Like a reminder to us both that we are on borrowed time.

"I know," I say, not able to form any other words.

"That's why I'm open to trying anything and everything. For you, sweetheart. For us. But at some point, I know that there will be nothing left to try, and I'm at peace with that. You and me always, right?" Mom grips my hand on the kitchen counter where I rest mine.

"You and me always, Mom... but it doesn't make it any easier," I murmur as I swallow back another wave of tears.

"No, maybe not. But seeing you flourish at work and smiling and happy is what really brings me joy," she says, and I give her a tight-lipped smile.

"I need to go to New York for a week," I tell her, watching her to gauge her reaction.

"That's fantastic! The city that never sleeps. Hopefully, you have just as nice a time as you did on the last trip there. Ohhh, you might meet a handsome man..." she coos, and I huff a laugh as I quickly brush away a stray tear that fell before she can see.

"Well, I'll be researching day spas and treatments so I'm not sure how many men hang around those places." Taking a deep breath, I pull myself together.

"What about at nighttime... you can maybe meet a man at a bar or something. Or maybe... Hudson can meet you there? Show you around the city a little more? I'm sure he knows some nice places to go," she says, wiggling her eyebrows at me, and I roll my eyes. I feel my cheeks heat at her comment, my lips still tingling from our kiss at my office.

"So you will be okay if I go?" I ask her, my body feeling weary, not wanting to entertain her about

Hudson. My mind is a swirling mess about him enough as it is.

"Of course. I feel great at the moment, and I have the support of many friends. The last thing I want is you saying no to opportunities because you think you should be here. Go, Lacy. Go and see the world. As I said, maybe Hudson—"

"You are clearly reading too many romance novels," I mumble.

"Oh, just imagine if he swept you off your feet!" I look at her, deadpan, and see that she's almost glowing with excitement.

"Not going to happen, Mom. But I promise that I will thoroughly enjoy the spa treatments and be nice and relaxed when I get back."

"Just promise me that you won't hold back on finding love, Lacy. Not on my account. Life is too short. We both know that." she says, squeezing my hand again, and I nod as I swallow down the bile that rises. I remain quiet, not able to promise her anything.

My shoulders lower slightly as she shuffles across the kitchen to put something in the trash as I finish what I was doing at the sink.

"Lacy, what is this?" she asks, and I look up, smiling, before I start to feel sick.

"Oh. Nothing. Just something from college. Junk mail." Walking toward her, I grab the letter I discarded earlier so she can't read it. But I'm not quick enough.

"It's a letter inviting you back..." she trails off, frowning as she reads it. "You didn't pass?" Her face is laced with concern, and I hold my breath.

"I passed. I passed every subject with flying colors... I just didn't pass it with him," I start to tell her. Because I did. I passed with an A average in every single subject.

"Except... statistics?"

My palms start to sweat, and I grab the letter from her hands and scrunch it up. Every month or so, he sends a letter. It's all formal, of course, all aboveboard, just like the text messages and the emails, all inviting me to repeat the very subject he teaches. Offering additional *support* to help me, saying that being in a classroom offers more to students than the online option I chose. He keeps them professional, not doing anything in writing that may link back to his behavior.

"Lacy? Please explain it to me." My mom's voice has changed. She knows I'm lying, but there's no way in hell I'm telling her anything about this.

"It's fine, Mom. Please, don't worry. I passed. I graduated. I completed my studies and got my degree. I just did the statistics part here at home remotely with an alternative professor when I came back early," I tell her, putting the lid back on the trash can and going over to the sink, wiping it down like a madwoman.

"So why is the professor inviting you back to complete it at a summer school program? The letter said that you are a star student who he would take great delight in having back for the summer," she questions, and my body shivers at the words. *Because he is infatuated with me.* The words are on the tip of my tongue, but I bite them back.

"I think he prefers his students to do the class face-to-face. You know, one of those old-school thinkers who believe that, even though I covered the same topics and same workload remotely, I didn't fully benefit from his teachings," I explain, because that is the only thing I can say that won't have her in tears and calling the police immediately. I don't need that stress in my life.

"Sounds a bit odd," Mom says, walking back to the dining table and taking a seat.

"It is. His office sends a letter every month or so. I have a feeling it might be tied to his bonus system within payroll or something." I huff a laugh, trying to make light of the situation and position the letters so she understands what they are about if she ever sees another one.

"Oh, of course, that makes sense. Like they don't already earn enough." She huffs, pulling out her knitting that she started this morning. Making a new scarf for the winter already. I run my hands under the cool water in the sink as I take in a few deep breaths.

Those letters have been coming for months. Each one more persistent than the last. Then there are the emails, the text messages. There's no point changing my number because I have a work cell, the number clear on our website, as is my email. Anyone just has to search online and they find my contact details.

I try not to think about it all. He's a man of power and status, and I'm a young woman from a small town without many means. I'm not foolish enough to think that I would win in the situation if I was to go public. I swallow roughly as I think about the last time I saw him. When he locked me in his office under the guise of a meeting. The look on his face will haunt me forever.

15

LACY

Water sprays me from the kitchen tap. The lettuce I'm washing to have a side salad with dinner now saturated and my t-shirt looking similar.

"Why are you jittery?" My mom watches me carefully from where she is sitting at the dining table. Ever since she found that letter earlier, I have been feeling off. The letters I constantly receive, the ongoing text messages and emails, lying to Mom... None of it feels good.

"I'm not," I say quickly, taking a deep breath to slow my racing heart. I think about Hudson again. My body seems to calm a little whenever I do. I get lost thinking about the way he stargazed with me, the way he bought me cookies, the way he grabbed the thorn from my skin with his teeth, how he kissed me.

"You have been fidgeting and dropping things all night, Lacy," my mom scolds me as I grab a kitchen cloth and wipe my white t-shirt. The wet material sticks to me a little where the water splashes hit me, but I don't care. It's just Mom and me and it isn't like she hasn't seen my bra before.

"There's just a lot going on at work," I tell her, which isn't a lie. The trip to New York is also on my mind. I need to put a roster together for daytime visitors and support people for her. I also need to cook some meals and put them in the freezer, ensure the cleaning and washing are all up to date, and do a grocery shop. Me being away for a week takes a lot of coordination.

"Is that why you keep dropping things and look flustered?" Mom asks, and I stop what I'm doing and look at her. Her lips purse a little.

I sigh, close my eyes, and take another deep breath, lowering my shoulders. I'm tired, cranky, and stressed.

"That's better," she says. "So are you thinking about Hudson?"

My eyes ping open and I look at her, seeing a wide grin on her face, and my shoulders are now back up near my ears.

"How did you know?" I mumble, somewhat surprised, but I might as well indulge her since she has mentioned him to me a few times already.

She scoffs. "Bit hard not to, honey. The man has been in town for only a month, been out here to the house, gave you his jacket to keep warm, which you so lovingly pressed for him the next morning. He's bringing me specialist medical attention from the city, which is happening rather quickly, and Rochelle told me today that he got you your favorite cookies," she says, raising an eyebrow. Damn Rochelle. This town talks more than parrots on speed.

"We are just friends." I chop the lettuce like it has done me dirty. I'm tense all over again. Hudson cares, I know he does, but we can't be anything. That's why I stopped it. His lips were so soft, so demanding, and I wanted to lean into it more, but I can't.

"He is a good man..." Mom says, and while I'm not looking at her, I can feel her gaze burn into my face. "I will forever be indebted to him..."

"What do you mean?" I ask her, my brow furrowed as I slice the lettuce, the knife slipping a little in my wet hand.

"He saved you that night, Lacy. He was the one who got you back for me." Her eyes water as her voice cracks. My breath pauses momentarily before I clear my throat and already want to remove the heaviness of the conversation.

"There's a lot to consider, Mom. He's an older, wealthy widower, who also happens to be a dad," I point out to her as I rub my eyes, the dizziness tonight worse than ever, and talking about all this isn't helping.

"Oh, little Harvey is such a delight. Susan talks about him constantly," Mom says, now smiling again. She brushed right over my other concerns, probably knowing I'm grasping at straws here. I can't help but smile too, though, because his son really is such a special kid.

"Harvey is great. They joined me at the diner the other week..." I tell her, trying to act like none of it matters when, deep down, I'm feeling a mixture of emotions.

"Hmmmm... Rochelle told me that as well," Mom murmurs.

"Why does everyone in this town talk so much?" I snap, and it's clear my mom doesn't like my tone by the look she gives me. I'm tired, the water on the lettuce is annoying me, New York is on my mind, and my hand keeps slipping as I chop harder.

"Are you okay, Lacy, really?" Her tone softens, and I pause. I don't need her worrying about me and some stupid schoolgirl crush I seem to have developed.

"Fine, Mom," I say, a little calmer. I wish the local community center had yoga or something, not that I would have time to go. But I'm just. So. Tired.

"So... Hudson?" she teases again, and I roll my eyes just as the knife slips from my hand and clatters to the floor.

"This stupid knife," I grumble, bending over and swiping it from the floor, the water on my hands making me miss the handle, and my hand sliding straight down, my palm slicing on the blade.

"Shit!" I curse, pulling up with a jolt, the pain instant. I squeeze my eyes closed, trying to breathe through the pain.

"Lacy!" my mom scolds with an angry frown at my language before her eyes rest on my hand, my white t-shirt now not only see-through but getting coated in red and her face morphs into shock.

"I'll call the doctor," she says, grabbing her cell next to her as she panics. I snatch the kitchen towel from the counter and wrap my hand, holding it tightly to my chest for comfort as the burning pain sears through my skin. It's all I can do to nod to her in agreement as I start to feel even more lightheaded.

I can hear Susan and Mom chatting in the living room as Hudson and I sit at the kitchen table.

"It's a pretty clean cut. Is there anything you're not perfect at?" he asks, grinning, his smile making my heart skip a beat. His doctor's bag lays open at our feet, my table now no longer set for dinner but as a makeshift hospital trolley with bandages, antiseptic, and thread.

"I like to ensure everything I do is done to the best of my ability," I say sarcastically, wondering why this is happening to me. He looks good, as always. His smile is warm, his hands gentle. He's slightly more casual than I've seen him before, but still very well put together. Everything just seems to match or work well on him. Me, on the other hand... I have my oldest threadbare jeans on, my white t-shirt now pink from the blood and slightly see-through from the water. Dried blood smears up my arm, my hair is haphazardly pulled back, and while I haven't looked at myself, I'm one hundred percent certain that my mascara is all smudged.

"Admirable. Although apparently texting people back isn't one of the things you do?" Hudson says, looking at me with a raised eyebrow, and I nearly wince with guilt.

"I was just busy," I murmur my poor excuse, and he grins.

"Hmmmm, does it take you that long to get back to everyone who texts you or just me?" He doesn't seem upset, still smiling, almost like he is enjoying teasing me about it.

I go with the truth. "Just you," I tell him, my lips curving into a smile as his widens.

"Well, one thing you should know about me, Lacy, is that when I want something, I'm persistent."

My breath catches as his smile gives way to a look that almost burns down my entire facade. As he looks at me like he wants nothing more than to pick me up and make a meal out of me right here on this kitchen table, my heart pounds, stomach flips, and I will my mouth to move.

"Good to know," I whisper to him as he removes his gaze from me and focuses back on my hand.

"Now, I hope that you can refrain from any further accidents with sharp objects. Not that I mind mending you. You are my favorite patient," he says, looking at me with a sexy-as-sin smirk before giving me a wink as he starts his final stitch.

"Can't promise anything," I tease, and he chuckles. It's contagious. It feels nice to smile. These small snippets of what life could be like make me ache with longing. I love them and despise them in equal parts.

"There," he says with finality, looking at his handi-work. "Those stitches will need to stay in for about a week. I will bandage it for you, but you need to keep it clean and dry for a good few days." He cups my hand, inspecting where he stitched. My hand is small in his, his embrace warm, and my whole body flushes at the contact.

"I will do my best," I tell him to get my mind back on the issue. I can't lie. I have washing to do, dishes too, so it's bound to get wet.

"I hope that you do. Maybe I should do daily house calls? Make sure you are doing what you are told?" he murmurs, looking at me under his brow, already knowing I won't rest it and will continue to use it in every way he is telling me not to. My hand still rests in his. I haven't moved and neither has he, and I don't miss the way his thumb strums along my palm as he contemplates.

"Do you not trust me?" I tease, a smile dancing on my lips.

"Ohhhh, I do. I trust you wholeheartedly. But I know you don't put yourself first, so that might be something I step in and do. I kinda like the idea of taking care of you," he says, and I swallow as I take a shaky breath. I've never had anyone take care of me. I wouldn't even know what that felt like.

"Thank you, Hudson," I say seriously, appreciating him coming and putting me back together. The pain is now almost gone due to a light numbing cream he used on my hand. I would like to tell him he didn't have to come, but as the town doctor, he kind of did. "I'm sure I'll be fine."

"The cream should help tonight. I think your thumbs will still work to text me, you know, in case you ever want to get back to my messages."

I bite my lip and smile. Him calling me out for ignoring his messages feels like our own little inside joke. It's nice to have something between us. I look up at him, and his eyes don't leave mine. He moves his leg then, his knee brushing against my own, and my breath quickens at our closeness.

"Dinner is ruined," I comment with a sigh, looking

over my shoulder at the kitchen behind me. His mother rushed in with him tonight, and while Hudson took me to the table to address my injury, Susan helped my mom who was in a flustered panic, before she kindly cleaned up the shredded lettuce and other ingredients that were either on the counter or the floor. I feel a deep pang of guilt looking at the sparkling clean kitchen, knowing I didn't do it and had guests in my home who did it for me. I now need to order Susan some flowers to say thank you, or maybe get her a little gift from the distillery and mentally add that to my never-ending to-do list. Victoria and Annabelle are working on some goat milk soaps at the moment, so that might be nice for her. My mind then flicks to the fact that I still need to scrounge around in the kitchen to put something else together before Mom gets too hungry. My own stomach now growls, it demanding food too.

"Don't worry about that. I handled it," he says, and my head whips back around so fast I almost stumble in my seat.

"What? What do you mean, handled it?" I ask in confusion, having no idea what he is talking about.

"When we got here and I saw everything, I called Rochelle. Asked her to bring something over for dinner and something you can just heat up for tomorrow night as well. I could see that you needed something and it should be here soon," he says casually, like it is the most natural thing in the world for someone to do as he looks at the time on his Rolex that shimmers under my dining room lights.

"You didn't have to do that." I'm equal parts appreciative and tentative. "How much was it? Let me get my purse." I move, about to stand, but his hold on my hand tightens, stopping me. I look at him, noticing his jaw pop.

"You need to eat, and I knew I didn't want you using this hand again tonight, so I took care of it." His hand comes to my face and pushes a hair from my cheek, curling it around my ear. *Took care of it.* I have no words, no idea what to say. I've never been in this position before. Guilt at not doing what I need to do for Mom, mixed in with a sprinkling of gratitude and uncertainty, makes a mess of my stomach as it sinks a little.

"Speak of the devil, here she is," Hudson says, standing at the sight of car lights shooting through the already darkening sky. My mind whirls, struggling to keep up with exactly what is happening as I watch Hudson go to my door. Opening it like he lives here, he meets Rochelle and grabs the bags before she makes a quick exit. The smell of her delicious homemade chicken soup encases my home and my mouth waters. He takes the bags to the kitchen and starts unpacking them, and I fidget, my nerves dancing. I can't let him help me like this, but before I can jump up, his mom rushes in.

"Let me get that ready for you all," Susan says with a broad smile and gets busy in the kitchen as Hudson sits back next to me, grabbing a bandage out of his bag. My body tenses. I don't like this. Susan is a guest; she shouldn't be in my kitchen, putting together our dinner. She's already done too much with the cleanup. Hudson shouldn't have ordered it, and I feel nauseous because I don't want to be in debt to anyone. This town talks. Too much. The last thing I need is people discussing my finances now as well.

"Relax. It's just chicken soup. It's already hot so it will take her two minutes to put some in bowls for you and your mom," Hudson says as he gently wraps the bandage around my hand. Clearly, I'm an open book because he knew exactly what I was thinking, and I can't move because he has my hand hostage.

"She doesn't need to worry. I could have done it," I tell him, not wanting to sound ungrateful, but feeling really uncomfortable having all the attention and assistance.

"Not with this hand, you can't. Besides, I'm pretty sure she's going to make you a week's worth of pot roast once we leave here." He grins, knowing that I hate all this help, yet my mouth waters slightly, because Susan makes the best pot roast I've ever eaten. I look down and see the bandage nice and thick around my hand and frown.

"I'm not going to be able to do anything with this," I say to him, my hand now firmly wrapped.

"That is my plan." With a smirk, he finishes off the bandage as his mom delivers a bowl of soup over to us before taking one to my mother in the living room and leaving us to it again. My stomach rumbles at the smell. Rochelle is the best cook in town and her chicken soup is no exception.

"Hungry?" Hudson asks with a small smile, clearly hearing my stomach.

"No, I'm fine," I lie through my teeth as my stomach rumbles embarrassingly loudly.

"Liar," he says with a chuckle, clearly enjoying himself. "Here, let me help you." He moves the bowl closer. I go to grab the spoon and stop. The hand I hurt is my right one, the hand I use for everything, and there's absolutely no way I will be able to grip a spoon and feed myself soup with this bandaged hand. I go to grab the spoon in my left hand instead, but that feels so uncoordinated I already know that I will miss my mouth more times than I will meet it. Spilling soup on my already mess of a top in front of Hudson is about as enticing as slicing my hand on that blade again.

"I... I can't..." I stutter, frustrated, hungry, yet stubborn enough to keep trying.

"Let me feed you," Hudson says, sweeping up the spoon and dunking it into the bowl. I suck in a sharp breath and feel a little dizzy again.

"No. It's fine. I can do it." But it's too late, the spoon is filled with soup and lifted to my face, waiting for me.

"Be a good girl and open your mouth, Lacy," he says in a deep tone, and my eyes snap to his. Heat swirls between us. His overt flirting takes on a new level of seduction, and my mouth waters, wanting to take anything he serves. We watch each other closely for a moment, my insides taking flight as my heart rate increases before I do exactly what he says. I open my mouth, and he serves me the spoon. I move deliberately, my eyes hooked on his, swallowing the warm, tasty soup. His lips part with both appreciation and admiration, his eyes now hooked on my mouth as he takes back the spoon.

I lick my lips, running my tongue along my bottom lip slowly, and see his jaw clench. The air around us has shifted. The tension is thick, and he's silent as he fills the spoon again and repeats the motion.

"That's my girl," he soothes, his voice deep, almost a growl. My body reacts to him immediately, my heart thudding, my skin buzzing. The pleasure I feel from doing what he tells me is somewhat relaxing in a life where I usually need to make all the decisions and must carry the load myself. I've never been anyone's girl, but right now, I really want to be his.

The soup hits my tongue, and I hum at the flavors. "This is the best soup I have ever had," I murmur before I open my eyes and see him staring back at me. Heat swirls in his gaze, and his intense stare has my pussy pulsing in time with my heartbeat right here at the dinner table.

His eyes don't move from mine as he fills the spoon again, bringing it to my lips.

"Good girl," he drawls. "Nearly done."

"You are enjoying this, aren't you?" I ask him, my tone much breathier than I intended.

"I am. Very much. I could watch you swallow all day. The way your throat moves. Your neck is so delicate..." he says, continuing to feed me while I flush at his words.

"I like you feeding me," I whisper, and it feels like the tension has spiked one hundred degrees as his nostrils flare and his gaze fills with wanting.

"Be a good girl and finish this soup, and I might do it again sometime."

We continue, sitting at the table in silence. I finish the soup, him watching me, being gentle, his movements purposeful and ensuring I eat all of it. Just as he asked me to.

"Thank you," I say as he pushes the empty bowl to the side. Then he grabs my hand again, running his fingers up and down the inside of my wrist.

"What are you doing Thursday night?" Hudson asks, and I balk a little, not expecting that question. I sit, shocked for a moment, as it dawns on me that he's asking me out.

"Ummm…" I think out loud, caught off guard, my body and mind clearly still on the soup experience, and as he sits smirking at me, I realize that was his intention all along. Catching me by surprise so I couldn't make an excuse. *Cooking, cleaning, helping Mom, working,* they all flow through my head at a rapid pace.

"I'm busy," I say with vigor, because I want to go out with him, but I just can't say the words. They feel too foreign on my tongue, and after what I just experienced at my dining table, I'm not sure how we could keep our hands to ourselves for a one-on-one date. I'm clearly losing my mind, and I need to tame my feelings; otherwise, I will be complete putty in his hands.

"You are. With me," he says, nodding, almost challenging me to disagree. I bite my bottom lip, really wanting to say yes before my eyes flick to the living room, thinking about my mother, and my body sinks again.

"I told you, I don't date," I say, pleased with my strength to reject him. Again. Even though everything in my body is pushing me to do the opposite.

"I will pick you up at seven." He continues like he didn't hear me.

"I can't, I have to—"

"I will bring my mom over to sit with yours, so you

don't have to worry about her," he says, and my body hums. *I took care of it.* His words from earlier sneak back into my brain.

"But..." I start to say, although it is futile.

"I have already booked it." Now I am intrigued.

"Booked it?" I ask tentatively, a smile coming to my lips, and he smirks. He knows that I'm all in. I think he knew all along.

"*Beetlejuice* at the theater in town," he says, his hand still holding mine, his fingers strumming up the inside of my wrist, almost like he is trying to calm me, scared that I'll bolt.

"*Beetlejuice*?" I question, the conversation moving too quickly for me to really grasp.

"I'll be here at seven." He nods, then stands and looks down at me. The action makes me mimic him, my head nodding in agreement almost automatically, and his smile widens. *Did I just agree to a date with Hudson Hamilton?*

"Good girl. That wasn't so hard, was it?" he murmurs as his hand cups my jaw gently, clearly knowing that I struggle with putting myself first. I look up at him from where I remain sitting, wide-eyed, and his gaze doesn't falter from mine. In this position, looking up at him, I want to do whatever he tells me to, just so I can hear him call me a good girl again. Makes me crave another kiss from him.

"I'm not sure yet. Ask me Thursday night," I grumble, feeling like a brat, but with a smile on my face and my head spinning. His thumb runs over my jaw gently before he lets go.

"I look forward to it. Now no more using this hand for a day or two. Keep it dry." He starts to pack up his medical gear.

"I need to drive," I say to him, leaning back in my chair, because there's no way I can remain at home doing nothing.

His brow furrows as he thinks. "Fine, but not too much. Go slow and be careful when you grip the wheel."

I nod. I like how he doesn't tell me what to do. I can tell he would prefer I didn't use it, but he's letting me decide.

"Mom? I'm ready," he calls out, and we hear a scuffling noise. We both turn to look toward the living room, seeing our mothers right near the door, clambering to get back, clearly eavesdropping on our entire conversation.

I roll my eyes, and my cheeks ignite with heat. The Whispers rumor mill is no doubt now in overdrive.

16

HUDSON

I dressed a little more casually tonight. Jeans and a shirt, a look I know that I'll probably adopt full-time soon, the suits of the city not really fitting in too well around Whispers. The more time I spend here, the more I feel like the boy who left all those years ago. The slight accent is back, I'm driving a truck, and my smile is permanent. My life finally feels like it's clicking back into place.

"Popcorn, as requested," I tell Lacy as I grab the large box from the candy bar, along with a soda each, passing one to her.

"Mmmmm... that freshly popped smell," she hums, her eyes closed as she takes a deep breath. I noticed she does that a lot. She appreciates the little things. She doesn't need the latest designer bags or clothes; she's not materialistic. She enjoys every moment for what it is. It's probably why people naturally gravitate to her. She also savors her food. The cherry and cherry stem, the sundae, the cookies, and now the popcorn. *The soup.* That heated exchange the other night is one of the most intense things I've experienced with a woman fully clothed.

"I'm beginning to think you might be a bit of a food-ie?" I tease as we start walking to the cinema. I'm already imagining the restaurants that I could take her to back in LA or even New York, maybe Paris. She would love them.

"Give me sweets under the stars, and I'll be a happy girl," she says, smiling, and I laugh. I feel good. This feels good. Being with her is easy, light, fun. Casual, not pressured, she looks amazing, and it feels right. Better than any other date has ever been.

"I can't remember the last time I was here at this cinema," I say, looking around the art deco inspired, aging decor. I came here a bit as a kid, but I preferred the outdoors. I look at the old fortune teller machine in the corner, remembering bringing my first date here back when I was a teenager and paying for a fortune.

"Me neither, although I would have thought it would be busier than this," she says with a little shrug, and I grin.

"What was the last movie you watched?" I ask her quickly.

"Hmmm... I can't remember. That's how long it has been." She laughs at herself. My grin widens. I love seeing her laugh, and as we walk together, I catch my reflection in the glass wall. I can't help but notice how happy and relaxed I am around this woman.

"Here, let me," I say, grabbing the door to the cinema and holding it open as we walk through.

"Clearly, *Beetlejuice* is not very popular..." she murmurs, looking around.

"It's very popular. It's a classic," I tell her, walking down the aisle to find a seat.

"But no one else is here." She looks at me like I am crazy.

"I know. I booked the whole place just for us tonight."

Her steps stop short as complete shock overtakes her face.

"Huh?" she says, wide-eyed and her mouth agape, and I grin harder. She's so fucking cute.

"Well..." I say, stepping toward her, smiling. The feeling that she is going to bolt at a moment's notice is something I feel constantly with her. It keeps me on my toes. I don't usually have to work hard for female attention. It has always come easy, both before and after my late wife. So she makes me think a little more and work a little harder, and I like that. I even had to be smart about how I asked her out. I tried to catch her off guard so she didn't make an excuse. I know she's busy, and I know she has a lot on her plate, but she needs to see that she can take a break sometimes, and if she is willing to do that with me, then I'm a very fucking happy man.

"I think we both know what this town is like. If others were here, then they wouldn't be watching the movie." I know full well that people would come and just look at us, watching our every move before telling their friends and family and making Lacy and me hot town gossip for weeks. Although my mother tells me people are already starting to talk.

"But... I mean... I was going to pay you for my ticket... half the popcorn." As she fumbles over her words, I can feel her start to panic as her shoulders tighten. I frown, because there is no way in hell she is paying for anything.

"My treat tonight." I grab her elbow gently and keep her walking so she doesn't have time to think about it. I'm starting to learn that Lacy hates being indebted to someone, either financially or emotionally. The look on her face when my mom cleaned her kitchen for five minutes earlier in the week was almost comical. I rented this place for the entire night so we could relax. It wasn't a lot of money, so I also made a ten-thousand-dollar donation to the local drama and theater club too. They had to bring the film in especially for me because it's so old.

"But I owe you for the cookies, for helping me with my hand, for the soup..." she trails off, a slight blush now coating her cheeks as she thinks about that night. I can see her internal struggle. She has paid her way her entire life, and she's uncomfortable with it being any other way.

"We are not keeping score, Lacy. I asked you out. I pay. I'm also going to pay for a lot more things. This is the first of many for you and me, and just so you know in advance, I'm old school. I pay for the dates, and I will damn well get you anything you want on those dates," I tell her, hoping that she knows exactly how this is going to go. Brow furrowed, she searches my eyes and takes a breath.

"Thank you. It's probably one of the nicest things anyone has ever done for me," she says, softening. I don't like that statement because a woman like Lacy should have the world. She gives so much to everyone else; I'm surprised no one else has swept her off her feet before now.

"One of?" I'm intrigued, keen to know what rates on her list.

"Well, I also got my favorite cookies delivered, so there's that," she says, a cheeky smile coming to her face.

"Hmmm, that Connor ate," I grumble, hating the fact that he sat in her office with her, eating her favorite cookies. Jealousy coils, the feeling entirely new and never having appeared before I stepped foot back here in Whispers.

"He has a sweet tooth too. But the distillery restaurant is trialing a new dessert menu this week, so I know he'll be busy with the chef taste testing until his heart's content for days."

"I think Harvey's class is coming to the distillery for a tour?" I tell her, remembering, as the two of us continue shuffling into the row and take our seats right in the middle, a completely unobstructed view.

"Yes. School tours are so much fun. I'll be there. Connor and I both usually do question time with the kids that come through."

"Harvey has been to the distillery a lot before, so he might get bored. But at least he will have some familiar faces with you and Connor."

"Is he doing okay? Are you concerned?" Lacy asks, seemingly perceptive.

"I'm not concerned. I think he's fine. It's just a big move to come here where he needs to make new friends, and I think he is doing okay, but it's hard to know for sure," I tell her honestly.

"I'll keep an eye on him. See how he is with his classmates," she offers.

I nod, appreciating the offer.

"You do realize… that the fact you hired out the entire complex tonight will fuel the rumor mill for weeks, right?" She side-eyes me, her grin contagious. I look at her, taking in her face up this close. Her natural pout, her big brown eyes, pink cheeks, hair pulled into a ponytail. She seems more relaxed now, knowing her mom is fine, and the two of us only have to worry about each other. My eyes travel down her body and back up. She's stunning, and I'm royally fucked.

"I don't care that people know we are together tonight, but I prefer them not to stare at us all night while we try to watch a movie." I continue to admire her next to me, our arms touching as I put the popcorn in the middle to share.

"They wouldn't stare," Lacy says, looking at me with a knowing little grin that makes me want to do really dirty things to her.

"When I start feeding you your popcorn, they might," I say, and her eyes widen slightly, which has my dick jumping in my pants. The idea of feeding her is now front and center, a new kink clearly unlocked for me.

"My hand is fine now," she says, and she's right. I took the bandage off and checked it before we left. She still has the stitches in, but it almost has full movement back, the cut healing perfectly.

"I like feeding you." I pinch a piece of popcorn from the box and bring it to her lips. She pauses, looking up at me with intrigue, before she opens her pouty lips. The salt dusts her lower lip before she opens wider, her tongue darting out, and I push it in farther for her lips to close around it, my fingers getting caught. I swallow as I watch her taste the buttery salt left on her lips. Her eyes are wide as I put my fingers to my lips and suck the salty remains into my own mouth. I see her chest rise and fall rapidly, and a deep growl rumbles in my chest in approval.

"Good girl," I murmur. The praise comes to me quickly, as does my satisfied smile, and her body seems to relax even further at my words.

"They will be looking at you, not me, if you are feeding me like that..." she says, a little breathy and with a slight sass in her tone that has me grinning even wider.

"You are too beautiful for them not to stare at."

Our eyes don't waver from each other's as I lean toward her slowly.

"Hudson." It's barely a whisper from her lips, and I edge forward some more, wanting them on mine. She lifts her hand, running it up my arm, and I know we're on the same page.

"I love it when you say my name like that, Lacy baby," I tell her before my lips brush lightly against hers and the whole world ceases to exist. It's chaste, a blink-and-miss-it kind of kiss, but it tells me everything I need to know about this woman, and that is I want more of her and she wants more of me. I move my lips slowly against hers tenderly, enjoying every second before I pull away and look at her. Our noses nearly touch, and when her lips quirk up in a small smile, my head almost explodes from my chest.

"You had a bit of salt," I say, grinning, obviously lying as I give her a wink.

"Did you get it all or need to try again?" she teases me back, and I laugh. I love getting to know the real Lacy, and more and more of her personality comes through whenever she is with me.

"I admit, I do have a slight fascination with your lips." I could seriously watch this woman eat and lick her lips all day. It's a turn-on.

"Hmmm... is that something I need to be concerned about?" she asks, this teasing conversation making me feel so damn good.

"You don't need to be concerned about anything with me. But... *Beetlejuice,* on the other hand..." I say, getting us back on track. While I want to sit here and kiss her all night, I know there is a guy up in the camera box waiting for my signal to start the movie.

"This better be good. You really talked it up," she grumbles playfully, and I lift my hand up and give him a wave and then a thumbs-up, and with a giggle from my girl beside me, the lights go down, the movie starts, and my grin never leaves my face.

"Beetlejuice, Beetlejuice, Beetlejuice!" Lacy says, smiling and laughing as we make our way out of the movie theater into the night and back to my truck.

"Told you it was good. Classic films, I love them," I tell her, walking beside her. It's a little cool out so I wrap my arm around her middle and keep her close, feeling good as she leans into me, wanting my touch just as much.

"I wonder if we can see it tonight," she says, coming to

a stop and looking up. I watch her. Her ponytail cascades down her back, the ends of it brushing my hand, which I have firmly around her waist, her eyes wide as she looks at the night sky.

"See what?" I ask, looking up, wondering what she is talking about.

"The Heart Nebula."

I grin, knowing she's looking for something amazing.

"Do you see that?" She points upward, and my eyes follow her hand.

"I see a bunch of stars..." I murmur, wishing I could see what she obviously does.

"Those stars there, they're called the Ursa Major, also known as the Great Bear. It's the third largest constellation in the sky and the largest in the northern hemisphere."

I can't see shit, but watching her take it all in with glee is worth it.

"A great bear, huh?" I say, looking back up, trying to see it. I can just make it out, but it takes a lot of creativity, and that is something I lack. "Tell me your favorite animal?" I ask her, wanting to know the small things and the big things, everything about this woman.

"Butterflies," she says, and now I'm intrigued.

"Really? Why?" I ask her as we start to walk back to the truck again. Our steps are slow, and I move my hand from her back and grab her hand, entwining her fingers with my own. The streets are deserted. The town is asleep. There is no one around at this time of night, so I take my time. Her dainty fingers wrap with mine just as tight, and again, the stupid grin I've had all night doesn't waver.

"Because they start slow, like a caterpillar, and then they take flight. I feel like I was a caterpillar coming back after college, and now I feel like I'm in the cocoon, ready to take flight but still waiting." She's right. I feel like the more she lets me in, the more I get to see the real Lacy. From her quick wit, her little flirtatious moments, her complete honesty. I can see her blooming more and more right in front of me.

"How did you find college?" I ask her, waiting to hear all the juicy details of parties and maybe sorority gossip. But as I look over at her, her face falls before she masks it.

"It was fine. I just put my head down. Studied. Then came home early to be with Mom."

I don't know how I know, but I have a feeling college wasn't the experience that she was expecting it to be. For a student on a full scholarship, it can be hard, especially at an Ivy League. But there's something in what she isn't saying that has my senses on alert. I'm about to ask her some more about which college she went to and her experience, but she shifts the conversation.

"What about you? What animal is your favorite?" She turns to look at me, giving me her full attention, and I bask in it.

"Giraffe," I tell her, smiling, and she giggles. The sound zips around my body like an electrical current.

"Why?" Her eyes glisten. We are only talking about animals, but this is the most fun I have had in a long time.

"They have a unique long neck so they are super tall

and also very handsome," I say in my most distinguished English accent voice as I stretch my neck up tall, and she stops walking to laugh harder. Her head flies back, her mouth wide, her eyes closed, and it's the sweetest sight. My heart thuds, looking at her exposed neck, wanting to run my lips up and down her bare skin.

"You are so beautiful, Lacy." The words leave me before I even realize what I've said, and her laughter fades. She looks a little unsure, and I notice her chest rising and falling more quickly.

"Hudson..." The way she says my name, I'm not sure if it's in warning or wanting, but either way, I like my name on her lips.

"You are one of the most beautiful women I have ever met," I tell her, stepping closer, and I hear her sharp intake of breath. Our toes are touching as I gaze down at her, my hands finding either side of her waist. I watch her swallow before I feel her hands coast up my forearms and rest near my elbows, staying close.

"They sleep standing up, you know," she says quietly, and my brow crumples, confused.

"What does?" I ask. I lost concentration when my eyes landed on her lips, the perfect pout, the pretty pink.

"Giraffes." The small grin on her face is playful, and I smile because, of course, she knows. Her intelligence is one of the things I'm learning more about.

"They do." I nod, thinking I read something like that.

"They also have a big heart," she adds, looking into my eyes.

"One of the biggest," I agree. And for a moment, we stand there, only looking at each other in silence. Her with curiosity and me with a longing I've never experienced.

"Are you going to kiss me?" she whispers, almost teasingly, as the cool night air clouds from her lips. My heart stutters at that sweet question.

"Would that be alright with you?" I ask, trying to take things slow when all I want to do is the complete opposite.

"Yes..." she says in a breath that I don't let her finish before my lips are on hers, and I pull her tight against me.

Her hands dig into my arms to keep steady as my hands wrap her up, pulling her body against me, and sealing her lips to mine, so much so, she's on her tiptoes. Her lips are soft, and I taste the saltiness from our popcorn as they move against mine. I run a hand up her side, bringing it to cup her jaw, tilting her head a little just as my tongue slides across her bottom lip and she opens up for me.

My tongue tangles with hers as desire swirls within me. Her hold on me increases, but she doesn't have to worry because at this point, I'm going to struggle to let her go, already itching to have more of her. As her body softens in my hold, I kiss her like I haven't kissed anyone in years. Our kiss in her office was electric, the chaste kiss in the cinema earlier was teasingly perfect, but this, with Lacy giving me back as much as I'm giving her, is all-encompassing and there is no turning back for me now. I'm in heaven.

"Wow..." she says quietly as we pull away slightly before I peck another few kisses on her cheek.

"Yeah, wow..." I agree, murmuring the words against her cheek, not yet ready to pull away completely.

"Giraffes are good kissers too," she quips, and now it is my turn to laugh. Her quick wit is enough to set me off, and it feels good. I keep her close to me and walk her to the truck, opening the door and getting her inside, realizing that the kiss was great, but not enough. My ache for her is now burning, and I have no chance of simmering it down. Not after tonight, and I just hope she feels the same.

17

LACY

I walk out to the bottle room and survey the kids.

He looks like he is having a great time.

Of course he is, Tanner promised him ice cream. Does he have friends?

He has a friend. They are laughing at Connor.

Also, are we texting right now? Have your thumbs fallen off and working entirely on their own without you? Do you need a doctor?

I laugh as I read his response. This feels good. Feels right. I'm not sure why I waited so long to text him back after all these months.

My thumbs are perfectly fine.

> Hang on. Is this the real Lacy? Because the real Lacy doesn't text me back usually.

Ha ha, very funny.

> One of my many appealing qualities as I am sure you are starting to learn.

That and getting rid of the excess salt from my lips...

I hold my breath, biting my lip as I wait. I see the bubble dance on the screen as he replies. I haven't really flirted like this before. It's new. Exciting. Fun.

> Jesus, Lacy, now all I can think about is your lips. I have patients to see!

I will leave you with that image, then.

Before I can think about it, I lift my cell and take a quick selfie of me pouting a kiss and send it to him.

> You're killing me...

I pocket my cell and look back at little Harvey. Hudson's question has my heart clenching. I know what it's like to not have many friends. I also know what it's like to be raised by a single parent. Father's Day at school every year was my most despised day. Mom even kept me home from school on more than one occasion, just so I didn't have to sit there by myself, while everyone else got to do show-and-tell and play games with their dads. So

I'm happy that Harvey is giggling with another boy, whom I see with Nikki at the diner occasionally, so assume he is her child.

The movie night with Hudson was great. If just for a little while, I felt like a normal girl. He was a gentleman and swept me off my feet, if I am honest. I was giddy and a little bit smitten and Mom was more than okay when I got home, which made me feel better about everything. She was better than okay actually, and full of questions about Hudson and me, none of which I was prepared to answer. Because I just don't know. It feels good to be with him, and the date was perfect. But it also doesn't feel real. I'm hesitant to give myself over to it because my life has always been unsettled. Just when I seem to have a handle on things in my life, they change on a dime, and usually not for the better.

Now, a few days later, life has resumed as normal, except for this new nervous energy. I shouldn't get my hopes up, but it's hard not to when the man hires out an entire movie complex for your first official date. So I have buried myself in the everyday. Hudson has been busy at the hospital, and I've been busy preparing for my New York trip, so we haven't seen each other again. But even now, I touch my lips, remembering the searing kiss we shared, and my stomach flips.

"So here are the machines we use to put the labels on the bottles," Connor says, walking to the far side of a machine that's not operating at the moment. The kids follow him like he is the pied piper, shuffling around to get a look. I search through their faces until I spot Harvey again, looking at Connor and taking it all in, just like the rest of them, even though he's seen it a few times already.

I wait in the wings until Connor is finished and then step up to the group as they all take their time looking at everything, the school tour now complete, before they all go into the restaurant for ice cream, compliments of Tanner.

"Lacy!" Harvey spots me the minute I walk toward them and runs forward, giving me a hug. My heart swells.

"Hey, buddy," I say, giving him a quick cuddle in greeting. I try to ensure I give him my full attention whenever he is here with Hudson or at my place when Susan brings him over because being an only child is lonely. I know all too well.

"Hey, why didn't I get a cuddle that big?" Connor asks him as he steps toward us.

"Because Lacy is my favorite," Harvey says honestly as he stands close to me, and my eyebrows rise. Harvey looks at me. "Plus, you give me those yummy candies from your desk," he whispers, and I laugh, remembering the last time he was here months ago, I did have a bowl of candy on my desk.

"So you just like me for my candy?" I tease him, and he shakes his head, laughing.

"Are you missing LA, or are you happy to be here with the cool kids in Whispers?" Connor asks him, scuffing his hair in the process.

"I love it here. I don't ever want to go back," Harvey says, and my eyebrows rise for a second time. It's great that he loves it, but I thought it would take him a bit longer than a month or so to settle in.

"What about your friends back there? Your family back there?" Connor asks him, grinning.

"Aunt Melody is coming to town soon," he says with a little shrug, and Connor and I look at each other over the top of his head.

"Oh yeah? Are you excited to see her?" Connor prods, clearly just as interested in the response as I am.

"Not really."

"Why not?" I ask him, now intrigued.

"She treats me like a little kid," he mumbles, and Connor laughs.

"That's because you are a little kid," Connor says, scruffing his hair again.

"No, you're not, you are a fine young man, and we love having you in Whispers with us," I tell him. Even though we're joking, little kids don't always get the humor in our words, and I feel like Harvey needs to have some confidence instilled in him.

"Thanks, Lacy. I gotta go. I want to get to the front of the ice cream line," he says, chirping up immediately before running back to his class.

"That was interesting," Connor says to me as we both watch him, already chatting with another young boy in his class, the two of them laughing together, seemingly best friends.

"A box arrived for you, Lacy. I put it on your desk," Tanner says as he walks into the room, his larger profile looking humorously giant against the small children.

"Thanks, boss," I say to him, and he gives me the evil eye, hating me calling him boss, but that is what he is, and I like to humor him.

"Okay! Who's ready for ice cream?" Tanner's voice booms into the room, and all the kids immediately squeal and laugh and run to him, following him into the restaurant where a large buffet of ice cream and syrups now wait.

"Coming?" Connor asks as he starts to follow the crowd.

"You go ahead. I will go and check what the delivery is. It might be those new bottle samples we are waiting on," I tell him, and he nods.

"Let me know if it is, and I will come take a look," he says, walking backward until he is out of sight, the big kid now going to join the little kids with their afternoon delight.

I head to my office, smiling, thinking of the kids and little Harvey, before I make a mental note to get more candy to keep here for when he comes back for a visit. I see the box on my desk Tanner left and frown, because it is too small to be bottle samples, and I don't think I ordered anything else.

"Open me outside." I read the label out loud before I pick up the box, the weight almost nonexistent. I walk out to the distillery garden, one of my favorite places here at work, knowing it's quiet and peaceful today with everyone inside with the kids.

My interest piqued, I open the box, setting it on the garden seat next to me, and pull out another smaller white box from inside it. The white box feels cool, and I notice an ice pack in the bottom of the packing box.

"What is this?" I murmur to myself, having no idea what the hell I ordered or what this could be. I grab the smaller box and put it on my lap, opening it carefully, and see a small white envelope inside. Pulling it out, I gasp.

Two monarch butterflies.

I open the envelope and wait, seeing them start to wriggle and slowly flutter out. They are a little slow as they flutter around my head, and I watch in awe as they fly around my face. One lands on my nose for a few moments while the other sits on my hand. I hold my breath, not wanting to move as my eyes start to sting in disbelief, happiness, and I feel somewhat overcome. They are the most beautiful things I have ever seen. I watch as they slowly fly toward the lavender plant nearby, and I grab the note from the box and open it.

You already have your wings, Lacy. Now all you need to do is fly.

Hudson.

I sink into my seat and struggle to breathe. *Holy shit.* Hudson bought me butterflies.

18

HUDSON

I look at the time, nerves dancing in my chest, knowing that the delivery I had organized was just dropped off to the distillery. It has been a few days since our date, and I have purposefully kept busy, because if I don't, I'm likely to want to see her every damn day. Our little text banter just now has me floating on cloud nine, but I need to keep cool. If I move too fast, it will have her running from me. I need to go slow and steady with Lacy.

"So your date went well, then?" my brother, Huxley, says from the other end of the phone. He has been trying to get it out of me for the entire call, my mother obviously filling him in on the details that she knows.

"It was great," I say, not wanting to deep dive into it with him just yet.

"And..." he teases, and I laugh at him, trying to relax my wound-up body, but my knee is bouncing nervously under my desk.

"Shit, was that a laugh? Did you just laugh?" my brother teases again.

"I laugh all the time." I scoff at him as I shuffle some paperwork to distract myself.

"You haven't laughed like that in a long time," he says honestly, and I pause, frowning. He's right. The amount of smiling and laughing I have been doing since I moved back to Whispers has far surpassed anything in the last few years. The realization of that fact is somewhat sobering. I never regret anything in life, but I now understand that I haven't been myself for a long time, and it feels good to be back.

"I think I'm coming out the other side of things." I sigh, leaning back in my chair. "Amanda was great, obviously. I learned to love her, and we went through a lot. Shit, I have Harvey because of her, but..." I pause, trying to gather my thoughts.

"But what?" Huxley pushes me, and I roll my head to release the built-up tension in my shoulders.

"I just didn't have this instant power pull toward her like I find with Lacy," I admit. "I can't explain it. I just find Lacy so refreshing, so interesting, so fun to be around, and so engaging." *And smart, sexy, witty, caring—God, the list goes on.*

"You married Amanda because it was the right thing to do. You promised her that you will look after Harvey, and you loved her as best you could in the time you had together. But now you are older, maybe a little bit wiser. You know what you want, what you need, and if Lacy is making you feel again, then I say go for it," my brother tells me, and I think about his words.

"You don't think age is a problem here? I mean, she is fresh out of college," I tell him, scrubbing my face, knowing that is something the town is going to really sink their teeth into.

"What is she? Twenty-three, twenty-four? I don't know her well, but I know her well enough to say that she is more mature than most thirty-year-olds I meet. She has her head on right. She's smart, confident, not to mention, totally stunning. She is the whole package, and I think you would be stupid to let her go."

"Harvey loves her too." My son talks about her all the time, and knowing he is at the distillery with her now fills me with joy.

"So you have already introduced them?" my brother asks. By the tone in his voice, I can picture him leaning back in his office chair with a smirk on his face.

"No, they've met before, through Mom mostly, I think." Seeing their connection to each other is another thing that makes this so much easier. It won't be weird or awkward to talk about the fact I have a son and introduce them because that is a bridge that has already been crossed.

"Well, that's one battle you don't need to even worry about, then," Huxley says, and I nod, even though he can't see me.

"What about Amanda's family? Something tells me they won't like me moving on, especially with someone so young." I say the next thing on my mind, because while I never broadcasted my previous dates to them, if I continue dating Lacy and bring Melody to Whispers to care for her mom, then my former in-laws are going to know about it all soon enough. I'm not entirely sure what they are going to think. Amanda was their pride and joy, and I feel like they will take it as a breach of trust or like I'm hurting Amanda's legacy or something.

"You just need to ask yourself if those people are going to continue to dictate your life, or whether you are going to live your life for how it is best for you and your son. They kept you in LA all this time, purely because they made you feel bad whenever you wanted to leave. They didn't want you to take Harvey away, even though they didn't seem to give a fuck about him. But I can tell you now, I think you already know the answer."

I think on this point and, again, he's right. Her family has dictated life for me since Amanda passed, and I just haven't really seen it until now. Their constant calls, their intrusions at Harvey's school, calling the nannies constantly, yet simultaneously never wanting to spend any quality time with him.

"It's early days yet," I tell him, pulling away from the seriousness of this conversation. We have been on one date. I don't want to get ahead of myself.

"Maybe... so where are you taking her next?" my brother asks, and I scoff.

"She's a foodie... She's going to New York for work soon..." There are great restaurants in New York. I have a penthouse there that I use sparingly throughout the year.

"Dinner in the city, I love it." The decision is obviously made in his mind. I don't admit to him that I have already called a few surrounding doctors to see if they have availability to cover for me for a few days. Not ideal, since I just arrived here over a month ago, but they were more than willing, so at least the town will be covered medically while I try to win Lacy's heart.

"Alright, I need to go. I have ten minutes until my next appointment," I tell him, feeling a little more settled after speaking to him.

"It's good to hear you laugh again, Hudson. I've missed it."

"It is a good feeling," I tell him honestly, just as I hear commotion out the front.

"Ahh, I need to go, something is going on." I end the call quickly and stand up, on alert for an emergency. But before I can take a step, she's in my open doorway.

"Lacy?" I say, surprised to see her, the grin on my face instant as I look her over. She looks pale, her eyes wild, her breathing rapid. "Everything okay?" I ask, starting to panic slightly, wondering what's going on.

"You got me butterflies?" she says, panting like she has run a marathon. Her hair is disheveled, like she rushed here, and a slight pink tints her cheeks as her hands grip on to each side of the open doorway for support.

"I did." I nod, biting my inner cheek to stop my smile from widening. Pocketing my hands, I force myself to stand still, letting her lead because I'm not exactly sure where her head is at.

"Real butterflies. Two of them," she says again, almost to herself, like she can't wrap her mind around it.

"I did." I nod again with my heart in my throat, waiting.

"That's insane. You're insane. What are you doing to me?" she asks breathily, looking like she's feeling a mixture of shock, disbelief, panic, and confusion as to why anyone would do that for her, and my chest vibrates as I start to let go of my facade.

"Doing to you? Hell, Lacy baby, what are you doing to me?" I choke out, not able to stand still any longer. I stride toward her, and she meets me halfway before I grab her hand and pull her to me, sealing her against my chest.

"Hudson." She whispers my name, as she does each time we are together, before I seal my lips against hers and kiss the ever-loving hell out of her.

As I wrap my hands around her waist tight, her body melts into mine. I feel her soften immediately into my hold as my lips tackle hers thoroughly. I'm not holding back. We've been dancing around each other for a few weeks now. Visions of her with the cherry stem, looking after her mom, stargazing, the movies. All of it is now coming together and nothing feels better than having her in my arms.

Seeing her in my office, with a look that is full of both hope and fear, sets my chest on fire in a way it has never been before. She grabs me just as firmly as her hands run up my arms and loop around my neck, pulling me closer as I kiss her more passionately, feverishly, and she holds me to her. One of my hands moves to the back of her head, digging my fingers in her hair, tilting her head where I want her, ensuring she knows exactly how I feel as we both release matching moans into each other's mouths. Her hair is smooth and silky in my hand, her lips soft and plump against my own, her fingers playing with my hairline at the back of my neck, and her feminine softness is in complete contrast to how we're kissing. I slow my feverish kiss, wanting to take it all in. Her little sounds hit my lips like torture, and there's no way I can stay away from her anymore. This is just another moment to solidify that fact.

No more going slow. No more dancing around each other. She is my girl, and now I want the world to know.

19

———

LACY

My body is humming and it's startling. I've never felt like this before. Never felt so out of control, giving myself completely over to someone else like this. It's scary, exhilarating, and almost relieving, knowing that someone has me and I can just let go. As Hudson kisses me like I have never been kissed before, my body turns to mush in his hold, and I don't want to let him go.

"I've missed you..." Hudson murmurs against my lips, pulling back slightly, his eyes doing a quick search of my face. I swallow, barely able to form words. I'm glad he's holding my head because I'm not sure I can even stand up on my own. I finally understand what people mean when they say they go weak at the knees; I can't even feel mine, and I'm pretty sure my legs are quivering.

"It's only been a few days," I say, biting my bottom lip, trying to stop the grin overtaking my face.

"I feel like I've been waiting a while for you. For this," he says honestly, and I look into his eyes.

"You have only been in town for just over a month," I whisper, my head slowly coming back into activation, my body tingling all over as his large, warm hands hold me with ease.

"I have wanted you for longer than a month, Lacy. Baby, I have wanted you since the moment I saw you working that bar for Tanner all those months ago. Making drinks with a smile that lit up the whole damn place." A grin comes to his face, and I'm glad he's still holding on to me. This man continues to surprise me.

"Oh, I thought... I mean, you just left?" I ask him the question that has been loitering on my mind for what feels like an eternity. My insecurities heighten. We didn't talk much when he was home before the incident, but after what happened at Marie's Place, and him rescuing me and holding my hand all night when I got injured, he left soon after. "That night... you left without even saying goodbye."

If what I'm feeling is reciprocated, which I believe it is, then we need to get on the same page. I have too much at stake if I give him my time to be left wondering if he will up and leave again. This is all so far out of my usual comfort zone, it feels equal parts exciting and downright frightening. But we have a connection. I knew it the moment I saw him run into that shed at Marie's Place, and I felt it the moment he got back to town.

"Lacy, my feelings for you started the moment I saw you and they have only grown since." He huffs, the memory making him smile. "But I have a lot of baggage. There's an age difference. You're younger than me, just finished college, plus I have Harvey and a hell of a history."

My heart skips a beat as he raises very valid reasons why we shouldn't be standing here in each other's embrace. Frowning, I think about the weight of my own responsibilities feeling heavy, yet being here with him suddenly makes them all a little lighter than they have ever been. It feels right, even though on paper it shouldn't.

"But when I saw you in that shed at Marie's Place..." he trails off, not displaying any of the previous hesitations. "There was nothing on this earth that could've stopped me from getting to you. Getting you down from those ropes that held you so tight, getting you out of there as the fire lapped at my legs, helping you heal... and it fucking scared me," he says, and I hold my breath.

"I needed to go back to LA. I had to consider Harvey. He had school, his friends. I needed to get back to the hospital and work. I thought after everything that happened that a bit of distance might have been good. You didn't respond to any of my messages, so I felt it just wasn't the right time to declare my feelings. You needed to look after you. I needed to look after my son." Taking a big breath, his hands move to hold me tighter, almost like he is scared I'm going to run away from him.

"But when I made the decision to return to Whispers, I made it knowing that it was the right thing for Harvey and a good choice for me. What I didn't expect was the feelings that rushed back the minute I saw you." Smiling, his thumb brushes back and forth against my waist. I wait silently and let him finish, even though my heart is thudding.

"I should've stayed away from you. But I couldn't. I should've remained professional, consulted your mom and that is it. Nothing has changed. I'm still too old. I still have Harvey and a whole lot of baggage. But call me fucking selfish because, Lacy baby, there's no way I can't give us a go. I want to date you. I want to get to know you. I want to spoil you, spend quiet country nights with you. I want to stargaze with you and you to teach me all the galaxies that we can see," he says, his voice soothing, his hand running up and down my back, eyes looking at me in hope.

I swallow, my throat dry. I'm not sure I can even speak. He has put everything out in the open for me so I know I need to do the same.

"I have a lot on my shoulders. A lot to manage..." I start, and he nods. "I'm younger, as you said. I would guess a little less experienced in life too." He was probably having sex before I was even in school. "There are probably a million other things I should be doing rather than being here right now with you. And I'm sorry I didn't text you back, but..." I say, taking in a breath as his palm rubs up and down my back. The movement is soothing and exactly what I need to keep me calm. He always does that. Always seems to know exactly what I need.

"...but if I'm honest..." I say, my voice almost a whisper. "There isn't really anywhere else I want to be than right here, in your arms and with you."

We both sit in our words for a beat, and I take a deep

breath. We both have a myriad of reasons why we shouldn't even entertain dating each other. Yet we both want to. We both want to try this, and it's almost like all those other reasons are merely background noise at this point.

"I want to try, and Lacy baby... it has been a long fucking time since I have wanted to try with a woman. That's how I know I need to." No other man or boy I have ever dated has spoken so openly and honestly as this.

"So you want to try with me?" I ask him, my smile a little coy, my words almost teasing as the reality of this situation starts to settle.

"I want to try a lot of things with you, Lacy." His cheeky grin is now on full display, and I smile wide as my cheeks feel vibrant red at his words laced with innuendo, leaving no doubt exactly what he wants.

"Thank you for the butterflies," I whisper to him. Tears prick my eyes at the care and attention that he continues to bestow on me.

"Better than the cookies?" he asks, smiling.

"Not much can stand in the way of me and those cookies, but I think being given live butterflies is certainly one way to do that," I tell him, laughing a little, still in disbelief, before our noses brush, and his lips peck mine.

"Come here, let me take out your stitches while you're here," he says, wrapping his arms around my waist and lifting me from the ground.

"Hudson!" My voice comes out in half giggle, half scream at the unexpectedness as he carries me a few steps to his consulting bed like I weigh nothing. My hold on his biceps tightens before he has me sitting me on the edge of the bed. The sound of my laughter is almost foreign to my ears, because while I joke around at work with Connor and Tanner, and have a great time with my best friend, Victoria, laughing like this, with a man whose hands I never want off my body, is entirely new.

"Don't move," he warns before he quickly kisses my lips again, then steps away to gather a few things he needs and places them on the bed next to me.

"Is this going to hurt?" I ask as he lifts my palm and inspects the stitches.

"I'll never hurt you, Lacy." His voice is steady and dependable, and I look up and see him watching me. Those monarch butterflies I released earlier have now taken flight in my stomach, and I swallow.

"Okay," I whisper with a nod, before he picks up my hand and gets to work. As he snips the thread with ease, I hardly feel it at all. His hold on me is soft, yet completely in control. Just like that night at Marie's Place, Hudson's hold is a safe, dependable place to be.

"All done. Good girl," Hudson says, and at his words, heat travels down my chest and straight between my legs. My traitorous body is totally off today with these new feelings I'm allowing to surface. With the thread all removed from my palm, and his warm hand holding mine, he lifts my hand to his lips and kisses my small pink scar. I start to feel a little dizzy and I know it isn't from the cut anymore.

"Thank you," I say to him as he packs away a few of his things before coming back to where I remain sitting on the edge of the bed. I'm not entirely sure my legs work anymore or if I'll fall to the ground the minute I jump off.

"There is a new moon this Friday," he says, and I nod in agreement. It's the best time to stargaze, so I watch the moon cycle pretty closely. "I have this little patch on my ranch that has the best views of the sky at night. Mom can come over and be with your mom so she isn't on her own."

Taking a breath, I give myself time to stress about everything and then calm my racing thoughts before I reply. He has thought about everything and that's starting to become a common theme with Hudson. He seems to have the answer to all my questions before I ask them. I'm starting to realize that when he removes what would ordinarily be barriers for me, it allows me to just be me. And I haven't been that girl for a very long time. I don't even really know who she is. But with Hudson, I see snippets of her, and now I'm really excited to let her blossom.

"I'd like that." I'm not able to help the small smile that dances on my lips, both excited for another date with Hudson and prideful for putting myself first for once. Although the worry about Mom still lingers and the guilt about having Susan over again to sit with her hangs heavy in my heart. But I know it's now time. My mom has been telling me for years that I need to get out and do normal things. Date, meet people. Now with Hudson, I think I'm finally ready to just give it all a go. Be all in and see where it takes me.

"I read somewhere that new moons are one of the best times for stargazing," he says, his smirk now wide, and I blink up at him as my body melts into his so naturally it should be startling. It's then I understand that he has been reading my book.

"Someone has been doing their homework?" I nod in agreement, my lips quirking.

"Maybe a little," he murmurs as he stands in front of me, his hands running up my thighs and resting on my waist as he lowers his head to mine. My hands move automatically as I assert myself more, and I cup his jaw, bringing his mouth to meet my own. Our kiss starts slow, almost like we're taking our time, ensuring it's all real and happening. But his hands circle my waist tighter, and he pulls my body closer to his as our tongues tangle, our movements becoming more intense. I pull his face even closer, wanting him, and wanting him to know that I do. As he deepens the kiss, my body heats, the urge I have to jump his bones increasing with every swipe of his tongue against mine. The two of us are panting as we slow down, and he rests his forehead against mine.

"I should let you get back to work," I tell him, looking up at him from under my lashes. It's just after lunch, and I'm pretty sure I saw a few patients waiting in the reception for him when I pushed my way through earlier.

"Hmmm... you too." Lifting his lips to my forehead, he kisses me quickly as I drop my hands down his arms. Hudson clears his throat and straightens, running a hand through his hair, and I see him flick into professional mode before looking at me cheekily and shaking his head and smiling wide at the situation. I swallow and take a breath.

He's right. My wings are growing, I can feel them. Now all I need to do is fly.

20

HUDSON

"This is so beautiful out here," Lacy says from next to me. She seems so tiny in my truck, but she looks good. Better than good. I'm not sure how or when exactly it happened, but it's almost like she's in a new skin. Her eyes are sparkling, her smile now constant. I see a spark of the woman who caught my eye at Tanner's bar many months ago, and I really like it. She gazes out the windows at my family property as we drive around and pride swirls in my chest. I have spent a bit of time here over the years, holidays and quick getaways, and I paid for half of it all, so I like that she appreciates it. I picked her up less than thirty minutes ago, dropping my mom off to sit with Lacy's mom for the evening, the two of them talking about some movie or TV show they were going to watch.

"It's peaceful. I love it," I tell her, grinning as I reach out with my spare hand and grab hers. Everything is feeling perfect about now. We are in my new truck, I'm driving us over my land, I'm not on call tonight. Every week, a doctor from one of the nearby towns sleeps over at the hospital and does the night shift so I have a break. Which means I can relax tonight as well.

"How is your hand feeling?" I ask her. Having looked at it quickly back at her place, I already know it's healing well, the scar still pink but it should get lighter with every passing day. It doesn't sit well with me that she hurt herself, but accidents happen.

"Fine. A little itchy, a little tight. But otherwise, it feels normal," she says, opening and closing her palm where it sits on mine between us. I take another quick look before my attention's back on the road, my hold on hers remaining because I just don't want to let go. She moves her hand, turning it to hold on to mine, our fingers gripping together with increasing familiarity that feels good.

"Good," I tell her, trying to watch where I'm driving but finding it difficult.

"I bet Harvey loves running around this place," she says, looking at me and smiling. I'm glad my son brings as much joy to her as he does me. Being a single dad is hard, but also my most cherished role so meeting a woman who respects that is important.

"He loves it. Literally falls into bed every night exhausted." I laugh, thinking about my son who fell asleep not long after dinner last night with mud still on his face.

"Were you like that as a kid?" she asks.

"Yeah. Huxley, Connor, and I would always be running around and getting into trouble. Usually at Tanner's distillery," I tell her, and she smiles. "What about you? Get up to mischief growing up?"

"No." She sighs. "I mean, when I was little, I was such a girly girl, so tea parties with my dolls was what I gravitated to. Fishing, camping, and outdoor activities weren't really my thing. I got bullied a bit in school. I guess I was just different than the other kids. The older I got, the more responsibilities I had at home, and kids can be mean. Jolene, the woman from the diner, she was my main bully, something she still seems to carry until this day for some unknown reason. When the kids from school would go swimming at the mineral springs or to the diner for milkshakes, I would be home with Mom," she says, and I suck in air, realizing that this woman has been a caretaker for a long damn time. I know from my work that caring for a family member or friend can be challenging. Without the right support in place, those responsibilities can take over and start affecting caretakers' health and well-being and limit their ability to participate in paid work, family life, and social and community activities. I'm seeing that firsthand with Lacy. It's why I now broach what I have done this week.

"So, in regard to those responsibilities..." I start, pausing for a moment, not sure how she will react. "I have been doing some research this week on that caretaker option I was telling you about. There's a woman I found in Williamstown. She is a home carer. Someone who comes into your home and helps with the basics to alleviate any responsibilities on the families."

"Alleviate?" she questions, her tone more inquisitive than angry, so I continue.

"She is fully qualified, first aid trained and all that. Her name is Jennifer. Her primary role is to help around the house as an additional set of hands. So things like meal preparation, housework, grocery shopping, taking your mom out for shopping, walks, appointments, that kind of thing," I tell her as I turn up the hill to our destination.

"I looked into that once a few years ago, but I could never find anyone." No wonder she has been doing everything herself; she probably thought that this type of support wasn't available to her. But a lot can happen in a few years and the nearby town of Williamstown continues to grow with people and with new sets of skills.

"She has been a home carer for about five years in Williamstown and has great qualifications. If you are open to it, I can have you meet her?" I ask, hopeful that she is willing. Support like this would be a game changer to Lacy; I'm sure of it.

"I think it will feel weird to have someone else in our home..." she says tentatively, but I can tell she is thinking about it.

"It does no harm to meet her. Maybe have a coffee with her and then see how you feel? I think any support you can get at home is going to beneficial, not just for you but for your mom too. I'm sure she would love someone new to talk to and get to know. She must feel isolated at times." While it's true, it's probably a low blow. I know if anything gets Lacy over the line, it will be the help she can give her mom.

"Maybe you're right... Okay. Thank you. I will meet her and see what happens." She gives me a small smile, and I grin widely at her. The trust Lacy has put in me feels equal parts fantastic and terrifying, but she is starting to open up about life, and the fact that she's open to receiving help goes to show exactly how exhausted she is.

"We're here," I say, pulling up and parking. It's a small hill at the back of the ranch, and up here, you can see our entire property. Decades ago, this land wasn't worth much, but my parents farmed it, and it was where my brother and I grew up. Now it sits at the start of what the locals call Billionaires Boulevard, a long road that winds through the back of Whispers, elevated with views of the town. The properties next to us are out of sight, as our land borders are marked with thick pines offering security, privacy, and protection from the elements.

"Wow, this is amazing," Lacy says, sitting forward, looking out the windshield. The sun is setting, the orange-pink sky low on the horizon. I jump out of the truck and run around to her door.

"C'mon. Let me show you the property." I take her hand, helping her out of the truck. She struggles a little so I wrap my arm around her waist. "Here," I say, gliding her body down, me standing close enough that I can feel her curves pressing into the front of my chest. Her feet hit the ground and tiptoe with my own.

"Smooth moves, Doctor," she teases, and I grin like a lovesick puppy.

"It's just the beginning, Lacy baby." My words have heat, and I see her pupils dilate as she bites her bottom lip. A move that almost makes me feral.

"I look forward to the rest, then," she whispers, looking up at me under her eyelashes, her cheeks tinted pink.

"Hmmmm, you're killing me, looking at me like that," I say, my voice hoarse. Stepping back, I give us some space and keep my hand in hers. I walk with her a few steps to the edge of the hill, just before the grass starts to slope down.

"So this is all yours?" she asks, stepping in front of me and looking out to the west. As she takes in the panoramic view of the property, I take the time to admire her a little. Her dark hair is down in soft waves, her makeup minimal, jeans, boots, and a sweater on. Simple. Easy. And sexy as hell.

"Over until the pines," I say, standing next to her. My thumb continues to run over her hand, and I can't stop. Touching her is all I want to do. I take a deep breath to pull myself together. It was *never* like this with Amanda. We had fun. Lots of fun. We were both independent and my work was busy. It was a no-strings relationship for months, until strings attached themselves to us permanently in the way of Harvey. I feel the fresh cool air hit my lungs, and this time, there is a small floral aroma mixed with it. Lacy's fragrance. It smells nice.

"The river is down there." I point, loosening my grip on her hand and smoothing my arm around her back instead, bringing her close to my side and guiding her on where to look. "It runs right around here to the east."

"It's really flowing today."

I feel her body move into mine a little. It isn't unlike how we stood, looking at the stars the other night. She fits against me perfectly. It feels right, she feels right. Like it is meant to be.

"Lots of fish. A great spot for fishing," I tell her, and she nods, looking over it all.

"Mom and Dad's place is over there. Huxley and I live there." I point to the large place across the way. Her eyebrows rise a little. It's huge. Magnificent, really. All timber and glass, everything oversized. Vastly different from where she lives. I've noticed her house needs a bit of work. Something I might look into for her.

"What is that?" she asks, pointing to a flattened spot, large trees all around, a pool already dug out. My builder, Griffin, has just poured the concrete slab for the house.

"That will be my new place," I tell her, and her head whips around to look at me.

"New place?" she asks, and I smile at her shock.

"Huxley is spending more and more time here, and while the house is big enough for both of us, I kinda want my own place. Something just for Harvey and me," I explain. "Something more permanent." I need her to know that I'm not going anywhere.

"It looks like it is going to be big?" she asks, looking back over at the concrete slab that is tucked away a little more, bordered by larger trees. The tranquility that space offers is in complete contrast to the city. I can't wait to make it my new home.

"It is. I want a lot of space. It was something lacking for me in LA. Out here, I just feel so much better, more at ease."

"I get that. That's how I feel when I stargaze. Like everything is alright in the world."

"Speaking of which, let's get set up before it gets too dark," I suggest as the sun is almost down.

The back of the truck is full of blankets, cushions, and a picnic basket. I pull it all down as I lay out a few blankets and as Lacy places the large cushions, I grab a few more blankets to cover us later.

"Don't tell me... Rochelle?" she asks as she looks at the food that I pull out, the two of us now sitting on the ground, with a mix of cashmere and mohair blankets around us to keep us warm. The large cushions at our backs allow us to sit back and relax in comfort.

"Yeah. I got a few of the cookies you like, as well as some different things. She has the best food in town. Probably even better than my mom's, but don't tell her I said that," I say, which makes her laugh.

"So true. She has cooked for this town for years. It really is comfort food," Lacy says, the two of us digging in.

"Wow, it's so peaceful here..." Lacy says, staring out into the distance as we eat. She has a serene look on her face, and I'm glad I can bring some quiet to her world. I know her days are hectic, and I can visibly see her shoulders lower the longer we sit here. The night sky really is her peace.

"Whispers is a great part of the world."

"What about Harvey? I know he loves Whispers, but a small town doesn't offer kids the same things the city can, right?" Lacy watches me, waiting for my answer.

"Well, you and I both turned out okay and we grew up here," I say, smiling, enjoying seeing her smile back. "I think Whispers offers him more than the city, actually. He can still get a great education, even better if you think about all the outdoor activities he now gets to do. Plus, he'll join the Whispers baseball team and try other sports."

She's trying to sound me out, ensuring that I'm staying, not yet believing that I am.

"And, of course, we can't forget that he is going to fly your jet," she says playfully, and I chuckle.

"Hmmm, I feel like I already regret that conversation," I tell her, finishing my sandwich, shaking my head at my son's antics.

"It's a wonder he isn't asking you about it every day," she says through a giggle.

"Oh, believe me, he is. Let's pack up. The sun will be totally gone in a few minutes, and I don't want to miss the highly educational lesson I'm sure you are going to give me tonight."

"There will be a test at the end," she teases as we quickly pack up our picnic.

"I'm ready for it." I've read and reread the book she gave me already, and while I am nowhere near an expert, I hope I can at least put the theory I've learned to good use. We get busy getting the blankets around us as the midnight-blue night sky takes over and the temperature drops a little.

"Come here," I tell her, putting some large pillows behind us and lying down on my back, my arm stretched out, wanting her to lie next to me.

"It's still a little too early. The stars are starting to show, but not in full brightness yet," she says, tucking into my side, my arm under her head.

"So when did you discover a love for the stars?" Although I can't see her face, I feel her smile.

"Mom has been sick since I was little. One night was a particularly bad night. She had to go into the hospital, and while everyone was busy attending to her, I slipped outside. I just needed to get away. The noise, the smells, the conversation. I was about twelve or thirteen, and I was panicking and just needed to escape. So I went outside and sat on a bench near the back door of the hospital," she explains, and I nod, knowing where she is talking about. "It was so peaceful. Everything was still. The birds were asleep, no people, no cars, no noise. After a little while, I looked up. I got lost in the stars that night. I think I stayed there for about an hour before someone came and got me. From that night and pretty much every night since, I have stepped outside and looked up."

I lean over, placing my lips on her forehead, keeping her close.

"Everyone needs a stress reliever, time away, it's good. Healthy," I tell her, appreciating that she has this as a hobby of sorts.

"I looked at a lot of starry nights after what happened at Marie's Place," she admits, and my heart thuds.

"I had a lot of sleepless nights after that as well," I tell her quietly, the conversation turning a little more serious.

"I don't think I have ever been so scared before in my life than I was that night."

I look down at her, trying to see her expression.

"To be honest, me neither."

"But you work in medicine, deal with life-or-death situations all the time?" she questions, looking up at me, confused.

"All true. I worked a few years in the emergency

department, and that was full of different situations night after night, but seeing you tied in that shed will be burned into my brain for a long time."

"I wasn't scared for me that night..." she says, and I wait, listening, wanting her to talk about it.

"I was mostly scared for my mom." She swallows roughly. I know this is hard for her to talk about.

"Your mom?" I question, my brow furrowed, wondering where her head is at.

"She only has me. If that night was my last, I was so worried about who would take care of her, look after her." The one time that you would think she would be afraid for herself, and she still thinks of others. God, this woman is so fucking beautiful.

"Your mom is resilient, Lacy. She can do a lot of things without support. She has a good community around her. But I know what you mean, because I wasn't scared for me either that night."

"No?" she asks, her eyes on mine, searching.

"I was so scared that I wouldn't be able to save you. So scared that I couldn't get you down from that rope quick enough." It feels so good to talk about this, cathartic, like clearing the air.

"But you did," she says, her smile small but there.

"I did. There was no way I was leaving you in there. You were getting out with me. That was something I knew for certain."

"Look! A shooting star!" Lacy says quickly, and my head whips around, catching the last moment of it, looking amazing in the midnight-blue sky.

"What is your wish?" I ask her, her eyes now meeting mine.

"I can't tell. Otherwise, it doesn't come true," she says cheekily, and I laugh as we go back to looking up at the sky, my body humming, wanting to know all her wishes so I can turn them into my to-do list.

21

LACY

There's no breeze. The birds are asleep, and my body is cocooned in a soft cashmere makeshift bed. It should be hard lying here on the ground. I expected bugs or at least the calls of wild animals, but instead the ground is softened by a range of blankets and cushions, and Hudson's body is keeping my internal thermostat high and my heart racing.

I feel Hudson's cell phone vibrate, and he looks at it quickly.

"It's my mom," he says, and I'm immediately on edge.

"Is everything alright?" I ask, trying to sit up and he smiles.

"Everything is fine. She is just telling me that they started another show and have finished the chocolate chip ice cream already. Apparently, it's a series, and they want to binge-watch another one tonight, so we have a little bit more time together before you turn into a pump-kin," he says, grinning, and I huff out a laugh as the fight-

or-flight stress I felt just now dissipates from my body. I lie back down, snuggling into his warm embrace once again.

Taking a deep breath, I look back up. My eyes connect with the myriad of bright stars we can see tonight in the midnight-blue sky. I try to think of a time when I didn't jolt when the phone rang unexpectedly or when I wasn't worried for my mom, but nothing comes to mind. I know she is safe, well looked after, and probably having the time of her life watching her old movies with one of her best friends, knowing that I'm out with Hudson. I run my hand along Hudson's chest, and he curls me into him. Swallowing roughly, I feel his ridges and his solid frame under his button-down before my gaze flicks back up to the sky.

"That one there. See how they connect? It's called the Big Dipper," I tell him, pointing up to the sky as my heart bounces around in my chest. We have been here for about an hour, talking and dissecting the stars.

"There's the Little Dipper, right?" he asks, pointing up as well, and I smile.

"You are right again, Doctor Hamilton," I tease. He already knows so much about the stars. "You have been reading a lot," I say, turning my head to look into his eyes. We are snuggled in close, so close our noses almost touch.

"Hmmm, I had a good teacher." His playful voice deepens, his eyes searching my face. I see him look at my lips and back at me, and my nerves skyrocket as my stomach flip-flops onto itself.

"Kiss me." The words leave me before I even realize I'm going to say them, and he doesn't hesitate. He lowers his face an inch before his lips meet mine. He kisses me slowly at first, gently caressing my lips with his own in a sensual dance. I lean against him when I feel his hand cup my jaw, tilting my head up a little before his tongue sweeps across my lip and darts inside. My insides quiver, but I want him so badly. The more time I spend with him, the more I feel like me. Just Lacy. Just a regular woman. And right now, I just want Hudson.

My heart is pumping as I turn onto my side to face him completely. I run my hand around his waist to his back, and his arm underneath me holds me closer, sealing my front to his. Our tongues tangle as my lips tingle, and my body hums before my leg slowly crosses over his.

"Lacy... baby," he moans, making my pussy throb. His kisses become firmer, his hand cupping my face, moving my head exactly where he needs me to consume me fully. It's quiet except for little moans which I now realize are coming from me, my body almost vibrating in need.

"Hudson..." His name is a mere whisper off my tongue as he adjusts slightly as his mouth peppers my jaw with kisses before he moves farther south, kissing my neck. A shiver rolls down my spine, and my nipples peak as he nibbles on that spot right behind my ear where my neck meets my shoulder, the spot that has me turning to liquid in his hold. I have nothing else on my mind but him, his touch, the way he's embracing my body.

"God, you are beautiful," he murmurs against my

skin, his breath a light caress. Our legs entwine with each other's, and I can feel him hard against my hips, my underwear growing damp. Any inhibitions I have had fall to the wayside, my body almost on autopilot as it craves his touch. Needing some friction, my hips move against his, just as his denim-clad thigh lifts like he knows what I need. I grind down on him, seeking something, anything, that will provide some relief to my throbbing clit.

He moves back to my lips, our kisses now more demanding, and my hips move involuntarily against him. A low growl rumbles from his chest, but his lips don't move from mine as his hand smooths from my jaw down my body, taking his time, feeling the curves of my shoulders, skimming across my front, cupping my breasts before he grazes the hem of my sweater and his fingers skirt across the bare skin at my waist.

"I want to touch you," he says on a breath, and I nod against his lips. "I need your words, Lacy baby," he says, brushing his nose across my jaw, his lips not far behind.

"Yes... Hudson..." I almost pant the words, feeling needy for his touch. It's been a long time since I was in this position with a man. In fact, every other partner I have had was a mere boy when compared to someone like Hudson. Hudson is taller and broader than any other man I have been with, and from what I can gauge from the hardness pressed against my belly, he's bigger elsewhere too. Not that my history is extensive. I haven't even orgasmed with a man before. That joy can only be achieved by my own hand.

"I love my name on your lips." His hand skims underneath my top and up my bare torso, my skin tingling as he cups my breast on the outside of my bra. My body arches into his warm touch automatically as I move my own hand to the front of his jeans, letting my fingers drag across his skin at his belt, then dipping beneath a little, and I feel another shiver ripple across his body.

"I love your hands on my body," I whisper, biting my bottom lip so I don't start purring like a cat in heat.

I don't know if it's the fact that we're way up here in isolation on his property, whether it's being with him and in his arms, or if it's because I'm in my safe space under the stars, but I sit up abruptly and grab my sweater at the hem, whipping it from my body and leaving me just in jeans and my bra.

"Fuck," Hudson groans, and then he is on me in under a second. His lips crash into mine as his body covers mine, settling me on my back and positioning himself between my parted legs. I feel all of him now and my hips move immediately, rubbing against his hardened length, and even with our jeans still a barrier, it's already amazing. Brandishing my lips, he runs his down my neck, my head falling back and exposing my neck to him as he peppers kisses along my skin, moving down to my chest, pulling the cup of my bra down and taking my nipple in his mouth.

"Ahhh, Hudson. Mmmmm..." I whimper, jutting out my chest as he sucks on my nipple and his hand molds my other breast. Skin pebbling with goosebumps, my heart races. My usual busy mind is empty, my mind solely on this moment, on him, and instead of thinking about all the things I need to do, the only thoughts I have are wanting more of this, more of him.

Moving his mouth to my other breast, his tongue laps at my nipple as his hand cups my curved waist, squeezing me tight like he can't get enough or like he is ensuring I'm real, before lowering to the waist of my jeans.

"I want... I..." I pant out, my body now on fire as my hand grabs at his shirt. "Off..." I say, not making any sense, but he knows exactly what I want as he sits up on his knees, looking down at me, and grabs his shirt at the back of his neck. As he whips it straight over his head and off his body, I lie stunned for a moment and take in his naked torso. I wasn't sure what I was expecting, but it wasn't what I'm seeing now. I blink a few times like I am trying to fix blurry eyesight, but the visual remains the same.

"Surprised?" he asks cheekily, still sitting up on his knees in front of me. I lift onto my elbows to get a better view. His hand drops to my face and rubs his knuckles up and down my jaw, and it's then I realize I am staring open-mouthed at him.

"Like I said, it's good to have a stress reliever... Stars are your hobby, this is mine," he says, and my eyes flick from his, back to the canvas of art I'm seeing covering his entire chest area. It's dark, so I can't make out all the tattoos he has, but there are many. Staying clear of the neckline, they finish just above his wrists, so in his business attire you would not even know any of this is underneath. It's a total contradiction between the smart, sophisticated doctor everyone sees. But it makes him immediately more approachable to a girl like me, and I like it. A lot.

Without thinking, I sit up, lean forward, and put my lips to his skin. I kiss him softly and slowly, across his pecs, his muscles so taut; clearly, he isn't eating ice cream sundaes every week or indulging in cookies from the diner on a regular basis either. He is hot, hard, his muscles defined, and he hisses as my tongue darts out. I lick him, and his hand cups the back of my head, tilting me up as he leans over and looks at me from above. When I flick out my tongue, licking his nipple, he leans over, kissing me again, even more ravenously. As he does, my hands move to his belt, and I pull it open in my haste, wanting to explore the rest of him. His grip on the back of my head tightens as he pulls the hair at my nape, my lips opening in unison for his tongue to assault my mouth. I'm totally and utterly in this moment. I love letting him lead like this, moving my head where he wants to, gripping on to my hair so tightly the sting is small but welcome. It's nice to have someone else take control. My day-to-day life is so scheduled and so overmanaged, giving myself over like this is like my own private medicine.

"Lie back." His voice is rough, his command clear, and I move automatically, doing exactly what he says. I'm breathless as I lie back onto the soft blankets, him on his knees, looking down at me. His finger trails over my bare skin, skimming between my breasts and landing at the button on my jeans.

"I want my lips on you, Lacy," he says, but it sounds more like a growl.

"Yes... Yessss..." I whisper, panting in a way I don't even recognize. I feel like a deprived woman who has been waiting for this moment for years, and that isn't too far from the truth. I trust Hudson, and under the quiet night sky, there is nowhere else I want to be but here.

Opening my jeans, he lowers the zipper and pulls the denim from my hips, straight down my legs in one almost fluid motion. The cool air hits my skin, and I slowly move my body against the soft blanket at my back, trying to combat the coolness on my front.

"Shit," Hudson grits out. "You are a fucking vision." His eyes travel up and down the length of me, now in nothing but my matching set of underwear. He takes his time, drinking me in, giving me a moment to catch my breath. The underwear I'm wearing was a gift from Victoria. She told me men love lace, and I have never had an occasion to wear the matching set until now. At this moment, I have never been more grateful to my friend because this set is my one and only pair of nice underwear and it's been sitting in the back of my drawer for months.

Getting naked and turned on by a billionaire under the night sky on his multimillion-dollar ranch was never something I ever thought would happen to me. His finger hits the hem of my underwear, ducking underneath and skimming my skin at my hip. The soft touch makes my skin quiver as he breezes across my ticklish spot, before he grips my hip tighter as he lowers his head to mine.

"I want you to touch me," I tell him, needing him to know I want him. I want this.

"Ohhh, baby, I plan to do more than touch," he

murmurs against my lips with a sexy-as-sin smirk on his face before he kisses down my body, his hands trailing down my sides.

I should be cold, shivering, the night air almost frigid, but I'm burning up, desire swirling in my body like it never has before. Hudson's body sinks onto mine, and my legs open on either side of him instantly. When his lips hit my lace underwear, I gasp. It has literally been years since a man has had his mouth on me. His large warm hand grabs my ankle and then smooths up my leg, pushing me open wider before he sinks his fingers under the lace again, pulling the wet fabric to the side.

"Oh God." I should be embarrassed by my neediness, how turned on I am, but I can't process that as I anticipate his touch. It's like I'm vibrating, strung tight with anticipation, yet melting like butter for more of him. He is taking his time, which is killing me, my body in a heightened state.

"You are glistening in the moonlight, baby," he says, his mouth so close to me, I can feel his warm breath on my inner thigh.

I whimper in agreement, knowing how wet I am for him. I feel like I am pulsating, the need to have his lips on me almost making me combust.

"Such a pretty pussy," he murmurs quietly as his fingers drag up my center, his touch soft before his lips press onto me, and I almost jolt up from the blanket.

"Hudson!" I gasp at the contact, and his grip firms from where his hands are now laced around the backs of my upper thighs.

His responding hum vibrates around my center, and

my body arches, my hips already moving against his mouth as he seals his lips to my clit.

"Oh God... Ohh, Hudson, right there." My moans are uncontrollable. I had no idea how wound tight I was. With one hand, I grip on to the soft cashmere at my side, pulling the material into a white-knuckled grip as Hudson circles my clit with his tongue before sucking on it, the pattern repeating itself over and over, getting faster and faster with every swipe.

"You taste so good, Lacy," he groans, licking a strip along my opening, and the compliment makes me bite my bottom lip. I feel amazing with his mouth on my body.

"Yes! Oh God, yes..." I moan, my body almost out of control as my hips grind against his face, and his hands grip on to me tighter. I wonder briefly if I'm suffocating him, but I'm too far gone to really care. My mind is complete mush, and all I can think about is chasing my high. My other hand drops to the back of his head, and I dig my fingers into his hair, which elicits a rumble from his chest as his movement quickens.

"That's it, baby, take what you need," he says quickly before his lips are back on me and sucking, flicking, and swirling on my clit some more. I grind against his face, squirming, my confidence increasing.

"Hudson... it feels so good... too good," I say breathily, my eyes closed, my head feeling dizzy as my pussy pulsates under his tongue. He moves his hand then, and it sweeps across my thigh before he's pushing a finger inside me.

"Oh my God, oh my God..." I pant. I haven't really

watched porn, but I have a feeling this is exactly what they sound like. With no other noise around us, the property in darkness and nature asleep, my moans and pants and whimpers are vibrant in the air, but I can't stop them, and I don't even want to.

"Come on my tongue. Let go for me," Hudson tells me, as his tongue teases my clit again, his finger moving in and out with perfectly pressured thrusts as I push my head back into the soft blankets, feeling myself reach the peak.

"Oh God... oh God... oooooooh, Hudson!" I'm crying out within the next blink, letting out a little squeal, looking up at the stars as he provides me with my own. My body arches as Hudson's head remains buried, sucking on my clit, and my entire body shudders in his hold as I come. I'm breathless, quivering as Hudson slows his movements and peppers kisses to my clit and upper thighs before crawling up my body. I feel like I have spent a month at a day spa with how relaxed I am now.

He is still in his opened jeans, his hardness bigger than before, and he hovers over me, waiting for me to look at him. My cheeks heat as I slowly open my eyes, my body completely liquid, as it dawns on me that was my first orgasm a man has ever given me.

"You alright?" he asks, watching me carefully, a small grin dancing on his face.

"I'm better than alright," I whisper, my eyes hazy. As I look at him in a new light, a smile curls my lips. I run my hands through his hair, the softness in stark contrast to his hard body. "I want to feel you," I say quietly as my hand trails down his cheek, his shoulder, his skin warm under my touch.

I no longer feel like the daughter of a sick woman or the girl who was tied up and left for dead. I feel like Lacy. A smart, independent woman who knows exactly what she wants. And what she wants is staring right back at her.

22

———————

HUDSON

I watch her closely, seeing a flickering of emotions cross her eyes. My heart is thudding, my body hot and my dick so hard in my jeans it could split wood. But I wait. I have no idea how experienced she is with men, but after that orgasm barreled through her and onto my lips, I feel like it has been a long time for her.

"I want to do that again," she whispers so delicately it barely reaches me. As she smiles up at me, her whole face lights up, and I sink down to her and kiss her plush lips. I wasn't sure of a lot of things coming here tonight. I wasn't sure if she would open up to me; I wasn't sure if she wanted me as much as I wanted her, but right here, right now, all hesitation flies completely out the window.

"Damn, Lacy baby, I could do that every day of the week," I murmur, my nose nudging hers, and I see her biting her bottom lip, a dead giveaway she is thinking about something, so I pause for a moment. I watch her face; her eyes look a little glassy, and it's almost like her stresses are melting away right before my eyes. Those beautiful butterfly wings are spreading, and I feel Lacy the woman starting to bloom even more.

"I want to taste you." Her voice is so soft with her admission, even as my dick twitches in response, I need to make sure that's really what she wants.

"You don't have to," I say, shaking my head. I don't want her feeling like she has to repay me for anything.

"I want to," she says, more firmly this time, answering my internal question. I look at her, seeing if I can see any hesitation in her face. There is nothing but wanting, which heats my body from the inside out.

"I have been dreaming of having your lips on me," I admit, and her grin widens.

"Looks like we both get what we want, then." Sitting up quickly, she forces me to move and roll over onto my back as she straddles me. In nothing but her underwear, under the navy inked sky, this is a sight that will live rent free in my head for years to come. Bathed in nothing but the full moonlight, in lace, looking so innocent and perfect.

"You are fucking phenomenal, you know that baby?" I tell her, the endearment falling with ease from my lips. Her slight blush and her small smile tell me my words resonate somewhere within her. I run my hands up her bare thighs, both to keep her warm and to touch her, not able to stop and loving how soft she is.

"You keep showering me with your words and your gifts, Hudson, and I'm going to be one very spoiled woman." She runs her hands across my naked torso, and my skin prickles in the wake of her touch. She is right. I want to spoil her. Shower her with affection, lust, and gifts. I know she isn't someone who has had a lot of any of that, and I want to be the man who gives it all to her.

I admire her now, seeing that the strength she shows so much in her everyday life comes out in her sexual prowess. And while I know she hasn't had a boyfriend in a long time, thanks to the gossip I hear from my mother, I have a feeling Lacy is just as confident with herself in the bedroom as she is out of it.

"I want you to tell me about all this, but another time," she says, eyeing my chest, the colors and patterns swirling on my skin. They've been my own private endeavor. The creativity, the pain, all of it has helped me over the past few years. Her hands delicately move down my bare torso, her nails lightly scraping my skin, making me swallow a moan.

I push my jeans down as she lowers my underwear, and my dick is raging, popping straight out for her, and I revel in her sharp intake of breath. She bites her bottom lip again as her eyes remain glued to my cock, so I palm it, wrap my hand around myself, and pump. Having never been this hard before, I pray I don't come too soon.

"Isn't that my job?" she says, looking at me with one eyebrow raised in a challenge, and I smirk.

"Get to it then, baby. Wrap that pretty mouth around me and suck," I tell her, the words a little tougher than my usual, but her eyes widen slightly in delight, her hips moving against my upper thighs, trying to grab some friction again already. I've noticed she likes me telling her what to do. I have a feeling she has had to make a lot of decisions in her life up until now, and having someone else take the reins for her is something she leans into.

She shuffles down and replaces my hand with her own, and my breath catches as she touches me for the first time. Her hand is small, soft, and delicate against me, and I watch her lower her head before her tongue darts out and licks across my tip.

"Shit," I hiss, tensing my core, the anticipation of having her mouth on me pushing me to nearly my breaking point. One hand grips on to the blankets, the other resting behind my head.

"Mmmmm," she moans as she takes another lick, her hand holding me like a fucking lollipop for her enjoyment.

I growl deep and low, my hips wanting to thrust up, the urge to fuck her face racing to the surface, but I remain steady. She is teasing me, so I let her.

"Are you playing with me, Lacy baby?" I ask her, my teeth grinding, holding in the ache I have for her.

"Maybe..." she purrs against my skin like a fucking sex kitten, dragging her lips down my length and back. Seeing her as a seductress like this is a new need unlocked. She is sultry and tantalizing, and I now crave her in an entirely different way.

She leans over some more, taking the tip of me in her mouth, wrapping her lips around me so they are pouty on my cock and sucking. I groan at the feel of her warm, wet mouth. It's perfection, just like the rest of her.

"That's it..." I praise. I'm not classifying this as edging, but she's teasing me and is very close to the line. I'm trying very hard to keep it together in equal parts enjoyment and equal parts torture. Letting her lead, letting her set the pace.

"I like the way you taste," she says before taking me in a little deeper.

"Lacy, shit... baby..." I choke out. I should be ready for the feeling of her mouth on me, but I'm not. I love getting head. Most guys do. But the visual of Lacy in her underwear, out here under the stars, there isn't a time I could think of that has been better than this.

"Hudson," she moans, then takes me even deeper, and I lift my hips a little. Not able to hold on a moment longer, I hit the back of her throat.

"Fuck, baby..." As I watch her start to bob up and down on me, I'm a goner. Her long brown hair covers her face as she works me over, so I pull it up in my hand, holding it tightly at the back of her head.

"You look so pretty with my cock in your mouth." This feeling is overwhelming, and my dirty talk comes straight out. I see her wiggle her hips, again trying to find friction, and I smirk. *She likes me talking to her like this.*

She hums in appreciation on my cock, and it thickens even more as the vibrations wrap around my skin, prickling my balls.

"Fuck me," I groan again, as my teeth clench harder. My stomach muscles are working overtime, my abs tight as she goes deeper with every motion, but I can't avert my eyes from watching as I slide in and out of her mouth. She is tasting me thoroughly, moaning on my cock with eagerness, sucking, licking, and bobbing, her mouth a tool of magic.

All my senses have rushed to my cock as her hand slides over her curves and dips down her thighs.

"Jesus, baby, you are fucking amazing. Touch yourself,

Lacy... Is your pussy wet for me? Is it throbbing?" I ask her, breathless, wanting my lips on hers again but unable to move. She feels too fucking good sucking on my dick.

"Mmm-hmm." Nodding around me, her hips buckle, and I know she is touching herself.

"God, I want to taste you again already, your sweetness on my tongue..." I moan, my eyes almost rolling backward as I feel my balls tighten. "I'm going to come, baby... I'm going to come straight down your throat, and you are going to come on your fingers..." I warn her, and she doesn't stop, pushing me closer to ecstasy.

Sweat has broken out against my forehead, and my eyes are glued to her mouth before I flick them to her hips, seeing her hips moving against her hand, faster and faster as her moans muffle around my cock. I know she is close too.

"Holy shit. Baby, I'm coming... Fuuuuuuuck, fuck." Matching the speed of her own hips, mine thrust up, and I let go, not able to hang on a moment longer.

"Lacy!" I roar into the night sky, just as I hear her choked scream, her mouth and throat opening wider as they relax with her orgasm, and I come down her throat with one last thrust.

I lie, panting, my eyes open, looking at the stars she loves so much, trying to calm my racing heart. Lacy slowly pulls off me with a pop, gasping for air as I let go of her hair. Her hands run up my chest, and she slowly falls against me. Her body seals to mine, our skin coated in a light sheen of sweat as we both come down from our highs.

"That was amazing..." I say on a heavy exhale, my

hand coming to her head and stroking her hair, my body now liquid. "Good girl, Lacy baby," I tell her, and she sits up to look at me. I kiss her a little, my hands immediately lowering down her back, finding her ass as I grip on to it tight, getting a handful of lace and muscle. Her legs fall on either side of me, and while we are sated for now, I have a feeling that our need for each other is going to grow and my hunger to have her again is going to be harder to tamp down. Trailing my hand up her bare back, she peppers kisses to my lips and jaw until she gets to my ear.

"I like you calling me that," she whispers, like it is a secret, but there is no one around for miles, so it isn't like anyone can hear.

"Lacy baby?" I ask her, grinning into her hair, her face still buried near my ear, thinking of her nickname.

"Your good girl..." she admits, and a contented growl rumbles in my chest.

This night couldn't be more perfect.

23

HUDSON

"Maybe we need to stick this here?" Huxley says as we both look at the homemade poster that is Harvey's school science project. Huxley arrived this morning for a few days, and I'm sure if he knew this was on this agenda for today, he would have the plane flying in a totally different direction.

"No! The moon needs to go here next to the Earth, Uncle Huxe; otherwise, it isn't reeeaaal," Harvey tells him adamantly, schooling Huxley as my brother's eyes meet mine over the top of this solar system poster that we are trying to put together. Harvey drew and colored all the planets, so now all we need to do is stick them down in order from the sun. The gate intercom chimes, and Harvey runs to the small screen on the side wall to see who it is.

"Isn't he too young to be doing this kind of shit? We didn't do this until high school, I'm sure of it," Huxley grumbles.

"Is it too early for whiskey? I feel like I need a fucking whiskey," I say, scrubbing my face, wondering how in the world to get all these planets stuck down in the right order. I tried to search on my phone, but Harvey told me that was against the rules. He himself has no idea, so clearly he wasn't paying enough attention in class.

"Where the fuck does Uranus go? Who even named a fucking planet Uranus?" Huxley hisses to himself, before he plunks down in the dining chair, leaving me alone to look at the poster until Harvey comes back over.

"Who was that, buddy?" I ask, assuming it was either Mom or Dad.

"Lacy," he says, and my head whips up. It's been a few days since our night under the stars, and I've thought of little else since. We've talked a few times, but it's been rushed, between her meetings and my patients, but even now, I lick my lips, remembering the taste of her on my tongue.

"Lacy, huh?" Huxley says, now standing again, wiggling his eyebrows, and I roll my eyes at him and run my hands through my hair.

"I'll go get her. You two figure out what we are doing here," I say, stalking away from the dining table and heading to the front door. I try to walk normally, but my steps are rushed, as is the need to see her again.

I pull open the door, just as she steps from her car.

"Hey, you," I say, my grin instant as I jog down the steps from the front door to greet her.

"Hudson, you didn't have to, nor should you, be securing Jennifer for us," she says firmly, and I take a breath.

She doesn't look as angry as I was expecting, but hell, the two of them met the day after I told her about Jennifer and hit it off, so I had to act on it right away.

"She was in demand, and I know you mentioned that you all hit it off, so I wanted to secure her before anyone else did," I say honestly as the woman I haven't stopped thinking about stops right in front of me with her hands on her hips. I see her internal battle. The one that makes her slightly stubborn, not wanting my help, yet knowing that it's what's best.

"I don't need you to pay for that service. I'm capable of—"

I cut her off with a kiss. My lips meet hers, and everything in the world settles. I feel her shoulders lower as her body melts into mine, and I stifle the growl that builds in my chest from wanting her so badly.

Her hands slide around my middle as I cup her face, threading my fingers through her hair, deepening the kiss that I've desperately craved since I last saw her. Our night under the stars was fucking phenomenal. She is fucking phenomenal. Slowly pulling away, I look into her eyes.

"I know you are more than capable, Lacy. But I also know you have a lot on your mind and a lot to do, so I took care of it," I tell her, wanting to take care of her every day of the week. But I know she's independent, and if the determination in her gaze is anything to go by, then I know she will want to pay me back. Of which I won't accept.

She takes a deep breath. "I don't want to appear ungrateful. I appreciate it, I really do. But Mom and her care are my responsibility. I don't need handouts," she says, and I nod. I can appreciate that.

"So maybe you can do something for me in return?" I ask, knowing just the thing.

"Sure, anything," she says eagerly, and I smile. A million things run through my mind, but I go with the G-rated option.

"Come inside. I'll show you." Grabbing her hand, I guide her through the door to the mess on my kitchen counter.

"You know the name Uranus means the Greek God of the Sky," Lacy says as Huxley and I sit back, watching her and Harvey complete the poster. I hear Huxley stifle a cackle, clearly still an adolescent.

I knew she had a thing for stars, but planets are a whole different ballgame. The facts she spouts are all fascinating to me, but to Harvey as well as he looks at her with hearts in his eyes.

"I know, son, I know," I murmur to myself as I watch the two of them work together. It would've taken Lacy less than five minutes to have the cut-out planets in order for Harvey, but she took a seat next to him and the two of them have been talking about planets for almost an hour.

"You know, talking to yourself is the first sign of insanity," Huxley murmurs as his eyes flick between his phone, me, and my visitor.

"Shut up," I grumble, my eyes staying glued to Lacy

and Harvey. The vision of them together does something to my chest that I haven't felt before.

Lacy looks over and grins before she throws something at me, hitting me in the face with a ball of paper. Her eyes meet mine again briefly, and her cheeky smile is like an aphrodisiac as I bite my bottom lip, searing my gaze into hers before I unravel the paper to reveal a hidden message.

Stop looking at me like that, her scribble says, and I chuckle, looking back at her straightaway, my stare on her not wavering.

"They sure have a good connection," Huxley says quietly as I pocket the note.

"...so it's really cold and windy there. There is no way anyone can land a rocket on that planet," Lacy says to Harvey, and his eyes widen in wonder as he takes it all in.

"Fuck, I didn't know that," Huxley says, and I resist the urge to punch him in the arm.

"Do you know anything?" I tease him.

"Oh, I know my brother is in deep, deep, deep..." he singsongs, and I remain silent. I have no comeback because it's true.

"What are you still even doing here? I thought you flew down to help Dad with some paperwork or something?" I ask, because now that Lacy is here, I prefer Huxley not to be.

"Looks like they are finished. I'll take Harvey up to Mom and Dad's, give you guys some space." My brother says the most intelligent and helpful thing he has said all afternoon, as I see Lacy and Harvey start to pack up, and I give him a nod.

"Okay, so we're all done. Harvey, why don't you tell your dad what you learned today?" Lacy asks him, smiling.

Harvey grins at her like she hung the moon herself.

"The moon is shaped like a lemon. Venus spins backward, annnndddd..." he says as he thinks. "And Uranus is the coldest planet in the entire solar system." He nods at me, and my eyebrows hit my hairline.

"You learned all that in an hour? I'm impressed." I ruffle his hair and his cheeks pinken at the compliment. Lacy beams at him in pride, and I swear I feel my heart swell.

"Did you do astronomy at college, Lacy?" Huxley asks her, and she shakes her head.

"No. It's just a hobby."

"You went to an Ivy League, right? Willowstone?" Huxley asks. I knew she got a scholarship to a top college, but I had no idea she was in California, so close to me or at Willowstone. It's one of the best universities in the country, probably the world. I even have a few connections there.

"Ahh, yeah..." Her smile is forced and her eyes cloud over a little. A movement so subtle, no one else notices. But I do. "I'm glad to be home now, though, with Mom."

Huxley nods in understanding before looking at Harvey.

"Come on, bud. Let's go raid Grandma's kitchen. She said she was making your favorite cookies today," he says to Harvey.

"Yes! Thanks, Lacy. Can you come over again tomorrow?" Harvey asks Lacy, and she looks a little like a deer stuck in the headlights for a second.

"I can't tomorrow, but why don't we meet up for Sundae Saturday this week?" she suggests, glancing between my son and me, the two of us grinning at her stupidly. I have a feeling that he and I would meet her anywhere.

"Yes! I forgot about Sundae Saturday." Harvey fist-pumps the air before running out the door, my brother following him, looking confused, having no idea what any of it means.

"Harvey is really great. You must be so proud of him. He is so smart for his age," Lacy says as I step up to her. Now that we are alone, I slip my hand around her waist and walk her back until her ass hits the kitchen counter. Her eyes widen, breath catching as I close in on her, sealing her to me.

"He is and I am. Thank you. I had no idea about the planets," I say sheepishly as I brush the tip of my nose against hers. I hear her cell chime, and I watch as she digs it out from her bag on the counter. Her face turns a shade of white as she sees whatever's on the screen, body turning rigid.

"Lacy? Everything alright?" I ask, wondering if something is wrong with her mom. Her head turns quickly in my direction, and she looks startled, like she forgot I was standing right in front of her.

"Oh..." She exhales, shaking her head like she is waking up from a bad dream." Sorry. No, fine. Everything's fine. It was just... um... just a work thing." Shaking her head again, she puts her cell back in her bag, then faces me fully. Color returns to her face, and her grin is wide as she meets my eyes.

"Are you sure?" I ask her. For whatever reason, I can tell she is not being honest with me.

"Totally fine. So, we are still not even, Doctor Hamilton. Securing Jennifer was a big deal. More than just an hour of my time." She's back to teasing, and my body relaxes with hers. Lifting her head, she almost brushes her lips against mine, bringing them close, just not close enough. Thoughts of her call now move to the back of my mind. I can't help it. I'm not sure if it's just us being together, the date under the stars, or seeing her with my son, or all three, but Lacy has been slowly relaxing more and more around me, her confidence building, and I can see a sparkle in her eye that wasn't there before.

"I can think of other ways we can even the score," I whisper playfully as I duck in, taking her lips with mine. Her hands loop around my neck, and I pull her close. Kissing this woman is a new addiction I never want to stop.

Our lips move, my hands roam, and she makes these cute little moans that have my jeans tightening every second she is in my arms.

"They might be back in a minute," she says between kisses. Our pace quickens, neither of us wanting to stop.

"They will be a little while. We have time," I tell her as my hands run down her sides and back up again. Cupping her breasts as her head falls back, my lips meet her neck.

"Hudson," she breathes out, lifting her head to look at

me, her cheeks a little flushed, our breathing becoming rapid.

"I missed you, Lacy baby," I tell her as I lean in to kiss those perfect lips once again.

"I missed you too..." Her hands run up the back of my head, digging into my hair, massaging my scalp, and I groan into her mouth as my tongue becomes more demanding.

"I want you so much it's almost suffocating," I murmur, my lips tracing down her jaw, kissing every inch of her skin I can reach.

"I know the feeling," she moans as she moves her body a little, needing some friction, and I move my leg, positioning it between hers. "Anyone could walk in."

"Hmmmm... let them..." I say, not wanting to stop kissing her as her hips roll on my thigh, and I feel her warmth, her neediness for me now apparent. I know my brother won't be back in a hurry, and he and Harvey will probably eat all the cookies Mom cooks and not leave me even one. So I take my time, enjoying having Lacy in my arms.

"I really should get to work," she murmurs, not making any move to leave or pause our makeout session, and I smile against her lips.

"Yeah, you should probably go," I tell her, but her hands grip into my hair harder, and I pull her body tighter against mine.

Neither of us move. We stand in my kitchen, her pinned to the bench, her hips moving against mine, our lips tangling together, her body in my arms, and hell, she feels good. We don't stop kissing, but I let her relax in my arms, her head falling back again as I kiss her neck, smelling her sweet floral aroma. When I lick her skin teasingly, she giggles and squirms.

"Hmmm, ticklish?" I ask with a chuckle, moving my lips back across her jaw to her mouth.

"A little..." she says, her tone coy enough to have me wanting to find all her other ticklish spots. "But I like it... I like everything you do."

"Good to know." I put my lips to hers again as my stomach flutters, and we don't break, we don't waver, even though my dick strains against my zipper more and more with every grind of her delicious hips. This is the hottest makeout session I have had, and I'm in no hurry to finish.

This is perfect. She is perfect.

24

LACY

The bottle samples have arrived, and they look great.

"Is this what you had in mind?" Connor asks, and I smile.

"This is exactly what I had in mind," I confirm, my grin not faltering. Everything in my life seems to be more enjoyable. I'm happier, work is amazing, Mom is doing good, and I haven't had a nightmare in over a week.

"Lacy. A delivery for you," our receptionist says, walking in grinning with a large bouquet of flowers. Hudson and his gifts are now legendary in the office. As I stand to grab them from her, I see Connor smirking.

"Well, I will leave you to open your little love note from the doc. Good work on those bottles; they look amazing," Connor says, standing and walking out, leaving me giddy. Hudson seems to like spoiling me. My fingers move fast as soon as Connor is out the door, eager to see the note, because while the gifts are amazing, his words are what lights me up inside.

I rip open the envelope, looking again at the large bouquet of white roses. He knows I like to pick the fresh roses from the distillery garden, so it is a little odd, but I appreciate it just the same.

As I slide the card out of the envelope, my smile is wide as I read his message, before I gasp and my hands start to shake.

Lacy

I have loved the thrill of the chase, but I'm not playing anymore. You will be mine and I'm coming for you.

These are not from Hudson. Fear consumes my body, my hands trembling harshly as the note falls from my grasp. My eyes water as my breathing escalates, and the room starts to spin. I close my eyes and start to count, trying to calm my frantic breaths, and I grip on to my desk so I don't fall. It takes me a little while, but slowly it works, and my breathing regulates. As I open my eyes and look down at the flowers on my desk, I swallow the bile that rises, and with my sweaty palms, I grip on to the large heavy bouquet and walk quietly out of my office. No one is around, all of them in meetings, and my pace quickens as I run down the steps of the office and make my way to the back of the distillery to the large trash containers, the ones reserved for our large rubbish items, where no one else will even look.

A feral growl sounds from deep within me as I throw the flowers into the air, tears falling down my cheeks. I pant as I watch the bouquet rise up almost in slow motion for a moment before the flowers fall, landing in the large bin with bits of old barrels and other random building materials, until all that is left is me.

A panting and shaking mess.

I JUMP from the car and dash inside, frazzled. I'm running late and have been all day. I've felt off ever since the flower delivery this morning. My senses are heightened, jumping at every noise. Usually, I can push his messages to the back of my mind, but there was something about the note that was different. More demanding, more threatening. Like he is getting agitated. He probably thought that I would buckle and come back to school immediately, doing everything he's asking of me. Maybe no one has ever told him no before.

"Oh, there you are, Lacy," Patti says from the reception desk at the hospital as I push my way inside.

"Sorry!" I cringe, feeling terrible but still not myself.

"It's fine. Melody is here and is already with your mom," Patti says, standing, giving me that empathetic smile that I hate, and I walk swiftly to follow her down the hall.

Mom and Melody have had a few calls, and now I finally get to meet the doctor face-to-face. I'm trying to keep myself in check because the flutter of excitement dancing in my chest from the possibility that Melody will be our answer, the one who will save my mom, is hard to tamp down.

"I've got it, Patti." I hear Hudson and turn, seeing him step out from a room at the side, and I suddenly feel an overwhelming sense of relief and safety.

"No problem, Doc," Patti says before turning and walking back to the front desk.

"Hey," I murmur to him, releasing a heavy breath as my body relaxes.

"Hey, you," he says, his voice low, then he steps toward me and slides his hand around my waist, pulling me tight. I fall into him, tears already threatening and my hands already shaking. As I wrap my arms around him, I never want him to let me go.

"Lacy? Are you alright?" he asks, clearly concerned because my behavior is off.

"Just... hold me..." is all I get out, and I feel his hold around me tighten. His hands splay across my back, nearly every inch of my front covered and my back protected, and I bury my head in his chest and close my eyes. He rubs my back, his hand moving up and down slowly, and I just breathe.

"It will be fine. Your mom will be fine." He thinks I'm upset about Mom, and I should be. Guilt riddles me instantly. Here I am, worried about some random flower delivery, when my mom is literally fighting for her life. I clear my throat and pull back a little, looking around, because we are standing right in the middle of the corridor. Anyone can see us.

"Sorry, I've just had a big day." I give him a small grin, and he eyes me warily. He knows that isn't it, but he doesn't push, and I'm thankful.

"Besides, should we be this close at your place of employment, Doctor?" I tease as my hand runs up his arm, enjoying the feel of him, my frantic state already soothing the minute his hands touched my body.

"Hmmm, no one around who I can see…" he says before he bends his head and his lips hit mine. The kiss is soft and over too quickly, but it's enough to rid me of the swirls of anxiety I've been feeling all day and the immense fear I experienced this morning. "How are you?" he murmurs as he pulls back slightly, assessing my face.

"I'm good, even better for that amazing discussion we had in your kitchen yesterday. You?" I ask, pushing the topic onto him as I still feel my hands are a little jittery. It's been a long time since I was thoroughly kissed like that, and I can't hide my smile.

"Same, but I realize that there are many other rooms in my house I still need to show you," he says cheekily, and I giggle.

"I look forward to that, Doctor," I admit. "Do you still want to share a sundae with me on Saturday?"

"I want nothing more, especially if you do that sexy thing with the cherry stem in your mouth." He winks, quickly pecking me on my lips again. "We better go in. Your mom has been in with Melody for about fifteen minutes. I just had to take a call."

I nod, and Hudson knocks on the door of the consultation room.

"Enter," a stern female voice says before Hudson opens the door.

"Lacy's here," Hudson says, opening the door wide for me to step through.

I walk in, spotting Mom straightaway, smiling, and I get one in return.

"Sorry, I'm late," I say as I sweep in and look around.

My eyes settle on the woman sitting opposite my mom. I knew she was stunning, seeing her on the video call last week, but in reality, she is almost like Barbie. Blond hair, blue eyes, blinding white teeth, and even though she's wearing a loose white coat, I'm pretty sure her figure is amazing. The complete opposite of me.

"Hi, I'm Lacy," I say, extending my hand.

"I'm Doctor Wilkinson. Please take a seat," she says, and as Hudson closes the door, I sit in the empty seat next to Mom, feeling like I am in the principal's office at school, my hands already fidgeting in my lap. "As I was saying, Veronica, we have discussed this before on our video call, that there are no guarantees. I think we all know this is not a disease we can beat. However, partial remission is a correct diagnosis at this point and full remission is also possible. I would like to do a few more tests to check a few things," she says, and I frown.

"Of course, Lacy and I know the situation," Mom says as her hand grabs on to mine. The doctor looks at the movement before her eyes flick to mine.

Hudson pulls a chair up next to me and takes a seat with us and my mom practically beams at him.

"So..." Melody says, and the three of us look at her. "What I would like to do is run some tests, I can see your red blood count is a little low, so a potential transfusion may be needed."

"Transfusion?" I question, needing clarification, and I feel my mom's hand grip mine tighter. I take a deep breath, feeling my fight-or-flight starting to develop, so I try to calm my breaths. Then I feel Hudson's hand grabs my other hand, giving me a squeeze. I see Melody's eyes flick to the movement, before she looks sharply at Hudson, then her eyes rest back on me.

"What are you thinking?" Hudson asks her, and I look at him, grateful he's asking the questions as my mind is running and not connecting to many thoughts today.

"Veronica," Melody says, looking straight at my mom, ignoring Hudson and me. "I think it would be pertinent to run a few more diagnostic tests, because your red blood count isn't where I like it to be. It can be an indication that there's possibly some bleeding internally. At this stage, I want to ensure we do everything we can to support you, so we can look at blood transfusions from someone who shares the same blood type as you."

"I'll do it. We match. I'll give her mine," I say so quickly, my mother looks at me sharply, and Hudson's grip on my hand hardens.

"Lacy. Giving blood like this is a regular ongoing demand on the body," Hudson says, eyes full of concern.

"I can do it," I assure him before looking back at Melody. "I'm fit, young, healthy. I don't smoke, I don't drink a lot. I don't do drugs."

"Well, we can start the draw down from you almost immediately," Melody says, smiling, clearly happy with the outcome, before Hudson cuts her off.

"Lacy, we need to talk about this..."

"I want to. I can do this." My tone turns pleading. I need him to understand.

"Lacy, I don't want you to put yourself at risk for me," my mom says, also showing concern.

"There is no risk. Right, Doctor Wilkinson?" I ask, looking back at Melody. She looks from me to Hudson and then back to me again. Her face is set in a scowl, having transformed from her smile, and I notice her gaze once again flicking down at my hand that is clutched tight in Hudson's grasp. I swallow the slight intimidation and wait for her reply.

"The risk is minimal," she says with a nod, giving me her approval, albeit stiffly.

"See. No risk. I want to do this for you, Mom." Squeezing her hand, I hope she understands.

"Hudson?" My mom looks past me to the man on my left, who is holding my other hand so tight that it's near the point of going numb.

"I would like to check your blood levels," he says, and my shoulders tighten. I'm not used to people telling me what I can and can't do. But I take a breath, knowing it comes from a place of worry and my stress levels lower. He cares. He cares for me a lot, and I can see it in his eyes. He's worried for me, and for the first time in a long time, I'm comforted by the fact that someone is in my corner.

"I can do a full blood workup today, Lacy, as well, that will tell me how best to proceed," Melody jumps in, and I nod. She's a professional; she knows what the right and wrong ways are to go about something like this, so if she approves, then that is okay by me.

"Great. Let's do it," I agree instantly, wanting to get the ball rolling.

"Are you sure?" Mom asks.

"I'm sure, Mom. You and me always," I say our little slogan, and she smiles.

"Great. Well, Lacy, let's take a little blood today so we can run some of the tests. I'll put a rush on it and get those results back in twenty-four hours, and then, assuming we get the all clear, we can take the first donation pretty quickly," Melody explains, her tone curt but professional. I'm probably reading too much into it, but I get the distinct feeling she doesn't like me.

"How soon after does the transfusion happen for Mom?" I ask, feeling excited that this is happening. For too long, we've been just going back and forth for basic treatments, feeling like we're getting nowhere, and now we have a solid plan moving forward, which makes me feel more positive.

"I will assess her tests as well, but if it's what I am thinking, we will get a few donations from you initially, and then I think what's best is for your mom to go into the hospital for a few days to take in the transfusion. Because it's her first one and she can have some around-the-clock care. Williamstown will be more than equipped to proceed with both the donation from you and the transfusion for your mom. Hudson, you can manage those appointments for Veronica and Lacy, can't you?" she says, looking at Hudson, and I see him still frowning.

"Sure, we can handle all that locally." He nods once, not seeming too keen on any of this. I squeeze his hand in mine, and he looks at me quickly. When he gives me a small, sad smile, my heart thuds. I feel an overwhelming sense of connectedness to him, and I know he feels it too. I like him taking care of things for me. It's new, and I thought I would hate it, but having him here, wanting his opinion and taking care of me in the small ways he already has, is something that I'm coming to terms with and something that I realize that I not only cherish but also crave.

"Great. Well, I believe we are done. Lacy, let's grab some blood, and I can run those tests for you. Less worry for our local doctor here." She smiles, but I feel a slight hint of sarcasm in her tone directed at Hudson. I ignore it. Mom's health is the main thing and is all that matters.

25

HUDSON

I look at Lacy's blood test results and frown.

"She is more than a fine candidate," Melody says over the phone in a tone that indicates she's agitated, while I am gripping on to the phone like it has a death wish. She flew in here yesterday, did the consult, and flew straight back out. She didn't even have time to see Harvey after school.

"Her iron is too low... and her inflammatory markers look a little off." I tell her the same thing I've been saying for the past ten minutes since I got hold of her. Lacy had her tests done and Melody put a rush on them and got them back in twenty-four hours. While Lacy is fit and healthy, her iron is a little low, her blood pressure is a little high, and I just don't like it. Something feels off.

"Hudson, you asked me to come on board as the specialist. My recommendation is that Lacy is fit and healthy to donate and that a transfusion for Veronica is literally the only thing she hasn't tried at this point. But let's be honest, it may buy her a few extra months, at most." Melody huffs, and while most doctors have a dark sense of humor, Melody's flippancy is somewhat annoying.

"I understand that," I grit out. My inner turmoil about this is causing a pounding in my head.

"Great. But here is something I don't understand..." Melody says as I run my hands through my hair for the hundredth time today.

"What's that?" I ask, looking over Lacy's test results again and again, not wanting to miss anything.

"It seems that you are a little too close to this situation," Melody says, and I pause.

"I'm just trying to look at it from all angles. But you are the expert, and I wanted you here. Veronica is best friends with my mom. I wanted to create a little space between me and her care." I'm not interested in getting into this right now.

"Well, you are a good doctor, so I can believe that. But what I find hard to believe is the way you were holding Lacy's hand in the consultation room and why now you seem more concerned for Lacy's health than that of the patient you brought me in to consult with," Melody says, and I sigh.

"Veronica and Lacy are well-known in the community. Lacy is her primary caretaker..." I start to explain.

"Hudson. I don't need a community history lesson. I know what I saw. Amanda was not only my sister, but my best friend. But if you think you can fuck some young girl from a small town and that I'll be okay with that, then you're mistaken," she spits out.

My anger rises, and I swear if Melody wasn't the

amazing doctor she is, I would not be entertaining this completely inappropriate conversation. "Who I fuck is none of your business. Lacy, outside of the medical support you are giving to her mother, is none of your business. I appreciate you consulting on Veronica's health for me, but if you can't be professional about this and leave this personal bullshit at the door, I might be better to find someone else." I'm protective of Lacy, and there's no way Melody is bringing this bullshit to Whispers. I would like to think her professionalism would be at the forefront, but she was close to her sister, so I should have thought about this more.

"You got me to take time out of my busy schedule to consult for you, and that's what I'm doing. I would have appreciated a heads-up on the entire situation before I started with the consultation. However, what I don't expect is for you to undercut my opinion. In my opinion, Lacy is fine to donate blood to her mother. You either want me to manage this, or you don't, Hudson. Which one is it? Because I have better things to do with my time."

I sit forward and look at Lacy's file again. The numbers look fine, and even though I don't like it, it doesn't mean the facts are lying.

"Fine," I murmur in agreement. Medically speaking, she can. Maybe I'm just too protective and too close to this situation.

"Great. I'm going to manage this process moving forward. I will have my office talk to Williamstown Hospital and organize the donation immediately. We may need a few from Lacy as Veronica's tests did come back showing some issues. And as you know, we need to have some time in between, so the sooner we start, the better," Melody says, and I nod, even though she can't see me. I need to trust her.

"Okay, Melody, we will do it your way," I tell her, closing Lacy's file.

"Good, and Hudson?"

"Yes?" I ask, knowing she has more to say.

"I think you need to take a good, hard look at what you are doing. I always thought you were a smart man. But dating someone so young like Lacy, and Amanda has only been gone a short time..."

"Amanda has been gone for years..." I say, letting my words hang between us as my frustration simmers. I'm a widower, I know that, but how long do I need to remain single before moving on with my life? It's literally been over five years. I need to move on, and I have. I don't need her family's approval, and I find it astounding that I'm getting this attitude from her, considering her own father is a known philanderer and her mother a socialite who turns a blind eye.

"I need to go. I will keep you updated," she says, ignoring my statement, then the line goes dead. I throw my cell on my desk and sit back in my chair as the familiar feeling of despair settles in my chest.

I don't like it. But Melody is the specialist, and while her opinion on my private life is none of her business, I don't want to get in the way of her medical expertise.

I sit opposite Tanner and Connor at the bar. It's quiet tonight. Midweek is always like this, and after the day I have had, I needed a friend.

"Tough day at the office?" Connor asks, watching me closely.

"You could say that," I murmur, lifting the glass of whiskey to my lips, appreciating the burn.

"What's going on?" Tanner asks.

"I got a specialist in from of the city to consult on Lacy's mom," I tell them. It isn't a secret; practically the whole town already knows.

"Lacy said. Melody, right?" Connor asks, leaning back in the booth.

"Yeah," I say, trying to collect my thoughts, wondering if it was such a good idea after all.

"Lacy mentioned her time at work might be a little ad hoc for a while. She needs to give blood?" Tanner frowns.

"It's something for Veronica." I don't elaborate; they don't need details, and while I know they will keep everything confidential, I need to ensure I keep things private, not telling them anything Lacy hasn't already.

"So what's going on with you and Lacy?" Tanner asks, looking me dead in the eye.

"Are you two are a thing?" Connor follows up, and I look at them both.

"Yeah... yeah, we are." There's no point denying it.

"Don't fuck with her. She's my best employee ever. Plus, she's Victoria's best friend," Tanner warns, and I give him a nod.

"Not planning on it." I sip my whiskey as I think about her.

"Aw, double dates in your future, then, boys?" Connor quips, and I smirk. I'm relieved he has no interest in Lacy, even though I initially had reservations about that fact.

"Smart-ass. Just wait your turn," Tanner says with a chuckle, and I smile.

"What turn?" Connor huffs. He's never said anything, but he seems to like the single life.

"Your turn to be pussy-whipped," Tanner says, pointing at him.

"Never going to happen," Connor says, shaking his head like he is having the last laugh.

"Gee, I look forward to the day some woman puts you on your ass," I tell him, grinning.

"Lacy is pretty independent." Connor smirks before lifting his drink to his lips.

"She's smart too. Funny, caring, sexy as hell," I finish for him, smiling as I think about her while Tanner's hard stare hasn't wavered.

"Are you sure?" Tanner asks, and Connor looks at his father before looking back at me.

"I'm sure. I want her and I'm pretty sure she wants me." Lacy doesn't have a father in her life, and while Tanner isn't overly close with her, he is her boss and his girlfriend is best friends with Lacy, so I know he takes the care of her seriously.

"Good to see you back into dating," Connor says.

"Took me long enough." I smile, happy about my connection with Lacy and comfortable with how things are going, even though the conversation with Melody left a bad taste in my mouth.

"I think Dad holds that record," Connor jokes, and I laugh as Tanner grumbles.

"Fuck off, the both of you," Tanner murmurs, which has us both laughing even more.

"Pretty nice bunch of roses you sent her this week. Must have cost you a pretty penny," Connor says, and my smile falters.

"Roses?" I ask, my eyes narrowing, and his cheekiness mellows.

"Lacy got a flower delivery. We all thought it was from you."

"Not this time. I know she likes the roses in the distillery garden, so I never sent any..." I say, suddenly feeling off. If she isn't getting flowers from me, who the hell is sending her flowers?

"When did they arrive?" I ask, knowing Lacy has been off for a little bit lately, especially after witnessing her reaction to whatever she checked on her phone.

"The morning before her mom's hospital appointment," Connor says, and I look at Tanner, seeing him frowning.

"She has never had a delivery of that nature before," Tanner murmurs, and I shake my head. None of it makes sense.

I clear my throat. "It was probably from a friend," I say, my stomach feeling heavy, knowing that Lacy isn't seeing anyone else. But I know she is keeping something from me, and I need to figure out what that is.

"Well, we have the New York trip for Lacy coming up," Connor mentions, trying to change the subject slightly.

"About this New York trip..." I start, because I have

been meaning to talk to them both about it. And especially now. The next few months are not going to be great for Lacy, and I want to do everything I can to make her smile. I just wish I knew what was going on so I could fix it.

26

LACY

I look around the room. I feel a bit cold, but I take a deep breath and put my big girl panties on. I left Mom in the care of Jennifer this morning, after she made me a nice bowl of warm oats while I got ready, acting like the auntie I never had. It has been about a week since she came into our lives, and already there is a difference. I don't feel as rushed; I don't feel like I need to do everything, and my stress levels have lowered. Mom is happier, too. Jennifer shares her love for romance books, so I think they talk for hours about that.

I sped out the door this morning to get here, my usual Saturday routine disrupted to come to Williamstown to donate blood for the first time.

Hudson wanted to drive me, but I needed to do this on my own. Something he wasn't happy about, so he arranged a car and driver to bring me. I couldn't refute it because the shiny new car pulled up in my driveway just as I was walking out the door. His timing is impeccable.

"Well, this is not what I was expecting this morning."

I look up as Jolene walks in the door with a clipboard and a smirk. I forgot she worked here. In all the years Mom and I have been coming here, I have never once seen her. I see her mostly at the diner on Saturday afternoons, greeting me with her usual scowl.

"Hi, Jolene," I say, already tense, and now even more so as she flicks through my patient notes. I frown, not needing her to know any more about my personal business. Professionalism isn't one of her strongest qualities.

"I will be taking your donation today," she says in a curt tone, her bedside manner no better than her usual personality. I wonder briefly if I can press the call button and request someone else.

"Thank you." I decide to be cordial as I watch her hook up the needle and bag, getting everything ready. She at least seems to know what she is doing.

"This is your first time?" she asks, not looking at me, and I take a deep breath. It appears small talk is what we are doing, which is entirely new for us.

"Yes. It's for my mom," I tell her, although I'm sure she knows already.

"Guessed as much," she says as she puts a ribbon around my upper arm, pulling it tight. "Make a fist with your hand and squeeze a few times. I need to find your vein."

I do what she asks, my teeth biting down, anticipation of the sting getting to me.

"Great. Here we go," she says, and I look away as I feel the sharp sting in my elbow, but it eases almost as quickly as it occurs.

"All done. You just need to sit here for a moment. It

will take about five to ten minutes. I will be around, but press the call button if you need anything," she says, packing up her things and tidying up the side counter, not looking at me at all. Closing my eyes, I try to breathe.

I RACE INTO THE DINER, a little late, and as I push through the door, the bells chime, announcing my arrival.

"Ahhh, here she is. I was getting worried," Rochelle says, walking up to me, looking me over in concern.

"I'm here. Better late than never," I say, smiling, even though I feel a little lightheaded.

"Hudson is already here waiting," she says quietly, and I look over her shoulder, seeing Hudson's head down, frowning at his phone in a booth at the back.

"Thanks, Rochelle." Smiling, I notice the booth Jolene and her squad usually occupy now has other patrons.

"Anytime, sweetheart," she says, before getting back to work as I start to walk toward the booth.

"Hey," Hudson says, his face full of worry as he stands when he sees me, striding a few steps to meet me.

"Hi!" I say, bubbly and bright, which I notice eases his shoulders somewhat.

"You're alright? It all went okay?" He grabs my hand, pulling me to him and looking down at my face intently. His other hand runs around my waist to keep me close.

"All fine. It's just a bit of blood," I tell him, like he doesn't already know, and his lips thin, unimpressed.

"It is almost a pint of blood, Lacy. Eight percent of

your total blood volume," he reiterates, and I give him a small smile, even though I do still feel a bit dizzy.

"I'm fine." My hands rest on his chest. I don't need him to worry. I'm doing this for Mom, and a bit of light-headedness is not going to stop me.

"Well, you need sugar so I went ahead and got Rochelle to put together your sundae for you."

Stepping back, I see the sundae on the table already, two spoons waiting nearby.

"Ugh, that looks delicious. I'm starving." We slide into the booth, both grabbing our spoons.

"Did you eat today?" he asks as I pick out the cherry.

"Jennifer made me a delicious breakfast before I left, and I had a sandwich at the donation space."

"So, Jennifer has settled in this week?" Hudson asks as we dig in.

"She's a godsend. She's already like part of the furniture. She cooks, helps with Mom, and they're always chatting about something. I already love having her around."

"Sounds like she is just what you need," Hudson says, scooping up the ice cream.

"Thank you for finding her and locking her in. I know I said it before, but it really means a lot," I tell him honestly, and he gives me a small smile and nod. "This cherry is amazing." I twirl the stem, placing it on the napkin like I usually do.

"So no issues this morning? Everything went well?" he asks again.

I want to tell him giving blood is the least of my worries. I want to tell him that I spent the entire day so far looking over my shoulder, wondering if today is the day my worst nightmare comes to life. I have been doing research, and what I thought was purely infatuation is now obviously stalker behavior, and I barely want to think about it, let alone verbalize it.

"It was all fine. However, my nurse was Jolene," I tell him, rolling my eyes, keeping my real thoughts to myself.

"Oh, I bet that was fun," he says sarcastically. I have told him all about her and her school antics.

"She was surprisingly nice, actually." Nice might be pushing it; maybe *cordial* is more suited.

"I would hope so. She was at work. The care and attention patients need should be at the forefront of everything she does."

"Spoken like a true professional," I tease.

"I got you an extra cherry," he says, turning the sundae dish a little, where I spot an additional cherry on the side. I look at him and raise my eyebrow.

"An extra one? For me?" I ask, my grin now almost taking up my entire face.

"I like watching you eat it and twirling the stem with your tongue," he says, sitting back, and all the concern and lightheartedness we just had now boils down into a simmering heat that has swirled around us since our date.

"You want to feed me, Hudson?" I ask quietly. The diner is busy, but no one is looking at us or paying us any attention. Positioned at the back, we are away from prying eyes. The novelty of seeing us together is slowly starting to wear off, it seems.

He smirks. "Lacy baby, there's a lot I want to do to

you," he murmurs, and my pussy pulses. I move my hand and pick up the cherry by the stem and lift it to my mouth. I have always loved food, and while I don't have time to make elaborate meals or bake all weekend, I do like to enjoy eating different things.

"Put it in your mouth," he tells me, voice low, and I watch him watching me, our eyes glued. I do as he asks, and I dangle the cherry to my lips, my tongue darting out to grab it and pull it into my mouth. I bite down, then swallow the cherry juice, Hudson's eyes trailing the movement of my throat.

"Harvey is at a friend's house for a sleepover tonight," he says, his voice gravelly.

"He is?" I ask, just as my stomach flip-flops.

"I spoke to your mom earlier today. She said Jennifer is free to spend the night with her, so I organized her to sleep over at your place tonight." He continues, and I swallow the rest of the cherry and place the stem on my napkin. I look at him and take another deep breath as his words from weeks ago ring in my mind. *I took care of it.* So I nod in agreement, ready to follow him anywhere he wants to lead me.

"Come home with me?" he asks, and my breathing pauses before I smile. With him taking care of everything else, I only have to worry about me, and right now, there is nowhere else I want to be than with him. I feel a mixture of things—joy and happiness mixed with a healthy dose of trepidation. But he has waited for me. Waited for me to be at ease with him. At ease with leaving Mom, helped me morph into myself and become the woman I was always meant to be.

"Let's go," I say, and his grin is instant as is the way he stands and throws a few bills onto the table.

"My truck is right outside." Putting out his hand, I slip mine into it, stepping out of the booth. The remains of the Saturday sundae now forgotten.

27

HUDSON

I feel almost unhinged as I grab Lacy from the truck.

"Hudson!" she gasps, giggling as I lift her quickly from the seat. God, I love her giggle. She doesn't do it often, so when she does, I feel a rush of endorphins for making it happen.

"Let's go," I say, tone gruff, lifting her bridal style and walking her up the steps. I feel like the luckiest man alive with her in my arms.

"You are insane!" she squeals in delight, and my smile grows. I have been waiting so long for a woman like her. Someone not only smart, funny, and gorgeous, but who will accept me and all that I bring, including my little boy.

"Insane for you," I admit, setting her on her feet, then I open the door and pull her inside. As soon as we are across the threshold, my lips are on hers. My hands wrap around her waist, and I pull her to me. We are toe to toe, my lips consuming hers, and I feel her body soften in my hold as she melts into me.

"Mmmmm... Hudson..." My name is a mere whisper ghosting from her lips onto mine as her hands run up my shoulders before settling behind my neck. I kick the front door closed, then walk her backward, not once taking my lips from hers.

"Lacy baby," I groan, smoothing my hands down her hips to cup her ass, pulling her to me as I step her backward until her back meets the door.

My lips slide from hers, and I drag them down her jaw, her head pushing back as her hands run down my arms to my chest. Her fingers work at my shirt buttons as I pull at her top, wanting it off her, wanting to see her.

"Let me," she says as I pull back just an inch, and she grabs the hem of her top, pulling it from her frame. Following suit, I rip the remaining buttons from my shirt as I pull it open and off my shoulders.

We don't wait before her hands land on my bare torso, nails digging in as I cup her breast. Molding it in my palm, my lips slam back onto hers, my other hand gripping her face and keeping her close. Her lips are warm and wanting against my own as her hands hit my belt, undoing it quickly.

"Are you sure you want this, Lacy?" I ask, because even though I know she does, I want to hear it.

"Yes. I want this. I want you," she says, her chest pushing against mine as my fingers unbutton her jeans. My breathing labored, my skin prickles at feeling her bare body next to mine.

"Are you sure?" she asks, cheeks flushed just as I drop my jeans, kicking off my boots in the process.

"Fuck, I have never wanted any woman more than I do you right now," I tell her honestly before I swallow her smile, my tongue tangling with hers. Lowering her zipper, I push her jeans over her fantastic ass, and she shimmies them down, her underwear going with them as I drop to my knees.

"Wow," she pants, seeing me kneeling before her. Her bare pussy is right in front of me, and my mouth waters at the sight. I lean forward and flatten my tongue, taking a taste of her that has me groaning. Looking up, I watch her head fall back against the wall as her hands thread through my hair.

"Oh shit," she breathes out, and I smile before I fully dive in. Her legs widen as she releases a whimper, leaning against the front door in nothing but a flimsy lace bra that does little to cover her round breasts. I lick her clit, circling it a little with my tongue as my hands glide up her bare legs, stopping at her ass, where I grab her tight and pull her to me.

I moan against her pussy, relishing the feel of her on my tongue, my lips, my face as her hips start to grind. God, I could eat her all day.

"Oh... yes... yessssss" She bites her lower lip before she starts to pant. Her fingers stretch on my scalp, pulling at my hair as her hips move more and more against my face. Her confidence with me rises each time we're together. She has grown her butterfly wings, and she's fucking magnificent with them.

I suck on her clit a little, teasing her before lapping her more, over and over in perfect rhythm.

"Shit, I'm close... Hudson." As her hips move faster, I

know she will explode soon so I flick her clit with my tongue, before I suck on it hard, feeling her legs tremble in my hold.

"Hudson! Oh my God, Hudson!" she screams as her whole body starts to shake, and she comes on my tongue right here against my front door. "Yes, yes... Oooh..." Her voice quivers as she comes down from her high, and I slow my pace, kissing her center, enjoying the feel of her on my face and lips. Her soft bare skin is so smooth and silky; it's my new addiction.

"I think your pussy is my new obsession," I tell her as I skirt my finger gently up and down her opening, not able to resist feeling her and admiring as her body convulses a little at my teasing touch.

"That is such a great stress reliever..." she moans as her head falls forward, and she looks down at me. I see her face free of tension, fears, and responsibilities, and I smile. I have taken the edge off, and now we get to have fun.

I stand, picking her up by her thighs, and I squeeze her ass in my palms as she hooks her legs around my waist, her bare pussy now warm against my pelvis.

"I can walk, you know..." she teases, and I kiss her bare shoulder.

"Don't care. I like to carry you."

Her lips find mine as I turn and run us upstairs. I can't see where I'm going, entirely consumed by this woman, but I find my room and walk inside before I peel her from me and throw her onto the bed.

"And throw me around?" She laughs, as I crawl onto

the bed after her. Quickly removing her bra, she tosses it across the room.

I pause, taking her in. Totally naked, on my bed, in my house.

"Hudson?" she questions, her gaze searching mine as I look back into her eyes. A new, more intent hunger unlocks at the need I see reflected back at me, and I'm immediately on her.

"Fuck, you are beautiful, Lacy," I tell her before my mouth captures hers.

Our movements become frantic, like we have been dying for each other for years, and I feel her hands coast down my chest to my waist, before they land on the waistband of my underwear, the last piece of clothing between us.

"You are so hard..." she murmurs against my lips as she pushes down my underwear. My cock springs up hard against my stomach, and before I understand what is happening, she wraps her hand around my length and gives me a few pumps.

"Lacy," I growl, pressing my forehead against hers as I look down at where she holds me. Precum already glistens as she runs her thumb over the tip, slowly pumping me some more.

"You are so big..." Her sweetly spoken words have me thickening more in her palm.

"Lacy," I say in a warning because I'm right on the edge. How can I not be? I have the perfect woman underneath me. Entirely naked. With limited reserves left, I lean over to my side table and grab a condom from the drawer as her hand continues to move up and down my shaft languidly, exploring, and it feels fucking amazing.

I sit back on my heels and rip open a condom, watching her watching me as I sheath myself.

"How's that no dating going for you?" I tease as I hover over her again, positioning myself between her legs. Feeling her warm, wet pussy, I slide my cock up and down her folds, the action already making her squirm and whimper.

"Is that what this is? Just another date?" she questions just as playfully as I edge inside her. She exhales shakily, and her head pushes back into the pillow as she welcomes me in inch by inch. I'm not a small man, and she has to stretch around me, but I grit my teeth, taking it slow.

"No, this is me making you mine," I say as I pull out a little and push back in, quicker this time. She bites her bottom lip just as I feel her hips lift to take me deeper, and I growl at her eagerness. It makes it harder for me to restrain myself.

"Yours?" she says breathily, looking back up at me, her hands gliding up my bare forearms to my shoulders, her fingers caressing my neck.

"Mine," I confirm, and she smiles as I thrust into her all the way.

"Hudson!" she gasps, her body arching into the mattress as her breasts push up against my naked chest. I lower my head and take her nipple into my mouth. "Make me yours."

Her pleading statement is like music to my ears, and my thrusts quicken as I scoop my hands around her waist, lifting her hips as I start to piston. Both of us moan in unison.

"Fuck, I love your pussy." Our skin slaps as her hands fly up above her head, using the headboard for leverage as her legs widen for me.

"Oooh, shit... Hudson... You're so deep, so good..."

"Wrap your legs around me, baby. Put them around my waist nice and tight," I tell her, and she does, her legs locking my hips in, as I move my hand and start to circle her clit with my thumb. Her panting increases as our hunger does, chasing our orgasms within each other.

She pants and moans as I continue to thrust into her, looking down at her perfect body. Her breasts bounce in time with my thrusts, her mouth dropped open, her head pushed back, and her fingers white-knuckled.

"There you go, just like that. Clench around my cock, baby," I murmur, feeling my release simmering just at the surface as she does just that. I'm not sure sex has ever felt this good.

Her eyes open and she looks right at me, her smile small as her panting increases.

"Yesssss," she whisper-moans, and I know she's close because her hips are moving rapidly against mine, the two of us so frantic the sounds of our skin slapping could almost be comical.

"So perfect. So fucking perfect. You going to come on my cock?" I grit out, barely able to say the words.

She hums, out of breath.

"Be a good girl, Lacy. Let go for me."

"Yes... Yes... Yes!" she screams as her head pushes

back into the mattress and her hips push flush against mine, pussy fluttering around me.

"Fuck," I shout, coming almost immediately as she does. "Damn, baby." I let go, my release so hard my vision turns fuzzy, but through it all, our eyes stay only on each other.

28

LACY

Hudson's body is warm and heavy lying on me, his hard breaths into my neck soothing. Our skin is coated in sweat, our hearts thumping madly, but for the first time in a long time, I'm truly happy.

"Lacy... Baby," he moans, kissing my shoulder, and my grin widens as he moves. "Give me a moment." Pecking my lips, he slides off the bed and into the bathroom, and I place my palm to my heart, resting it, hoping to calm it a little.

"You look happy?" he asks from where he is watching me in the doorway, and only now do I take the time to drink him in. I try to talk, but my mouth opens and no sound comes out as he stalks toward me, completely naked, and I get the full view of Doctor Hudson Hamilton.

"Cat got your tongue?" he teases as he slides back next to me, the condom now taken care of.

"I prefer dogs," I murmur, and he grins.

"Butterflies and dogs. I got it," he says, nodding, his smile genuine.

"And giraffes. I really like them," I say quietly as his hand coasts up my bare stomach and over my pebbling nipple. My body feels liquid, a soothing buzz simmering over my skin at his touch. I have just had two orgasms. Two. Never has that ever happened before, so I'm unsure how my body is burning up for him again already. But it is.

"Giraffes really like you too," he murmurs, then leans forward and kisses me, softly and tenderly, almost like we are trying to freeze this moment in time.

"So this is your room..." I comment as he leans up on his side, his head resting on his elbow, watching me. Going at my pace, just like he said we would.

"For the time being, until we move into our new place," he says, and I let my eyes wander. It's massive, the bed itself bigger than I even knew was possible to make. His windows are large, the late afternoon sun warming the room, and thick luxurious drapes hang on either side. The carpet is soft and warm underfoot, and the decor is what I think Victoria would call luxe minimalist in tones of grays and whites. Not to mention, the bed is the softest I have ever experienced.

"It's nice," I tell him, stretching out my limbs as he continues to draw soft circles on my chest, his hands never once leaving my skin.

"It looks better now that you are in it." His smirk is evident, delight dancing in his eyes. "I like having you in my bed, Lacy. I like spending time with you outside it as well," he says honestly.

"Well, that's good because I don't just share my special Saturday sundae with just anyone," I tease, and he laughs.

"Come, let's take a shower, then I want to cook you dinner."

I almost balk in disbelief. No one has cooked me dinner before. Not like this. Sure, some people drop off casseroles for Mom and me on occasion, especially when she's sick. And Jennifer is amazing in the kitchen. But outside of the chicken soup Hudson arranged from Rochelle the other week, it's been a long time since someone else cooked for me.

"Cook me dinner?" I wonder if I heard him right.

"Yeah. A king cooks for his queen. I might even feed it to you as well..." His words are laced with innuendo.

"You are a charmer, Doctor Hamilton." I sit up and he takes my hand, leading me into the bathroom, which is almost the same size as his bedroom.

"I meant what I said earlier, Lacy..." he says as he leans into the massive shower and turns on the water. I watch it steam up instantly and look around, wondering if this is a shower that caters to the elderly or disabled due to its size, but with the lack of handrails, I assume this is just how billionaires bathe. It makes my bathroom look like a kids' camp shower.

"And what was that?" I ask as I step into the water, heat encasing me immediately, and my muscles relax as I feel him step in behind me. His chest is hard against my back as the water cascades over us.

"You are mine," he murmurs in my ear, the feeling of his words and his breath coating my skin in goosebumps as I lean my head back against his chest.

"I like being yours..." I whisper, as his hands coast up and down my naked sides, his fingers skirting my curves, his lips peppering my shoulders. His hands run up my chest, and he cups my breasts, the water flowing down them as his fingers mold them in his strong palms.

"Good." He grabs the loofah and some soap and runs it across my body. It feels heavenly and calming, and I turn in his arms so I can do the same to him.

"You know you can tell me anything, right?" he asks, and I look at him and swallow. I need to. I need to tell him about college, my professor, but not yet. Not now.

"I know." I nod, smiling, trying to reassure him. I can tell he's concerned and maybe I didn't hide it well enough all this time. I clear my throat and look at his body.

"So, you need to tell me about these," I say, letting my hands skim across his naked torso, looking at the artwork that adorns his chest almost completely. He lifts his hands to lean against the wall behind me, almost caging me in. I continue to soap down his body, before I wrap my hands around his length, him feeling thick and heavy in my palm.

"Hmmmm. It's a bit hard to concentrate when your hands are on me like that." He's eyeing me like he wants to eat me whole, and I giggle but then feel a little woozy.

"Lacy?" Hudson's voice is harsh, and I look back up at him.

"Are you okay?" he asks, standing back a little, changing the heat of the water to be cooler.

"I'm okay," I say as I shake my head.

"Your pupils are a little dilated." Turning off the shower quickly, he grabs a towel.

"I just feel a little lightheaded," I tell him quietly as I rub my eyes, seeing spots.

"Here." Wrapping me in a large soft bath towel, he picks me up, feeling like I weigh nothing and am snuggled into a cloud.

"Carrying me again?" I try to tease, but the concern etched into his brow tells me he's not in the teasing mood anymore.

"Rest here. Let me get you some cool water," he says, striding around the room still entirely naked, water dripping from his frame, to a small fridge in a cupboard I didn't even notice earlier. Walking back, I see him cracking open the bottle of water as I take in a deep breath, my skin cooling and the spots leaving my vision.

"Here, drink," he says, sitting on the bed, and I take the bottle from him and do as he says.

"After your blood donation today, I should have been more careful. I'm sorry," he says, looking remorseful.

"I'm fine. A little lightheadedness is nothing new." I wave my hand at him to ease his concern.

"Nothing new?" he asks tentatively, and I balk.

"Sometimes I feel a little faint, but it's just because I'm so busy," I tell him, again trying to act like it's nothing, and his frown deepens.

"Your iron is a little low. I'm cooking you a steak for dinner."

I smile, and as he looks at me, assessing, his frown

eases, my pupils obviously now normal and the color back in my face. Crisis averted.

"Sounds delicious." I'm already feeling back to normal, and he makes me drink the rest of the water, his concerned frown now almost permanent, before we go downstairs for dinner.

29

LACY

I look into the freezer before I slam it shut and shuffle to my handbag at the kitchen counter.

"Okay, so I have lasagna and a casserole in there, and I've already portioned it out," I tell Jennifer as she looks at me from where she stands in the kitchen, giving me a small warm smile.

"We'll be totally fine. I can cook some fresh meals too," she says in that gentle tone she uses that makes my shoulders lower automatically. Jennifer has been with us for a few weeks now. My mom and I both agreed after Hudson went to the effort of finding her that we would trial it because I needed help. Turns out that it was the best trial we have ever done, and now Jennifer is almost part of the family. She and Mom get along so well it has given Mom an extra pep in her step and more energy than she had before. It has also alleviated so much from my plate, and I struggle to figure out what to do sometimes, because I'm so used to being busy every second of every day. Now I can work a little more, rest a little more, see Hudson a little more. It has been nice and has enabled me to just figure out what life is meant to be like. Giving me the space to breathe and be somewhat normal without the constant guilt that always plagues me. Although that still filters through most days.

"Thank you," I tell her, sighing in relief. It makes this work trip so much easier this time to know that she is here, twenty-four seven for the week.

"Take a breath, Lacy. I'm fine. I can look after myself. Besides, that lovely man of yours said he will be checking in on me," Mom says, obviously fishing for information, and I stop what I'm doing and look at her. She's right. She's looking better than she has ever looked. More color in her face, and she's walking around a lot more, making her own food and drinks, no longer needing me as much as she did just a few weeks ago. That's the way her health has been. Periods of pain, lethargy, sickness, then periods of wellness, energy, and life.

"Hudson is not... I mean, he is..." I struggle to label us because we are having fun, getting to know each other, and while we are exclusive, we haven't really talked about it all and "boyfriend" feels too adolescent, and "partner" feels too formal. "We are just getting to know each other. Just make sure you take your medications. Sleep well. Eat well," I say, drumming it into her.

"Lacy. I'm okay. Just go. Have a wonderful week. See the sights, drink the cocktails, and enjoy. Don't worry about me," she says, smiling, seemingly pleased to see me spread my wings.

"You heard her, she's fine. Tanner said he's going to

drop by tomorrow as well. So let's go!" Victoria says from the open front door where my suitcase waits.

"Oh, I do like that man. I'm such a lucky woman with both Hudson and Tanner now at my beck and call for the week," Mom says with a laugh, and Jennifer chuckles. I take a breath and lower my shoulders.

"Okay, I'm ready," I say, smiling at them both. More excited than stressed now, most likely due to the multiple orgasms that Hudson delivered to me last weekend. My pussy throbs even now, just thinking about it.

"Go! Enjoy the Big Apple. I can't wait to hear all about it." My mom grins before walking to me and giving me a hug, and then she and Jennifer scoot me out the door, while Victoria runs my bag to the truck, where she and Tanner are waiting.

"Thanks, Mom," I say, before giving her one last squeeze, and then I run out the door and jump into Tanner's truck.

"Have you got the itinerary for the week?" Tanner asks us as he drives us to his jet at Whispers airport.

"Check." I look through my iPad at the week's activities we have planned. It's a work trip, but mud wraps, massages, and facials at some of the city's best day spas can hardly be classed as work.

"That Jennifer is a godsend," Victoria comments, and I take a deep breath.

"Literally," I agree, thinking about her.

"What's her story anyway?" Victoria asks, and I smile.

"She is a widow, so she does some patient support work to bring in some casual hours. I'm lucky this week she doesn't have anything else going on so she is able to stay with Mom the entire week. She was happy to offer a discount since she will be eating our food and staying at our place," I tell her, happy with the arrangement.

"Lacy, no other work while you are in New York," Tanner says abruptly, and my head flicks up to look at him. His eyes hold on to the road, but I see his face is serious.

"What do you mean?" I frown.

"Have the week. Enjoy the spas and the research, but otherwise, I want you to have time off. No calls, no emails, no work. You have been working hard these past months, extra hours and whatnot. So when you are not researching the spas, go shopping, sleep in, do whatever it is you want to do." Tanner continues, and my eyebrows rise. "Do you have everything you need for the penthouse?" he asks Victoria, moving the conversations on quickly so I don't have time to answer. He looks at her briefly as we pull up to the jet on the tarmac.

"Yes. I have it all," she says with a nod.

"Call me when you get there," he says, looking at her, and I open my door, not needing to watch them kissing goodbye.

"Glad I caught you." I hear Hudson's voice as I slide out of the truck and look up, startled, seeing him in his signature suit, hands in pockets, watching me with a big grin on his face from the base of the jet stairs.

"Hey! What are you doing here?" I say, surprised, my smile instant as he walks to me, his hand circling my waist and pulling me close.

"I just needed to do this." Cupping my jaw, he tilts my chin up just as his mouth connects with mine. I grip onto his waist as we deepen the kiss, my heart rate escalating immediately, but with so much activity going on around us, the kiss is all too brief when we pull away from each other.

"I wanted to see you before you left. Say goodbye," he murmurs, his lips buried in my hair as he pulls me tight. I sigh. Contented and happy to be in his embrace, I wrap my hands around him and squeeze. For the first time that I can ever remember, things feel good. Mom is healthy, the support we have is helping, Hudson is sweeping me off my feet, and life is the best it's ever been. If only I could stop looking over my shoulder every hour...

"You've been busy too?" I ask him, knowing I was busy preparing for the trip and he had a few late-night emergencies at the hospital he had to work on. I'm not sure where he gets the stamina. He obviously doesn't have to work so I put it down to his small-town upbringing. The urge to help people in the community runs strong with most people around Whispers. We are a tight-knit community, and I think being born and raised here instilled that in Hudson. His need to help others and provide his skill here in the small town to those who need it drives him. He isn't a man who can just travel the world and lie on luxury yachts all day; he needs to contribute, and I think that is one of the things I like about him the most. His empathy for others, along with his work ethic.

"Life of a doctor. Nothing too dramatic, but night duty has kept me busy this week. Are you excited?" he asks, pulling back and looking down at me as I spot Tanner's people run to the trunk to grab our bags. Traveling via his private jet is a low-stress way to fly, and I'm completely grateful I get to experience it.

"I am." I smile. "Not sure which I am looking forward to the most. If it's massages, mud wraps, or hair spas?" I say teasingly, and he grins. I almost stumble as Hudson with a grin is a sight to see.

"Good. Don't worry about your mom. I will check on her every day too," he says, and I nearly swoon.

"Thank you, appreciate it," I tell him honestly.

"Oh, looky here," Victoria teases, coming to join us.

"Hey, Victoria," Hudson says, pulling away from me and greeting her.

"Tanner." He shakes hands with his friend.

"I should be surprised that you are here, but I'm not," Tanner says with a smirk, watching the two of us closely.

"Well, us girls need to go. Don't miss us too much, boys!" Victoria singsongs as she grabs my hand and pulls me along and out of Hudson's embrace.

"Bye!" I say to him with a bright smile, and he and Tanner stand next to each other, watching us go with clear longing in their eyes. Victoria and I run up the stairs and into the jet, and I take in a deep breath, feeling totally smitten. Stepping in, I make my way down the plane and fall into one of the large white soft leather seats.

"Lacy. This is for you." The hostess comes up and delivers a small box before she continues to organize the plane for takeoff.

"Oh, what is it?" Victoria asks, smiling, sitting in the seat opposite me, and even though I know I'm safe, my hands shake a little, and I'm too scared to open it.

"Well, don't just sit there, open it!" Victoria says excitedly, and I take a deep breath. Putting the small box on my lap, I pull it open. When I see what it is, my shoulders lower, relief filling me instantly as I laugh.

"What? What is it?" Victoria sits forward to get a glance as I pull out the small note.

For practice while you are away. Hudson.

"Is that a jar of cherries?" Victoria asks, looking confused.

"A jar of Maraschino cherries with the stem on. From Hudson."

"I don't understand, and we now have a few hours to kill, so let's get champagne and you can fill me in on all the details. A man like Hudson doesn't just come to the airport to say goodbye or give a jar of cherries for no reason."

"He shares my sundae..." I tell her, not having had the time to go into detail with her about Hudson and me before now.

She raises her eyebrow, intrigued. "Well, do tell..." She wiggles her eyebrows as the plane door closes and we prepare for takeoff.

"Ahhh, where do I start..." I groan while grinning, not able to stop the beaming smile I get when I think about him.

"You know I want all the delicious details."

"He is just..." I start to say, thinking of what I want to say. "He's just everything a girl could want. I mean, he is older and wiser and funny and clever and so caring."

"That ticks a lot of boxes," she says, taking a sip of champagne.

"It does, and he's obviously good with Mom and her

medical needs. But it's the way he is with me. He puts me first." As I verbalize my thoughts, I feel a jolt of realization and my body stills.

"You've never had that before, have you?" Victoria asks quietly, watching me carefully as I grapple with these overwhelming feelings.

Of course I know I'm my mom's number one priority, but she is sick, and her health has to come first. I have missed out on birthday parties, a few Christmases, school trips. Moving away to college was my first time ever where I put myself first and look how that turned out.

"I feel selfish just thinking about it," I tell her honestly, because it's such a first-world problem.

"Not at all. Lacy, you have been through so much," Victoria says, and I take a deep breath and nod, sipping the champagne and feeling the bubbles dance on my tongue, keeping my mouth closed. She doesn't know about college. No one does.

"It wasn't until I met Hudson that I felt like I was anyone's first choice or first thought or first anything."

"I can't imagine what that feels like," she says, sorrow in her eyes, and I give her a smile, not needing any more pity.

"It's fine. I'm used to it." I wave her off, trying to lighten the tone of the conversation, which got serious quickly.

"That's why you have been doing everything yourself, isn't it?" she asks, looking at me.

"What do you mean?" I take another sip, needing the liquid courage.

"Well, you felt like there was no one in your corner?

No one you could rely on? No one there to catch anything or do anything or handle anything."

I stay silent and give her a nod.

"Hmmm, and then sexy Hudson Hamilton came to town and swept you off your feet and is starting to make you feel like he could be the one who takes care of every-thing?" She says the same words Hudson has said to me a couple of times, and I swallow.

"I mean, I'm independent. I don't need a man..." I start to say.

"Maybe not. But you are allowed to want one. You are allowed to enjoy Hudson, spend time with him, laugh with him, have hot, sweaty sex with him..." she says, hitching her eyebrow, and I can't help the wide smile that spreads across my face at her words.

"I knew it! You've gotten down and dirty with the new doctor. Okay, I need details, and please do not skip anything, because this is normal, Lacy. Wanting a man, being giggly over a new romance, and you, my friend, deserve it more than anyone."

The guilt of putting myself first still lingers, but I know she's right. This is all normal and I deserve it just as much as anyone else.

So I tell her everything. I give her an update on my life, all the while holding the jar of cherries, not once thinking about the stress of leaving my mom, and my smile never leaves my face.

30

LACY

"Oh, we should totally get that," Victoria says to me as I try on a new little black dress. We have shopped and eaten our way around the city this week, all the while partaking in one spa treatment per day and making notes for the development of our own Whiteman's spa back at the distillery.

"Agree. It will match those hot black heels you got yesterday," Victoria's friend, Fiona, says from where she is sitting, bags at her feet from her own shopping today.

"It's a bit out of my price range..."

All week us girls have had a blast, and it's the most fun I've ever had. I've spoken to Mom every day and she's thriving. Apparently, Jennifer joined her at the knitting club in town, and the two of them have not only been knitting a new blanket for next winter, but Mom is now even more embedded into the community, meeting new ladies and old ones, bringing her more support than she's ever had.

"Not true. It's on sale," Victoria says, pulling at a sign

in the store that says thirty percent off everything. I smile. I've indulged more than I ordinarily would this week. On everything. I have a few new outfits, feel like I have put on ten pounds due to the restaurants we've been eating at thanks to the work expense account, and Fiona and Victoria took me to a moody cocktail bar last night. Fiona met some man here a while ago and was hopeful she might see him again. He didn't turn up, but we did make our way through a pretty extensive cocktail list, the slight thump in my head a reminder of our time.

"Okay, done. This is the last thing I'm buying, though. I have officially gone over budget," I tell them, my small savings taking a little hit, but nothing that I can't make up for once I get back to work.

"I think your new doctor will like seeing you in this," Fiona teases, and I smile as I look at my reflection. The dress fits like a glove, but that isn't what catches my eye. It's my face. The dark circles that were always around my eyes have lessened. My skin looks brighter, probably due to the facials and massages. My shoulders are lower and pushed back, posture tall, my body appearing more confident.

"From what I've heard, I think Hudson would prefer it off her body..." Victoria says under her breath, just loud enough for us to hear. I look at her quickly as Fiona giggles, and they seem like they have sort of private joke happening.

"Ahhh, anything you care to share?" I ask because, clearly, she knows something.

"Nope. Nothing. But we do need to get going. We have that other spa at three."

~

"Oh my God, I love my job..." I murmur to Victoria as the elevator takes us up to Tanner's penthouse after an afternoon of total bliss. The massage today covered me in warm oil, and I'm so relaxed I can barely keep my eyes open.

"Me too," she says as the elevator opens, and we walk inside.

"What's going on?" I balk, seeing all our bags packed and waiting near the door.

"Change of plans." Turning to look at me, she gives me a grin that looks mischievous and my fight-or-flight immediately kicks in.

"Victoria?" I ask, looking around, seeing nothing else amiss.

"Well, I'm going home," she says abruptly.

"What?" I ask, shocked. We only have a few more days, but I am surprised she is leaving early.

"I need to get back. Something has come up with Griffin and the new project we are working on, so my week of luxury has come to an end. I'm flying back in the jet today."

I pout because we're having so much fun. But like me, she works hard, and she loves her job in interiors, and if Griffin needs her on a project, she needs to be there.

"But what about our treatment tomorrow?" I ask, assuming I'll need to go it alone.

"Well... Connor is coming. He's going to do it while you have the last few days free of work to relax," she says, and I almost choke.

"Connor?" I almost shriek because that is the most ridiculous thing I have ever heard.

"Tanner made him. And your ride is waiting downstairs," she says coyly.

"Ride?" I ask, confused. My mind is still drifting off somewhere in relaxation land and not connecting properly.

"Just trust me." She steps toward me, hugging me quickly before she brushes down my hair and fixes my top. "Let's go," she says, grabbing her suitcase and wheeling it back into the elevator.

"For the record, I have no idea what is happening right now. My mind is firmly in the Bahamas with that coconut oil massage we just had," I say to her, just following her lead as I grab my bag, and we go back down. I assume I'll stay at a hotel somewhere. Although I do miss Hudson. These few days away have been amazing, but I'm longing to see Hudson, talk to him, touch him.

"It was a good massage," Victoria says as we watch our elevator descend.

"If you are taking the jet today, do I need to book my own flight home?" I ask as the elevator opens to the lobby, and we step out onto the polished marble.

"Ahhh, no... that's kinda taken care of..." she says, and I frown, before I look up and almost skid to a stop.

"Hudson?" I gasp at the man who is currently standing before us.

"Aaaaaand that is me out. Have a fun few days, you two," Victoria teases as she continues walking out of the lobby, into her waiting town car, giving me no chance to challenge her.

"What is going on?" I ask, looking back at Hudson.

"Well. Victoria had to head back, and I have a few days off after almost a week of night shifts kicking my ass, so I thought I would meet you here in the city, take you on another date." Walking toward me slowly, he looks at me expectantly.

"A date?" I ask, watching him, my mind finally connecting, and then I feel the oil in between my toes and almost scrunch my nose at how gross I must look right now. I'm going to kill Victoria. "But where will I stay?"

"With me. I've taken care of it," he says, stepping toward me and grabbing my hand, our toes almost touching. There are those words again. Those magical words that cloak me in a softness I have never experienced before. I look up at him, and he brings his fingers to my jaw, running them across my skin softly.

"You've taken care of it?" I confirm.

"I've taken care of it." He nods, a small smile dancing on his lips. I take in a breath, smell his cologne, and nod along with him.

"Okay," I breathe out, before he bends, his lips touching mine, and I melt, happy to be in his hold again.

HUDSON

Fuck, I have missed her. She's been gone only a few days, and I tried to give her space and not call her too often, knowing that she was on a girls' trip, but it killed me. The fact that she was miles away and I couldn't see her whenever I wanted to felt gut burning, and that's how I knew that this is serious. Lacy and I and whatever we're doing. There has been no other woman in my life who has me this needy.

My body has been itching for her, my dick permanently hard, which is a difficult task when I was dealing with farming accidents and sickness all week. It's one of the reasons I spoke to Tanner and Connor about this trip a while ago. They agreed that Lacy needed a break, and along with Victoria, this plan was hatched. I wasn't sure I could come to meet her until the last minute, but with me working too many hours and needing a visiting doctor to come in for a few days anyway, it was almost like the stars aligned. Harvey was also looking forward to spending the weekend with his grandparents, and when I dropped him off with them, I'm not sure who was more excited, him or my parents.

I smile as I think about Lacy when she came down in the elevator earlier today. I could see the shock on her face when she saw me, and while I know she's happy, I still wanted to give her the time and space to get everything sorted in her mind. So I remained a gentleman as we drove the short distance to my own penthouse, refraining from pouncing on her.

Here, on the Upper East Side, with uninterrupted views of Central Park, I had my staff pack the kitchen with food and stock the bar with whiskey and wine. I felt pride as I showed Lacy around my city home, watching her eyes alight with admiration for my high ceilings and polished finishes.

Now as the sun sets, I wait for her at my bar. Two fingers of Whiteman's in my hand, I shoot off a few emails on my cell as she gets ready for our date. I had a team of stylists from Saks do some shopping, and I filled half of my closet with clothes for her because I wasn't sure what she had brought with her. I had the second bedroom rearranged into a dressing room, so she had her own bathroom if she wanted and her own space to utilize. I have two other guest rooms, so it isn't like I needed the bed.

My plan is to take Lacy out for dinner at a Michelin star restaurant. I know she loves food, and it's one of the best in the city. So I ensured the stylist included some evening dresses, but also jeans and casual clothes for tomorrow. Victoria told me I needed options, so I did as Lacy's friend said and practically purchased the entire store. Her cell is here next to me, as is her purse and her lip gloss, and it vibrates, catching my attention. A number is on the screen, and it's somewhat familiar, but I can't place it as the ringing ends and goes to voicemail.

"Since you didn't tell me where we're going, I just picked a dress that I thought you would like." Her voice penetrates through the quietness of my open-plan living room, and I look up, needing to grip on to the bar in front of me for stability at the sight.

"I think I need to cancel our reservation," I murmur as I stand, throw back the remaining whiskey, then stride toward her.

"You don't like it?" she asks, frowning, looking down at herself.

"On the contrary. I just don't want any other man looking at you tonight, and in this dress, every pair of eyes in the city will be on you," I tell her as my eyes travel down her body and back up as I come to stand in front of her. She looks fucking breathtaking. The dress compliments her feminine shape, highlighting the curves of her hips, her voluptuous breasts, and her amazing ass.

"I can change?" she asks, a slight tease in her tone, and my nostrils flare as I look at her face. Her skin is fresh and glowing, makeup minimal, except for some bright-red lipstick, which I want coating my cock later. Under the light, her eyes dazzle and hair shines, slicked back into a tight low bun at the nape of her neck.

"You look stunning, Lacy," I tell her seriously, my voice deep as my eyes do another canvas of her body. The red satin dress is long, grazing the floor and skimming over her body like water. Held up by two thin straps over her shoulders, I can tell she isn't wearing a bra, and I reach out, smoothing my hand up the soft fabric at her hips, not feeling any underwear underneath either.

"It isn't really underwear friendly..." she whispers as I bow my head to meet hers, our noses almost touching.

"You are making it very hard for us to leave." I hold back a groan as my fingers walk up the fabric at her upper thigh.

"If we don't leave, we'll be late..." Her breath quickens as my nose nudges hers, but I keep my lips just an inch away from her glossy red pout. My eyes stay pinned on hers as my fingers gather the soft fabric in my hand, lifting it up her leg.

"I have missed you this week, Lacy baby," I croon as my fingers trail her warm skin, from her upper thigh to her hips, confirming she is not wearing anything under this dress.

"How much?" she teases, the warm breath of her words hitting my lips as they hover dangerously close to her own. I skirt my hand around the front of her hip to feel her bare pussy, and she whimpers at the soft touch.

"Just as much as you have missed me, it appears," I murmur as I slide my finger along her folds, feeling her wetness. I spread it around as she grabs on to my forearms for balance.

"Hudson... the dress..." she warns, but I wrap my other hand around her waist to hold on to her, my fingers now circling her clit. My pants grow tighter, my dick now rock solid.

"Don't move and the dress will be fine. Stay completely still, Lacy." I circle her clit over and over again, pulling breathy moans from her throat. Her forehead meets mine, her chest rising and falling more quickly.

"I can't..." she pants, as she leans forward into my hold, and I squeeze her tight.

"You can. Stand still. Feel my fingers fucking you." I push inside her warm center, first with one finger, then with two.

She moans, our eyes still pinned to each other, her panting, me gritting my teeth so hard they might crack.

"Fuck, I missed your pussy," I growl, swallowing as my mouth waters just thinking about it. My palm moves, rubbing against her clit, my fingers thrusting at a slow, sensual rhythm.

"It missed you too..." she breathes out, and I feel her body starting to shake in my arms.

"This is just to take the edge off, baby, until we get home later," I murmur, and I hear her take a sharp intake of breath as her head lolls back. She pants my name, gripping me tighter as I thrust harder and bring my lips to her ear. "I'm gonna make you come so hard you feel me for days."

"Hudson!" she cries out, her mouth opening in the perfect red 'O' as she grinds down on my hand. As she shakes and pulses, I pinch her clit, relishing how she comes undone in my hands.

"That's it... Good girl," I purr as her head falls forward and meets my forehead again. She whimpers when I remove my hand and let her dress flutter to the floor, her eyes opening to look right into mine. Bringing my hand to my mouth, I lick my fingers clean, watching a renewed hunger flare in her gaze.

"Now we are ready to go," I tell her with a smile, one she returns, and we walk out of the penthouse down to my waiting town car, her steps a little unsteady and me with a raging hard-on.

32

———

LACY

"So I'm guessing you love the dress?" I tease him as I hold his hand and step out of the car. This town car is luxurious, the driver in a proper suit, now parked right outside the restaurant. A small breeze skirts across my bare shoulders as Hudson hooks his fingers in mine and lifts my hand to his lips.

"I'm going to love it even more when I get to take it off you and see your beautiful body," he murmurs against my skin, just loud enough for me to hear, and the heat I felt before is now back with full force. I was flushed moments ago in the car and tried to put myself back together as best I could after he brought me to an orgasm with his fingers. It was unexpected, hot as hell, and left me feeling more relaxed than any massage ever could.

I still can't believe I have a few days off. I haven't taken any leave from the distillery since I started, and any spare moments I get, I'm managing things for Mom, so a day or two in the city with Hudson is really special. I have already spoken to Mom this afternoon, and she's doing well, so I'm letting myself just go with it all and enjoy every moment.

"There were a lot of dresses to choose from. You didn't have to buy all those clothes," I admonish him as we walk across the sidewalk. I frown a little, thinking about it all. The closet was full of female clothes, all new and still with tags. All in my size. I know Victoria helped him, but I still feel overwhelmed and left the tags on everything so they can be returned. The gifts are too much, too expensive, and not something I can ever pay back.

"Take what you want back to Whispers and leave the rest here for when we come back," he says like this is my life and we will just spend our time between the two places. My heart skips a beat at the thought. *Could this be my life?* The more time I spend with Hudson, the more I'm falling for him. The glimpses I'm getting of what it would be like doing life with him fill me with excitement and joy, from fancy dinners in New York to helping Harvey with homework back in Whispers. As the restaurant door opens and we step inside, I push those thoughts to the side.

"Mr. Hamilton. Welcome back, sir." A man in a three-piece suit greets us. "Right this way."

We follow him through the restaurant to a table for two down the back, away from prying eyes.

"People are looking at us," I murmur, my cheeks heating as every pair of eyes in the room turns our way. I look around and while we are dressed formally, so is everyone else.

"They are looking at you, wondering how I managed to get someone so young and beautiful on my arm,"

Hudson says, smiling like he doesn't have a care in the world. We haven't talked much about our age difference, primarily because it doesn't seem to matter to either of us anymore. But I'm aware of how young I look, and while thirty-six isn't old, Hudson does look a little older and certainly very distinguished, so people will come to their own natural conclusion on that.

"Are you flirting with me, Doctor Hamilton?" I toy with him as we arrive at our table. I like feeling like this. Carefree, natural. Just a girl with her man, enjoying life without the daily stresses that compress me in Whispers.

He holds out my chair for me to sit, and when I do, he leans over and kisses my bare shoulder. Shivers skitter around my body at the touch before he takes his own seat opposite me.

"Is it working?" he asks with a quirked eyebrow, and I laugh as the waiter leaves us with the menus.

"You don't need to flirt. You had me at *for good*," I tell him, the honesty whipping from me so suddenly, I feel my cheeks blush.

"For good?" he questions, confused.

"The first words you said when you were sitting in my armchair the first week you were home." Feeling nervous at my admission, my breath catches, and a feeling of warmth spreads through me. I watch Hudson thinking, his lips relaxing into a small smile and his eyes dancing in delight. I feel a little vulnerable, and I swallow roughly, waiting for his response.

"I wanted to see you that day. While I knew I needed to check your mom, it was you I really wanted to see," he says, and my mouth opens a little in surprise before I smile even wider.

"Champagne, sir?" The waiter appears at our side.

"I think so. I feel the need to celebrate," Hudson tells him. His eyes don't waver from mine as he grabs my hand in his on the table, his thumb brushing across my skin.

"What are we celebrating?" I ask as I take my glass and he takes his.

"To the start of something pretty special." Lifting his glass in a cheers, I copy him, my stomach fluttering at the look in his eyes.

"To the start of something special," I say, grinning like a fool. That's exactly what it feels like. The start of our lives together. I take a sip, the bubbles dancing on my tongue, and Hudson orders us dinner. Again, thinking of me and my needs by ordering us two steaks, because they are good for my iron levels.

I TAKE the last sip of the French champagne as I finish off my meal. I haven't eaten out at a restaurant like this before. In college, I worked at the local dive bar, and back home, the closest place to eat out is the diner or Whiteman's Bar. The restaurants Victoria and I visited this week were nice, but nothing like this. This restaurant is next level. If Jolene could see me now, her stare would be searing. She would be green with jealousy.

"Penny for your thoughts?" Hudson asks, leaning back in his chair and watching me closely.

I give him a small smile. "Just thinking about Whispers," I tell him honestly, and he smiles as his phone vibrates. He checks it quickly before his smile widens and he laughs.

"What?" I ask, smiling automatically.

"Connor. He hates me because I'm here with you and he has just flown in so he can do the treatment tomorrow and then spend the weekend."

I giggle at that, and Hudson looks at me curiously, his smile still wide. "What?"

"It's just..." I start to say, my laughter interrupting my words. "Tomorrow's treatment is a little different from the others." I'm already imagining Connor and what's going to happen tomorrow.

"Different?" Hudson asks, pocketing his phone. "Different how?" Sitting forward, he grabs my hand on the table, his focus entirely on me.

"Well, Victoria and I planned to try something totally out of left field... Tomorrow's treatment is a sound healing massage, followed by yoga flow at this small wellness center on the outskirts of town," I explain, and he pauses for a bit before he throws his head back and barks out a loud laugh.

I can't help but laugh along with him, and a few people nearby glance at us.

"Ohhh, I would pay money to be a fly on that wall," Hudson says, cackling, wiping his eyes.

"I just feel sorry for the therapist." Connor is going to hate every minute of it. "He's probably expecting an hour-long relaxation massage, not something like sound healing."

"Yoga is going to be like hell for him," Hudson agrees, still smirking.

"I'm surprised he came," I say, my hand now warm and tingling from his touch.

"Well, the Jets play tomorrow night, so he was keen to sit in his suite to watch the game," Hudson says, and I roll my eyes. Connor is such a boy. Whiskey, football, and women are his priorities. In that exact order.

"Dessert for you," the waiter interrupts, and I sit back as he places a small slice of cherry pie onto the middle of the table with a scoop of vanilla ice cream.

"Cherries?" I say to Hudson as the waiter leaves us again.

"Every time I think of cherries, I think of you." He picks up a spoon and points it at me.

"They are delicious," I tell him, grinning. The cherry pie before me looks amazing, and my mouth is already watering.

"You're delicious," he murmurs as I grab a spoon and take a bite. It tastes just as good as it looks, and the fire in Hudson's eyes burns me up in the best way.

"Hmmmm, there is that flirting again," I hum as we slowly eat the pie, the temperature between us only escalating.

"I'm not flirting, I'm being completely factual. There is nothing else I would rather eat," he says too smoothly, and I fail to breathe.

"Than me?" I ask quietly, my eyebrow raised.

"Than you," he confirms, his sexy smirk only growing at my shy reaction. I readjust in my seat as my pussy pulses at his words. He is so good at that, and now it's all I want.

"I think we should call it a night." Putting down my spoon, I wipe my lips teasingly slow with my napkin.

"Check, please?" Hudson says with a raise of his hand, and the waitstaff scramble. He stands immediately, eyes on mine as he takes my hand, and we are out the door in under ten seconds flat.

33

HUDSON

We push through the door to my penthouse like we have just been unleashed.

"This fucking dress," I growl, pulling it from her shoulders. The fabric is so light and dainty, it glides to the floor, leaving her completely fucking naked in nothing but a pair of gold strappy stilettos that do something to my insides that has my knees nearly buckling.

"You like the shoes too?" she hums, and my eyes flick from her feet to her eyes. The smug look of satisfaction is about to be fucked right off her face.

"You're teasing me," I growl. As I rip the dinner jacket from my shoulders and slam my lips into hers, her hands cup my face, pulling me to her.

"I like teasing you," she murmurs against my lips as I grab my shirt and rip it open, buttons flying across the room. I yank it from my body, not giving a shit that I just ruined it.

Her hands are already opening my belt, and I kick off

my shoes as our lips continue to consume each other, our need evident, like a palpable presence surrounding us. I've been hard for her since we left for the restaurant, and now I'm almost at the boiling point.

"I like everything about you," I groan as I kiss down her neck. She unzips my pants, and they quickly join her dress on the floor at our feet. I don't stop my lips as I kiss down her chest, taking a nipple in my mouth and sucking as she pushes down my underwear, me walking her farther into my penthouse. The two of us are now naked, the only thing on her body the high gold heels that I want digging into my back.

"Oh God, I need you..." she says with such a lustful desire as her eyes take me in, and I feel like the fucking Hulk.

"You've got me." I grip on to the back of her thighs, lifting her to me. Her legs wrap around my middle with ease as I walk us a few steps to the windows. The city lights sparkle below, and she inhales a sharp breath as the bare skin of her back touches the cool glass panel. Her nipples pebble, goosebumps littering her soft skin, her face glowing, and I can't wait another second to run my lips over every inch of her, licking, tasting, kissing all over.

"You're mine, Lacy baby. All mine," I grit out, feeling almost feral. The two of us are so urgent for each other we have left a trail of clothes on the ground in our wake, our hands gripping and exploring, lips kissing wherever we can reach as we pant. But the words are not a lie. She is mine. In every way possible. I'm completely enamored by this woman, feeling with certainty that she is the one. The one person who was put on this earth for me.

"Fuck me, Hudson," she begs, and that is all the invitation I need before I position myself at her core. Her legs tighten around me slightly, and I slide into her easily, feeling like I'm truly where I belong.

"Oh God," she exhales as her head falls back against the window, and I start to move in earnest. I'm demanding, my hips pushing against hers, the sensations almost overwhelming with her wrapped around me.

"So perfect, Lacy. You are so fucking perfect." My teeth gnash together when she moans beautifully in response, because I don't want to come too soon. I'm not sure if it was the champagne or the fact that we are somewhere new and different and out of Whispers, but she's totally relaxed tonight and getting more confident with me by the second. Her body jolts against the glass with every one of my thrusts, her hands threading into my hair, the familiar sting at my scalp turning me on even more.

"Hudson... Oh God, this feels so good," she moans and whimpers, her voice like a caress along every nerve ending. My cock thickens and throbs as our skin slaps together, the two of us chasing our high like the world is ending. It's then I realize we forgot a condom.

"Fuck, Lacy. Condom," I grit out, not stopping, but slowing my pace until her eyes meet mine again.

"Don't stop. Hudson, don't you dare stop." Her eyes are wild, cheeks flushed, and without another second of waiting, she's grinding against me for more.

"I'm clean," I tell her, wanting us to be safe.

"You are the only person I have been with since college. I'm on protection, though," she says, breathless, and I brush my lips against hers, our tongues dancing as my thrusting continues. Her body jolts in my arms where I hold her against the window as my hand smooths between us to find her clit, rewarding me with a dragged-out moan of my name.

Lights glitter outside, and I can't fathom the fact that the world carries on as normal while I'm gripping her ass, white-knuckled, not able to get close enough to her. I have her exactly where I need her, but I still want more. The understanding that I will never get enough of this woman dawns on me as my jaw clenches and my arms flex, feeling so much emotion and giving all to her. It has been a long time since I was bare with a woman, my late wife the last time, and I don't remember it feeling like this.

"So good, more. It's so good," Lacy whines, and I squeeze her ass in my palm, bringing her to meet me with every thrust. It's too much, and I know she will bruise, but her hips are joining mine, and I need to fulfill her need. When my fingers pinch, then circle her clit softly, in complete contrast to how we're fucking, her hand leaves my hair and slaps against the glass, body arching. She looks fucking amazing, and this is the hottest sex I have ever had in my entire fucking life.

"Hudson, you're gonna make me come. Please don't stop," she warns, and I smirk. Fuck yeah, she is.

"Me too, baby. You have me so damn hard," I moan, kissing up her neck, feeling my balls tighten as her hips move quickly against mine.

"Oh shit, Hudson," she pants, her voice a little higher pitched as her hand comes back and she grips on to my shoulders.

"Let go, baby. Let me feel you come on my cock," I grit out, and my words are enough to have her coming.

"Hudson!" she screams out into the penthouse, her fingers digging into my shoulders so hard I grimace, but I barely feel the pain as I come straight after her with a roar.

"Lacy!" I thrust into her, my hand clenching her ass as I come. The two of us pant, sweating and moaning, her head falling forward and resting against mine. We are silent for a moment, our rapid breathing all that we can hear as I kiss her lips tenderly.

"That was..." she says, barely able to get the words out. She now feels like jelly in my arms, and I huff a laugh because I can barely stand up as well.

"Amazing," I finish for her, keeping us together as I pull her back from the window.

"Do you think anyone saw us?" she asks almost timidly, glancing over her shoulder at the window as I walk her to the bedroom.

"I don't care. I want the world to know you are mine," I tell her, and her head whips around to look at me with the softest smile.

"And you are mine," she says seductively as I kick the bedroom door closed. Her words hold meaning, and as we look at each other, I know something has cemented between us. This is it. She is it. So with the night still young, I carry her to bed, knowing we both want more.

34

———————

LACY

"Are you ready to head home tomorrow?" Hudson asks me as we sit together on the sofa, looking out at the city lights surrounding us. With the fire on and soft music playing, I lean into his body, his arm draped around me, and I sink into this comfort. This is nice. The time we've spent together outside of Whispers has bonded us like we were always meant to be. I feel completely comfortable with him and have fallen more for the man who continues to sweep me off my feet. There is no turning back for me. He is it; I just know it.

"Yes, although," I say, stretching my limbs. My legs extend to their full length, yet still I can't hit the edge of the sofa, it's that big. "I could get used to this." Smiling, I release a content sigh. These past few days together in New York have been amazing. We've played tourists during the day and can't keep our hands off each other at night. It's like our own little private love bubble, and I've felt every bit the smitten woman I am.

"Mmm, it's nice for a break," he says, sipping on his glass of red wine.

"It's been wonderful. Thank you." Turning up and literally whisking me off my feet these past few days has been amazing. It's every girl's dream. Looking at him, really taking him in, something lingers in my mind, but I've been tentative to bring it up until now. "Can I ask you something?"

"Anything. I'm an open book for you," he says with a kiss to my head, and I smile as I find the courage.

"Tell me about your wife." My nerves swirl, not sure I'm ready to put myself through hearing all about the love of his life. But I feel if we are getting as serious as I think we are, then this is a bridge I need to cross.

"Amanda was..." he trails off, and I hold my breath. "She was the life of the party. We met at a mutual friend's place and got along well."

"Were the two of you together long?" I have no idea of his history, other than he was married, so the fact that he loved someone so much before makes me wonder if that is something he is capable of feeling again.

"We knew each other for about three months when she fell pregnant. It was a total surprise and scared both of us. We were pretty casual, just hanging out. But she wanted to keep the baby, and I wasn't about to leave her to face it all alone. So we had a shotgun wedding. We then found out she had cancer in her last trimester, and she died before Harvey turned one. I knew her for less than two years before she died. She was a great woman," he says, releasing a heavy breath, and I swallow past a lump in my throat. My chest hurts for his loss, and my stomach coils in what I think is jealousy, even though I have no right to feel that way.

I remain quiet, thinking it all through.

"She wasn't the one. Never was. As I said, we hooked up, went to a few parties with friends. Next thing I knew, she was pregnant with Harvey about three months after we started hanging out. It all happened pretty fast, and nothing was planned. Amanda was not in love with me either. We had a good time, got along well, but being together seriously and especially having a child together, none of that was what we wanted with the other," he says, and my jealous feelings of his late wife all dissipate in an instant. But it doesn't lessen how unfortunate the whole situation is, how badly I feel for her loss.

"I'm sorry. For both you and Harvey," I say genuinely.

"Harvey doesn't really know any different. It has always just been the two of us... until now." He's looking at me intently as our spare hands connect and our fingers intertwine.

"He is the sweetest boy. You have done a great job raising him," I tell him honestly.

"Do you want kids?" he asks me, and I take a breath.

"Yeah. I do. I love them," I say, and his smile widens, clearly happy with my answer.

"I have a question for you now."

I settle back against his body and take another sip of my wine, feeling good about what we are and how we're progressing.

"Sure. Anything," I say, wanting to be as open with him as he is with me.

"Tell me about your time at college," he says, and my

whole body stills. Fear ignites my blood, and my palms start to sweat. That is not what I was expecting. I thought he was going to ask more about my mom or even my upbringing with a single parent.

"I don't want you to tell me anything you are not comfortable with, but the few times we have touched on it, I get the feeling it wasn't the time of your life that you were expecting?" His hand rubs up and down my arm in a soothing motion. I swallow and nod, taking a steadying breath to calm my suddenly racing heart.

"I've never told anyone..." Sitting up again, I turn to look at him. I create a bit of distance, because I want to tell him; I just need to do it face-to-face. Again, his brow furrows, and I lean forward, putting my wineglass on the coffee table. I don't know what he will think of me after I explain this. The professor always said I wasn't to tell anyone, and I always blamed myself. Maybe Hudson will look at me differently. But I *need* to tell him. I firmly believe that for any close relationship to survive, you need honesty and openness. He just told me all about Amanda, so now I will do the same.

Hudson waits, his eyes searching my face, putting his glass down as well, obviously feeling the seriousness of this conversation. I clear my throat before I lay it all out there.

"The first few years were great. I met a couple of friends, had a few boyfriends. I mean, I studied hard and had a few part-time jobs to still help out Mom at home, but I guess it was exactly how you expect college to be," I tell him, and he nods. I take another breath and wring my hands together in my lap before he shuffles forward, grabbing my hands in his, anchoring me. Closing my eyes, I try to find the courage to push through this shame that crawls at my chest, before I open them again and look right at him.

"Go on." He encourages me with a softened tone, his face serious. I nod and take another breath.

"In my final year, things started to... change..."

He watches me carefully as I close my eyes and take another breath.

"There was this professor..." I say, and I feel his body harden, his grip on my hands firm. "He, um... he... It started when he asked me to stay back after class. He went through my marks with me on assignments. I thought it was a little weird at the time, because he didn't seem to do that with anyone else from my class, but I thought maybe it was because I was struggling with the class." I pause, and Hudson waits patiently.

"He offered to do some one-on-one tutoring, and at the time, I didn't question it. He's a leader in the college, very prestigious. It was somewhat of a privilege to be selected to get additional support. I didn't think anything of it." I try to breathe deep, my hands shaking a little in his hold.

"I stayed back after class, and he would go through a few things with me. But then..."

"Then what?" Hudson says, and I meet his murderous gaze. My heart sinks yet warms at his protectiveness.

"He just... Um... at first, I thought I was imagining things, but every week, whenever I stayed back after class, it kinda got a little more inappropriate each time. Initially, he just seemed to lean too close, but he had to look at my work over my shoulder, so it makes sense, right? I'd rationalize it like that. But the next session, he placed his hands on my shoulders, squeezing, and his hot breath would hit my neck as he got close. I didn't like it. Everything about it made me uneasy. My grades improved, though, and maybe he just worked like that, I didn't know." Feeling sick to my stomach, I watch as Hudson's jaw clenches.

"But then things progressed..."

"Progressed how?" he asks, and I swallow, wanting to vomit but pushing through.

"The weekly tutoring continued, and each week, he got more and more comfortable. He would pull up a chair and his leg would touch mine. Once, I was leaning over and writing something, and he grabbed my hair from behind and brushed it behind my back. I remember his fingers touching the bare skin at my neck," I say and shiver, just thinking about that creepy-crawly sensation. "Then one week, I passed a particularly hard test, and after class, he hugged me. It wasn't a quick congratulations kind of hug, but a long, drawn-out one. His hands held me too tight. I couldn't pull away, and to be honest, I was shocked, so I just stood still. His hands ran up and down my back, and he leaned down to whisper in my ear how proud he was of me."

"He was grooming you," Hudson bites out.

"I recognize that now... Just not at the time..." I say, shaking my head, not proud of myself. I'm usually so much smarter than this.

"One day, he kept me after class and asked me if I had a boyfriend. When I said no, he ran his hand down my face, then down my neck, before his fingers hit the top of my breast, and he told me that he thought I was beautiful." I push out a breath, hating reliving this. "I stepped away from him, held my books to my chest, and said I had to run before I was late to my next class. It was a total lie; I didn't have any class after his that day, but I couldn't stand being alone with him anymore. So I started to skip his class."

Hudson nods in understanding. "What an asshole."

"I skipped a few classes, my grades plummeted, and he sent me an email telling me to come to his office to talk about it, because if my grades continued as they were, then I was likely to fail his class. I was straight A student in almost every other class. I had to be because I was on a full scholarship. I couldn't fail. It wasn't an option," I explain, almost imploring Hudson to understand.

"Let me guess, he knew this? He knew that you were a scholarship kid?"

"I hadn't thought about that before, but yes. Yes, he would have seen that on my record." I nod. "So I went to his office to meet him and discuss my grades. I was panicking because I didn't want to fail, and I only had one semester left. I was so close to graduating. But I was also so scared..."

"What happened then?" Hudson asks, then gets up off the sofa and starts to pace the living room. I grab a cushion and bring it to my front, cuddling it before I continue.

"I went to his office and took a seat. He went through my grades, and none of it made sense. He said I was failing from the start of the semester, but that wasn't possible because I passed everything up until I started skipping. So he must have gone back through and lowered my grades. He told me that the only way those grades would be changed back so I could pass his class was if I showed him my gratitude," I say, and Hudson stops pacing to look right at me.

"What the fuck?" He's not happy about any of this, that much is clear. I squeeze the cushion tighter, feeling extremely vulnerable, my heart pounding, but I know I need to push through.

"I didn't know what to do or what to say, so I just sat there quietly. Scared. Shocked. My body almost couldn't move. I felt like a deer caught in headlights or something. He stood up and walked toward me, leaned over my chair, and ran his hands through my hair. Then he said that a good first step would be for me to get on my knees... and... and then he started to undo his belt." My voice quivers as my anxiety makes it feel like I'm shaking from the inside out. I squeeze my eyes shut, but it doesn't help because all I see is the visual of him that day. Hearing it all out loud makes me feel sick to the core. I've had it so bottled up for so long, my therapist the only person who knows.

Hudson remains quiet, staring at me in what looks like shock and rage.

"When I heard the clink of his belt, full-blown panic took over my body, and I bolted up from the chair. The movement caught him by surprise, because he stumbled back, not expecting it. His pants were around his ankles, so he kinda tripped but caught himself on the desk. It gave me enough room to rush past him to the door, but…" I have to pause as my eyes water.

Hudson rushes to me, kneeling on the floor at my feet, grabbing on to my hands and pulling me close to his chest as my tears start to fall.

"He had locked the door," I choke out. "I didn't realize he had. He must have done that when I walked in for the meeting. I just got it open when he slammed it shut and crowded me against the door. I could feel him… hard… on my back, and he buried his head into my neck and sniffed me. And then he said that I could go, but I wasn't to say a word to anyone; otherwise, my mother would not survive her next round of treatment and that he also expected to see me in class the following week." It isn't until I finish the story that I feel my cheeks are wet and I'm fully sobbing. Hudson holds me tight, rubbing his hands up and down my back.

"It's okay. I'm here, you're safe. Lacy baby, I've got you," he whispers, and my breaths calm little by little. Pulling back from him, I dry my eyes.

"I'm fine. It's just a lot to revisit," I explain, feeling that our romantic last night in New York is now ruined.

"What happened after that?" Hudson asks, and I shake my head.

"As soon as I left his office, I went straight to the administration team and told them I needed to finish my remaining subjects remotely due to my mother's ill health. It was all on record that I might need to do that anyway, given her condition, and so I swapped to all online professors, moved back home, and I never saw him again."

"So you never went back for your graduation ceremony?" Hudson asks, and I shake my head once more. Wearing the black robe and hat is a rite of passage for every college student, but there was no way I was setting foot back at that college.

"And you never told anyone?"

"There's no point. There are no witnesses, and no one would believe me over him," I say, my tone one of dejection.

"Is that who messaged you that day in my kitchen? You got a message and your face just went white," he asks, and I nod slowly. "Connor mentioned that you got flowers at the office?"

I swallow roughly and nod, knowing this is only going to upset him more.

"He sends me letters, emails..." I start to say, and Hudson's expression turns furious.

"He still contacts you?"

"All the time. Calls me, texts me, but the flowers were new. He hasn't done that before..." I tell him as nausea rolls through me.

"His behavior is escalating," Hudson says, thinking to himself for a moment.

The silence makes me nervous, so I can't help but blurt, "I'm sorry I didn't tell you earlier, I just—"

"Don't apologize. Everything in your own time, Lacy. But I'm here for you. I want you to know that."

I take in a deep breath, feeling a little lighter for sharing as I look into his eyes and see the support and protectiveness there.

"I know some people at that college. What was his name?"

"It doesn't matter. It's in the past. I don't want to ever think about it again. But I wanted to be honest with you."

"He is still trying to contact you, Lacy—hell, unwanted calls, emails, and now flowers. It isn't right."

I know what he is saying is true, but I just can't think about it. "I can't..." I whisper, my heart pounding.

"But what if he is doing this to someone else? Someone who doesn't have the courage to leave like you did?"

That has my pulse stuttering as goosebumps pepper my skin.

"I hadn't thought of that. But it's only my word against his. He's one of their top professors, and I'm just a scholarship kid."

Hudson's shoulders are rigid with tension as his eyes bore into mine with intention. "I will get everyone at that college fucking fired."

I'm shaking my head as I respond, unable to process all this. "I know how frustrating, horrible, and sick it is. But I just can't deal with it, with everything happening with Mom and work being so busy. Besides, it's just me against him. I can't win that battle."

"It's no longer just you, Lacy baby. You have me firmly in your corner. I'm here to support you with anything you need. I have access to the top lawyers, powerful people. I will make him pay. All I need is a name," Hudson says, and I think about his words.

"He wants me to go back, do a face-to-face semester over the summer." I huff a laugh because he might be a professor, but he is somewhat delusional if he thinks I will ever see him again.

"That's so out of line. You do know none of it is your fault. He was preying on you. Hell, he still is, by the sounds of it. I want to bury him. Just give me a name. Just say the word." He looks about ready to jump up off the sofa again and start calling the police himself.

"Let me think about it," I say quietly, needing time to sit with my thoughts and get a handle on my emotions. I don't want to dig up the past, but if there is another woman going through what I did, or even worse, then I wouldn't wish that on anyone.

"But Hudson... please, promise me you won't say or do anything? Promise me you won't tell a soul, and if I decide to do something about it, I will come to you, and we can do it together. But promise you won't do anything without me," I almost beg him.

Hudson sighs as he looks at me, perplexed and obviously struggling, before he nods.

"I promise. I won't do anything until you are ready."

I nod, grateful to now drop the subject. But I'm relieved I told him. There is nothing between us now. He knows all of me, and I know all of him.

35

———

LACY

I moan, feeling every inch of my sore muscles, but feeling well rested as the faint glow of light hits my eyes. It's our last morning in New York before we fly back to the reality of Whispers, my body, mind, and heart having all reached new heights these past few days.

Hudson has not only delivered more orgasms than I thought possible, but he has treated me like a princess. Wining and dining me, he's taken me out and about to enjoy some sights before curling up together each night. I told him all about my college reality and now there is nothing left that he doesn't know. I feel lighter for sharing, but I would be lying if I said I felt totally relaxed. I'm still on edge, wondering when the next note or gift will come.

I crack open my eyes, the soft-pink glow of the morning shining in from Hudson's bedroom windows. The same ones that look over Central Park in his amazing penthouse that I am not sure I ever want to leave.

"What are you doing?" I ask, seeing him perched up on an elbow, looking at me.

"Watching you sleep," he says softly as his hand lazily skims up and down my bare skin, from my hips to my breasts and back again. As I wake, the movement sends pulses to my center and my body stretches in response.

"That's not creepy or anything." I giggle.

"Hmmm, back to teasing me again already." Smirking, he leans forward and kisses me. "Good morning, baby," he murmurs against my lips as his hand travels from my chest down my stomach.

"Morning, Doctor," I say, smiling, but then gasp as his hand glides straight down to my center, his finger circling my clit.

"How are you feeling?" he asks, all the while his finger continues to circle, my body tingling beneath the touch.

"Hmmmmm... really good now..." I close my eyes on a moan, feeling warm all over.

"Does this make you feel good?" he asks as his tongue flicks my nipple, almost in time with his fingers.

"Yes," I say breathily as he pulls the nipple into his mouth, sucking and nibbling while his finger moves a little faster.

"Good." His lips drag to the other breast, doing the same thing, and I bite my bottom lip.

"Your fingers are made of magic," I pant out. My heart thumps harder when he slips a finger inside and presses against that special spot that has me whimpering.

"Your body is perfection." Kissing my breast, he molds the other one in his other hand, playing me like a musical instrument. It's like he's become a master of knowing exactly how to touch me.

"I could wake up like this every morning..." My body arches as I feel my orgasm closing in on me.

"I want to wake you up like this every morning," he murmurs against my skin as my hips start to move against his hand, building the friction in a way that has my eyes rolling back.

"Hudson!" I whisper-shout, and his finger works me overtime, knowing exactly what I need. He sucks on my nipple hard, thrusting his finger harder as his thumb strokes my clit with the perfect pressure, and I come quickly with another cry of his name.

"Good girl," he groans, and I melt into his mattress as he kisses up my chest to my lips. We lie together, naked and kissing, taking our time, in complete contrast to last night when we couldn't get to each other fast enough.

"Let's have a shower, then I need to feed you," he says, sitting and pulling me up with him. I lazily follow to the bathroom and his enormous shower, which is similar to the one he has in Whispers.

As the water coats us, I start to come out of my pleasured daze.

"Tell me about these." My hands glide from his shoulders down his torso. My fingertips graze each ridge of muscle in appreciation. It's clear Hudson works out regularly; his body may as well be sculpted. "What does this clock mean?" I ask, as my finger circles the clockface on his chest.

"Eleven thirty-five... It's the time Harvey was born," he says, soaping up his large hands before they rest on my shoulders. Spinning me around, he massages my muscles, and I groan in relaxation.

"What about the sunflowers?" I ask, looking up at him, and he smiles, enjoying my observations.

"My mother's favorite flowers," he admits.

"Hmmm, she has good taste. And these letters and numbers?" I frown as I try to make out the longitude and latitude crisscrossing his ribs.

"They are the geographic coordinates of Whispers."

Nodding, I look at another one, a familiar symbol that I can't quite place. "What's this?"

"A Caduceus for medicine." he says, and I hum as it's all making sense. His whole life history is inked onto his skin.

"Why? Why tattoos?" I ask curiously. I love them on him, but it's just not something I expected.

"I went a little numb when Amanda died. She was young, the loss was great. I was left with this tiny human and didn't really know what I was going to do. I needed to feel something again. To feel like me again," he explains, the two of us standing in front of each other, eyes not wavering from the other as the water streams down. There is nowhere to hide here from our vulnerabilities. "The tattoos were the one thing I felt like I could control. The pain of etching into my skin is the one thing that grounded me. A little like your stars," he says, and I smile even as tears glaze my eyes, understanding all too well.

"What's this one?" My hand smooths across his wet skin, my fingers skimming what looks like a flame.

"Marie's Place," he says, and my eyes flick back up to his as my heart stutters.

"I'm sure you've already been able to tell, but I tattoo things that represent periods in my life that have made an impact," he says as his hands move to my waist to hold me tighter, punctuating the fact that this tattoo has me within the ink. With my stomach fluttering, I look back at the flame, the memories of that night still there, but less damaging with him by my side. I lean forward and kiss it. I kiss it because we came out of the fire together. Alive. But also, I kiss it because he has something of me on his skin. Something we endured together.

"Any plans for more?" I ask, still taking in the fact that we've been connected through something so traumatic and are together like this now. I continue to look over the other images and decorations that adorn his skin.

"Hmmmm. If you keep touching and looking at me like you are, then I would say yes." Running his palm up my side, his thumb grazes my nipple, which is still peaked, until he moves higher to cup my jaw, tilting my head to look at me.

"I like touching you," I tell him as my back arches a little, my chest moving upward to get closer to him. I run my hand across his hips to massage his cock, relishing how he pulsates in my hand. He drops his grip from my jaw and rests it around my neck, tightening before his thumb brushes across my racing pulse.

"You're teasing me," he grits out as I pump him languidly, and I feel him thicken even more in my palm. Moving his hand into my wet hair, he pulls it, bringing my head away from his chest so I'm looking up at him before his lips claim mine. The kiss is hard, scorching, his grip on my hair causing pleasurable pain to my scalp as his other hand cups my ass, squeezes, and pulls me to him. Our bodies mesh against each other, the water cascading down us both as his rock-hard length presses into my stomach. Moaning into his mouth, I hold on to him, pulling away slightly to drop to my knees.

"Baby?" he asks, looking down at me with fire in his eyes, the water hitting the back of his shoulders.

"Hmmmm?" I say as my lips take in his tip and suck, smiling around him as a moan rumbles in his chest.

"Jesus. Put it in your mouth, baby," he murmurs as his hand rests against the wall behind me, his other hand running down into my hair again. I lean forward and take more of him, swirling my tongue like I do with the cherry stem, and I hear him moan again.

"Just like that... You suck my cock so well, baby." I look up into his eyes as I do it again, taking him deeper this time, feeling my clit tingle as his expression holds pure want for me. Seeing him like this brings out a whole new side of me. I've never been so excited to get on my knees for a man.

"Fuck yeah... That's it," he groans, lifting his hand to slap on the tiles behind me to join his other one. With his hands now plastered against the wall, I take control and run mine up the backs of his legs, resting them on his ass, pulling him into me as my pussy flutters. "Your mouth is magic. I'm not gonna last much longer."

There's a desperation in his tone that turns me on all over again, and I suck him down in earnest. His hips start to move in and out of my mouth with small thrusts, and I rub my thighs together, needing the friction.

"I'm going to come, baby," he warns as our pace

quickens, and I nod with a moan around him. He comes with a roar, panting as I swallow his release and slide him from my mouth to sit back on my heels. I'm smiling like a fool as I stare up at his awed face, something in his eyes quickly changing from hunger to adoration. Hudson is quick as he lifts me from the shower floor, straight up onto his body, my legs automatically hooking around his waist as I giggle.

"You're beautiful, Lacy. I am so glad I found you," he says, and my chest feels heavy as he kisses me with so much more than lust.

"I am glad you found me too," I whisper against his lips and circle my arms around him tight.

Hudson not only found me, but he made me into a butterfly.

36

HUDSON

I stride up and down my hallway, unable to stop moving. We got home from New York a few days ago, and I have been on edge ever since. Jumping back into work is all that's been able to keep my head on straight, but just barely. That changed this morning, though, when I woke up with an overwhelming need to get justice for Lacy. I've tried to set aside what she told me, my festering anger over what she's been through unable to be suppressed any longer.

"Dad, your turn!" Harvey yells, and I pace back down to the dining room, where there is a board game out and my parents and Harvey are sitting around the table.

My father frowns at me, so I plaster a fake smile on my face.

"Already my turn?" I ask, trying to act like I am having an awesome time.

"Here are the dice!" Harvey says, smiling as I take the dice from him and roll them on the board, moving my piece along.

"Next!" I say, handing the dice to my mother, who senses something is up as I turn and walk back down the hall, pulling at my hair. I hear her and Harvey giggling in the background, and I roll my head on my shoulders, trying to ease the tension that builds.

"Son," Dad says from behind me, his tone laced with concern.

"I'm fine. I just have some work things to do," I tell him, lying about where my stress comes from.

"Well, go do them. We'll take Harvey up to our place for afternoon tea," he says, and I nod in appreciation.

"Thanks, Dad," I say with a heavy exhale.

"You tell me if you need anything." He knows this isn't a work thing at all. If I can be half the father to Harvey that my dad is to me, that would be amazing.

He turns and walks back to the table before I hear him telling the others that he feels like ice cream and that Grandma has chocolate chip in her freezer. Harvey shouts in excitement before jumping up from the chair and racing out the door, my parents chuckling at him and following his fast-paced steps.

When they're gone, I continue my pacing, with my baby girl at the forefront of my mind. All I can think about is what kind of asshole would prey on innocent college kids who are from small towns and on scholarships. It's almost the perfect storm. Country kid without city knowledge or life experience or contacts, who genuinely believes the senior professors at their school are genuine and honest, who can't afford to fail even one test as their grades are connected to their funding. The whole thing reeks of a power imbalance and must be a gold mine for those who, like Lacy's professor, want to take advantage of young people while they have no real support system.

I struggle with wanting to hire private detectives to search every motherfucking professor on that campus so I can find the man responsible, and keeping this to myself as Lacy has requested.

It is unlike me. My medical profession and ethics instill that I help, not harm, yet for the first time ever, I want to do some damage. I can't. I promised her I wouldn't. But the bitterness on my tongue is not abating and the heaviness in my gut is not diminishing.

The ringing of my cell grabs my attention, and I frown when I see the name on the screen.

"Hudson?" he says as I pick up before I even talk.

"Hello, sir. Nice to hear from you," I say to Gordon, Amanda's father, the man I haven't seen or spoken to for years. I still remember him on our wedding day. He wore a scowl on his face the entire time, like he was at his daughter's funeral, not her wedding. He left pretty quickly after the formalities. I remember Amanda said at the time he had to rush to work commitments, which I found strange, but now, knowing what kind of philandering asshole he is, it's clear he just had a better offer.

"Yes. Melody has told me that you are back in Whispers," he says, straight to the point—not asking how Harvey or I are, not entertaining any type of casual banter—and I roll my eyes. He clearly doesn't give a shit about his grandson. We have been here for months, and this is the first call.

"Yes. We moved a while back. It's nice to give Harvey

some fresh air and space to run around," I tell him, my already agitated state increasing.

"Well, Gloria and I were thinking we would come out to see you. She misses the boy." Even though his tone is arrogant, I don't miss the fact that he said his wife misses her grandchild, but he doesn't mention himself.

"Of course, you are always welcome to come to Whispers," I tell him through gritted teeth. Entertaining them at the ranch for a few days is my idea of hell.

"Great, well, I will organize a few things," he says, although what he really means is his assistants will organize a trip, and he will tag along purely for his wife. I'm not sure what agreement they have, because as far as I can see, she is well aware of his desire to have other women. I can only assume either it's a money thing or they are in an open marriage. Either way, it isn't my business.

"Looking forward to it," I say, keeping things neutral. He's not a man who is overly warm at the best of times, so I don't feel the need to be that way either. I'm about to say goodbye when another thought hits me.

"Actually, before you go, sir?"

"What is it?" he asks, sounding annoyed, like he hasn't got the time, even though he called me.

"I'm just wondering where you are lecturing these days?" I try to ask casually, like I'm making small talk, which is something we have never done.

"Willowstone. Why?" There's an edge to his tone I don't miss, and my eyebrows rise.

I know I shouldn't ask, but he is a good contact, having been in the education system for years.

"Just wondering who I need to speak to in order to report a crime against a student?" I can call the university directly, but I would rather go through personal channels. Things move quicker that way.

"Pfft. Stop wasting my time. Clearly, you have too much time on your hands these days, Hudson. You need to move back to the city." His arrogance hits me immediately. That and the fact that he doesn't answer or acknowledge my question.

I scoff, about to ask another question to get further information, but the call ends without even a goodbye.

The fucker hung up on me.

Rolling my phone in my hand, I think about Lacy. I don't want to talk about it with her until she is ready, and I don't want to push her, but the whole thing makes me upset.

It doesn't take much more spiraling thoughts from me to press my contacts and make the call I've been debating.

"Hudson. How's things?" Sawyer, Tanner's lawyer from the city, who is often in Whispers, answers almost immediately. His upbeat tone is much more refreshing than the last call.

"Sawyer. I'm doing good. And you?" I ask as I pace again, wondering if I'm doing the right thing.

"Fine. But Tanner has me looking at the contracts for Victoria's goat milk soap business. Apparently, it has picked up and they are really busy. That and my asshole of a brother is in Capri with that new leading lady of his," he says, huffing, and I smile. From what I see on social media, my friend is living his best life in the South of France.

"When are you in Whispers next? I need some advice," I say, taking in a breath. I feel bad for a beat that I am doing this behind Lacy's back, but it's just advice. All confidential, and if I can get things ready for when she wants to make a move, it will be all the easier for her.

"I will be there soon, actually. Within the next few weeks."

Relieved, I nod, even though he can't see me.

"Great. I would love an hour of your time if you can spare it," I tell him.

"No problem. I can make it work. Everything okay?" he asks, and I drop my head.

"Hopefully. I just need some advice on a personal matter." I keep it simple, not wanting to delve into it on the phone.

"Okay, well, I will speak to you then," he says, and we say our pleasant goodbyes before I end the call.

I look out the window toward my parents' house, where my son is, wanting to join them but still feeling uneasy. I made Lacy a promise, and for the first time in my life, I'm not sure I can keep it.

37

LACY

I rush into the diner, my Saturday morning blood donation all done. It's been a week since New York, and aside from seeing Hudson most days, my life has gone back to being somewhat normal. Hudson and I flew back in his private jet and then both hit the ground running with work. Now as I get back into my routine, we decided to meet here for the weekly sundae together, my mom resting and getting ready for a big week as her first transfusion nears.

"The boys are already here waiting for you," Rochelle says to me the minute I walk in, and I hold my breath and glance around. In the far corner of the room, I spot Hudson and Harvey sitting in a booth, both looking at me expectantly. My smile grows as my shoulders relax, just being around them.

The looks Hudson and I are getting are less and less as the locals are now so used to seeing us together. That, plus our mothers have been settling the rumor mill for us, knowing that I hate being the topic of conversation in this town. Even though it has been happening for most of my life.

"Thanks, Rochelle." I offer her a smile, and her cheeky wink makes me laugh.

"I've missed that laugh, darlin'. It's good to hear it again," she says before walking off and refilling the coffees for patrons nearby. I swallow, thinking of her words. These past weeks with Hudson have been like I am walking on air. He calls me and checks in with me every day, and when I get his sweet text messages, I can't stop smiling. I feel so much different, so much better, more like a version of me I want to be since he came into my life. My to-do list is full but not as long because we now have Jennifer, and work is still busy but even more exciting because I love working on our new projects. I don't feel as wound tight anymore, and I like that I have someone else to talk to about it all. I'm still on edge, though. Still waiting for something that I know is coming, yet I have no idea what *he* is going to do next. My nerves are frayed, jumping at noises during the night. The only time I feel safe is when I'm with Hudson.

"Well, if it isn't Miss Perfect walking in to get her weekly ice cream," Jolene snarks, sitting close by in a booth with her team of gremlins. I didn't see her at the hospital this morning, so she clearly has the day off.

"Hi, Jolene," I say, looking at her, then at the gaggle of girls around her. I don't see these girls much and haven't spent any time with them since school. But they are here, every Saturday, just like I am, and on occasion seem to like ruffling my feathers.

"I see the new doctor is here with you again. So it

must be true," she says, and the girls next to her giggle, making me frown.

"What's true?" I have no idea what she thinks she knows, but Hudson and I spending time together is topical. There isn't much else to chat about around Whispers at the moment, so we are an easy target.

"Oh nothing, just people talk is all." She's dangling the carrot in front of me, waiting for me to snatch it. I should ignore her and walk away. That is what I usually do. But I can't.

"What are they saying?" I bite out, and her smile widens at my clear frustration.

"Rumor is, there's some fancy doctor coming from the city to see your mom," she says, and I nod. She's probably the one spreading the rumor, given she has access to my medical files.

"What of it?" I ask, my frown only deepening because I can tell there's something more.

"It isn't news that you can't afford something like that..."

Her posse sniggers, and I take a breath as my spine stiffens.

"Just spit it out already." I'm getting sick of her games. We were not friendly in school, and we aren't friendly now.

"You're sleeping with the new doctor to get upgraded medical care. At least, that's what people are saying. You're paying for your mom's care with sex," she says, sitting back and smiling wide, her eyes glistening wickedly as my heart almost splits in two.

"What?" I can barely speak with how my chest tightens. I can't get enough air in my lungs, and my feet are frozen solid to the ground. I'm unable to move.

"I mean, I never really picked you for a sexual favors kind of girl, Lacy; you were always so frigid at school." Jolene smirks, and her friends laugh louder. I feel like I'm climbing a mountain, unable to ever reach the top. This is what it was like in school, with these barbs thrown at me almost daily.

I expected gossip. I expected small-town chitchat. But I didn't expect outright lies. I feel like my body is crumbling underneath me as I look around the diner. *Is this what everyone thinks? Is this what they're all saying about me?*

"What's up, Lacy? Cat got your tongue?" Jolene teases again, relishing my clear distress. Palms sweaty, my heart races, my mouth going dry.

My eyes flick to the back of the diner, and I see Harvey and Hudson both waiting for me. Hudson frowns, his eyes flicking from me to the booth of women and back again, clearly aware that something isn't right. My spine straightens, and I take in a breath. I know the truth, as does he, and at seeing him, newfound confidence runs through my shoulders and pulls them back to hold my head high. I clear my throat and look back at Jolene.

"It's all getting a bit old, isn't it, Jolene?" I ask with narrowed eyes. How the hell does she work at the hospital with this kind of attitude?

"What is?" She smirks, like she has the upper hand.

"This pick-on-Lacy attitude you've got. Seriously, you've been doing it since fifth grade. I think it's time you move on, get a new hobby. This infatuation you have with me is getting kinda embarrassing for you." I look her up and down. Her face turns red, not used to me talking back, and I walk away without another word, not giving her a chance to respond. My knees feel wobbly, but for the first time in a long time, I don't care anymore. I don't care what she thinks or what she says. It's almost like a heavy weight has lifted.

"Hey, you two," I say with a smile, walking up to the booth where Hudson and Harvey sit. My hands are a little jittery, and I'm thankful that I have a bag to hold.

"Hey, baby," Hudson murmurs, standing. "Everything alright?" His hand automatically cups my waist, pulling me to him as his lips meet my temple. I release a breath I didn't realize I was holding and melt a little into his hold. Smelling his cologne and feeling his secure touch, my body starts to calm. As I look around, everyone in the diner is looking at us. Rochelle eyes me from behind the counter with a smile on her face, and Bob from the hardware store grins over his coffee mug. Everyone looks happy to see me happy, and for once, I appreciate it.

"Don't worry about all the eyes... They're going to talk no matter what we do or don't do," he whispers in my ear, his thumb brushing across my back.

"I know," I grumble like a sulking teenager, and he laughs.

"Brat," he says, pinching my skin at my waist playfully, and I laugh, feeling light for the first time in a long while. I realize it's him. He's given me confidence to face this. All the counseling I've done, all the talks with Mom or Victoria, they've all been great, but it's Hudson who's been able to break down a wall I didn't think was possible. His time, his words, his attention and affection have instilled a new confidence in me that I knew I always had, but had buried, too busy and too exhausted to bring out before. I was already smitten, and I realize I'm falling hard for this man.

"Hey, Lacy!" Harvey says loudly, his excitement clear, jolting me from my thoughts.

"Hi, Harvey." I give him a bright smile as I slide into the booth opposite them.

"What's that?" Harvey spots the bag in my hands, sitting up a little, as the red logo of Tony's Toy World on it gives it away.

"Oh, something I just picked up. Want to see?" I ask, hoping I have done the right thing. My eyes flick to Hudson, who looks confused. Perhaps I should have asked him first. I have never been in this situation before to know if I am overstepping. I bite my bottom lip, not so confident in my choices this morning.

"Been shopping?" Hudson asks, his eyebrows high, and I take a breath.

"It's something I thought perhaps we could do together," I say, looking at them both as I put the bag on the table and slide out the box.

"It's the model airplane I wanted!" Harvey yells, jumping up immediately and grabbing the box in his hands. Everyone in the diner looks our way again. I knew he would be excited, but shit, I should have expected this enthusiastic of a reaction. I smile back at them, ignoring Jolene and her posse and focusing on the people who matter.

"You didn't have to do that," Hudson tells me quietly, holding my hand on the table and giving it a squeeze

"I wanted to. I know Harvey loves planes." I shrug. I should have spent the money on getting Mom a new blanket for her knees or maybe on the screen door, but instead I went to Tony's Toy World and picked up the plane, knowing how much it would mean to Harvey. I can get the new blanket for Mom next week and the screen door will be fine until next month.

"Can we do it? Can you come over tonight and we can do it together?" Harvey says, his eyes wide, face still plastered with surprise and shock.

"Oh, I..." I start to say, because while I thought we could do it together, I hadn't planned on it being tonight. My eyes flick to Hudson to gauge his reaction. I should have probably asked him before I brought his son something. I'm not totally sure of the rules around this kind of thing. I think it's a nice gesture, but many parents may feel differently. But his smile is warm, the love in his eyes that he has for his son obvious, and when he flicks his gaze my way, it doesn't falter.

"Come over tonight. Let me cook you dinner?" Hudson offers, and I take a deep breath. I'm trying to balance all my responsibilities, but the guilt I'm feeling for leaving Mom at any time is eating me inside.

"Please, Lacy? Pleeeaasssee," Harvey says, bouncing in his seat, and I laugh lightly. I have no idea how I'm meant to turn him down, let alone his handsome father, whose eyes haven't moved from me the entire time I've been here.

So I find myself nodding with just as much giddiness.

"Okay. Sounds fun." I take a deep breath and quickly run through my mental to-do list. I know Mom will be fine to spend tonight alone. She has her cell, and I'm not too far away. Jennifer and I have ensured her independence has grown these past few weeks, and I know she likes to have some alone time. She will probably appreciate me being out of the house tonight.

"Great. Let's get our afternoon treat, and then we can take you home, pack you an overnight bag, and bring you to the ranch," Hudson says, leaning back, happy that the decision is now made.

"I got your usuals," Rochelle says, sliding up to the table, with one sundae and one brownie, both with extra cream today.

"Thanks, Rochelle, they look delicious." Hudson gives her a broad smile, and I think I see her blush.

"Anytime, Doc. Looks like a nice gift you got there, little Harvey."

"Lacy got it for me!" Harvey says excitedly, and I suddenly see spots in my vision. I blink them away as I hold on to the table tightly, feeling a little faint.

"Did she now?" Rochelle says, smiling, and I can tell she is pocketing that information for later. Probably to tell my mother or share it with her friends down at the community center, where she plays a weekly game of bridge. Although I don't know how much bridge they all play; it's more like one big gossip session in front of a deck of cards, if you ask me.

"Harvey is very spoiled, and Lacy is very generous," Hudson says, watching me, before he curls his fingers in mine, still on display on the table. Rochelle notices the move immediately, and her smile widens even more, like we have just given her the best gift.

"Treats are on the house today," she says, grabbing the menu cards.

"You don't have to do that." I frown, confused. Over the years, Rochelle has treated me on the house a few times. Typically, when I have come in super sad after one of Mom's particularly bad weeks. But today, that isn't the case.

"Oh, nonsense. It's nice to see young love blossom. You don't see a lot of that around here." Her eyes twinkle, her lips twitching before she steps away.

"She has had one too many coffees today, I think," I quip, before I let go of Hudson and grab my spoon, the sundae in front of me teasing me. My vision has cleared up, but I'm a little nauseous. Maybe my blood sugar is low.

"So how was this morning?" Hudson asks, eyeing me carefully.

"It was fine. Just like the last time, over pretty quickly."

"Any dizziness? Fatigue?" he asks in his doctor voice, and I roll my eyes.

"I am fine, Hudson," I say, grinning as I wave him off. I don't need him worrying about me. I'm already feeling better as it is, anyway.

"Are you going to eat that cherry?" Hudson asks, one eyebrow rising with a sexy smirk on his lips. I swallow, my eyes flicking to his son, who is completely oblivious to our flirty banter.

"You want to watch?" I ask quietly, my tone laced with

a trace of seduction, my eyebrow quirking to meet his in a challenge.

He doesn't say anything, but he leans back, throws his arm over the back of the booth, and his eyes hook on me as Harvey shovels in his brownie next to us. Hudson's jaw ticks, and flames heat my insides, my stress from everyone's eyes on us before now all forgotten.

"Put it in your mouth." His request almost comes out as a demand, and I swallow before I grab the cherry stem, letting the glossy red ball dangle before I place it in my lips and taste it. I suck the juices, dropping it into my mouth, and as I do, I hear a small rumble from the man sitting opposite me, whose eyes are burning into my own.

He waits and watches as my tongue darts around in my mouth, and I swallow the fruit before I grab the stem from my lips, perfectly tied, and place it on my napkin.

"I have a new admiration for cherries," Hudson murmurs as he sits forward again, grabbing his spoon, our little show for two over.

"They are my favorite," I tease, smirking.

"And you are mine," he says quietly as he digs into my sundae, and my stomach flutters at the sincerity in those words. My weekly treat is now one I share with a man I think I am falling in love with.

38

HUDSON

As I finish cleaning the kitchen, I watch Lacy and Harvey at the dining table as they open the model plane. Their interaction comes easily, and it has been a long time since I've had any woman as close to my son as Lacy is right now. His own mother loved him more than anything, but he was only a baby when we lost her, so he has never really had a female in that role before. You would think they have known each other for years and do this every day. Harvey is completely at ease in her presence and Lacy is laughing, clearly enjoying herself, and a new feeling of contentment rests in my chest. Like this could possibly be something. This could possibly be my life here in Whispers.

"I think it's bedtime, buddy," I call out to Harvey, walking over to where they sit.

"But Daaaaaddddd," he whines, not happy because we haven't had any time to put this plane together, but it's late, and he has been running around all day. Just when I'm about to tell him no arguing, I spot him yawning.

"Bedtime," I say again, my voice lowering as I walk over to him.

"We can start it tomorrow," Lacy says to him, her smile soft. The light shines on her glossy red lips, and all I can think about is her tongue and that fucking cherry from today. I need to order a box of them so every time she comes over, I can watch her eat them and tie the stem. It's the perfect foreplay for me, and even now, thinking back to it has me half-hard.

"Can Lacy tuck me in?" Harvey asks, and I pause. He has never asked for anyone else to tuck him in before. Not even Grandma. I look at Lacy, knowing she doesn't need another thing to add to her list, but before I can say anything, she smiles at my son, and I see him melt.

"I would love to," Lacy says, then looks at me. I have no idea how I can resist either of them at this point. As Harvey walks down the hall to his room, my body is humming for her.

"Come on, we can both do it," I tell her, holding out my hand for her, and she takes it. Her delicate fingers entwine with mine, and we follow Harvey down the hall to his room. I'm surprised to see him already changed and crawling into bed. He's obviously more tired than I thought.

"Can we do the plane after breakfast, Lacy?" Harvey asks, his eyes half closing.

"Sure thing. Now you get some sleep because we will need full brain power for the model plane tomorrow," Lacy says, stepping forward and pulling up his blankets, tucking them around his shoulders. "Good night, Harvey," I hear her whisper before she steps back.

"Good night, buddy." I kiss his forehead, his breathing already deep, eyes fully closed. Huffing a laugh, I shake my head as we step out of the room, and I close his door.

"He really is adorable," Lacy says as we walk together back down the hall.

"Thank you for the plane. You didn't need to buy it, but I know Harvey loves it." I wrap my hand around her middle and pull her to me. Holding her close, toe to toe, we face each other.

"I knew he would love it." She looks up at me, and now that Harvey is down, there is only one person on my mind.

"I like it. I also like you, Miss Jones," I murmur as I bend down, putting my lips to hers. The kiss is soft, a little tease, for her or for me, I'm not sure.

"Well, that's good because I like you too, Doctor Hamilton." Her tone is light and sassy, and I smile as our lips touch again. Moving my hands around her tighter, I pull her to me, sealing my lips to hers, and I feel her body mold into mine. Her hands run up my arms and hug my neck as her body arches slightly.

"Let's go," I say against her mouth before I bend and pick her up and muffle her surprised scream with another kiss. As I grab her ass and lift her to my waist, her legs curl around me perfectly. She cups my jaw with her palm and her thumb rubs across my stubble, her soft skin in complete contrast. Any tension I hold starts to fall away.

"Do you need anything else before I lock you in my

room for the night?" I ask as my lips find hers again and I kiss her slowly.

"No. Just you. I just need you," she whispers, shaking her head a little as I squeeze her ass in my hands, my jeans tightening just by having her in my arms like this.

"Good. Because you've got me." And then I'm moving, hitting the stairs and running straight up them to my room on the other side of the house as Harvey.

"Hudson!" she squeals, her grip tightening around my neck to hold on, but there is no way I would let her fall. My palm is flat on her back, the other still grabbing her ass in these sexy-as-sin jeans she wears.

"Are you practicing?" I tease, before I lower my head and suck on her neck, my steps not faltering.

"Practicing?" she asks breathily as her head falls to the side, letting me bite and suck on her skin. As I walk across the threshold and into my bedroom, her hips grind on mine with a moan.

"Practicing yelling my name," I tell her as I toss her onto my bed.

"Hudson!" she yelps in a mix of excitement and shock. I close the door behind me and stalk toward her, her eyes glistening as she sits up onto her knees to greet me.

"I like having you in my bed, Lacy baby," I tell her as I lean down and kiss her slowly. As I do, I grab the hem of her sweater, and she sits back, lifting her arms so I can sweep the knit straight over her head.

"I just like being where you are," she says quietly. I sure as hell want her with me every day, and if I could make that happen ASAP, I would. She waits, watching me as my eyes bore into hers.

"You are everything I never knew I needed." I cup her jaw, searching her eyes as I swallow roughly, my feelings coming in thick and hot. "I thought I knew what life was about. I had Harvey, I was successful at work. I have money, the jet, real estate. I have everything I could ever want or need. But I still remember the first time I saw you." My other hand runs through her hair and her hands settle on my chest, still up on her knees on the mattress, with me standing on the floor right in front of her.

"I was such a mess that day you came to the house." She huffs a laugh at herself, and I shake my head.

"Not that day," I say, and her face falls a little.

"At Marie's Place, when I was tied to the..." she starts to say, and I interrupt her.

"Not that day either."

Her eyebrows dip a little in confusion, and I smile.

"You had on these jeans..." I murmur as my hand lowers, and I cup her ass because I fucking love her in these jeans. "And a black Whiteman's Whiskey T-shirt with the gold logo emblazoned on the front. It was fitted, and your curves in that outfit were fucking phenomenal." I groan, the memory of her working the bar for Tanner still fresh in my mind like it was yesterday, not over six months ago.

"Just like me for my body, huh?" she teases.

"You had your hair back in a ponytail..." I run my hand through her hair again, the soft threads coating my fingers and falling freely. "Your eyes were big and bright.

And your smile..." I say, my words left hanging. Her face changes then into an expression of more disbelief of what I remember and the impact she has had on me. "Your smile that night, Lacy, it could light up the whole damn town," I whisper to her, and I see her eyes start to glisten. "You were like an angel, baby. And I knew that night... I knew that you were without a doubt put on this earth just for me."

Three little words dance at the end of my tongue. I want to say them. I want to tell her. But I refrain.

"I came back for you," I admit, chest tight with emotion. "That night in the hospital, you were asleep, I was holding your hand. I knew, Lacy. I knew then where I needed to be."

"Hudson," she breathes, and I lean down and kiss her. Sealing our words, cementing this moment in our minds, I wrap her body close. With my hand still cupping her jaw, I move her mouth where I need it to deepen our kiss, and her hands dig into my shirt at my chest, holding on just as tight.

I never want to stop kissing her, and I hope I never have to.

39

LACY

I look around, heart racing. It's dark, I smell gasoline.

"Victoria?" I try to yell for my friend, seeing her slumped over, tied by rope.

"No!" My mouth is dry and sore and covered in rope, my shouts and screams sounding like mere murmurs. I wriggle, my arms tied above my head and sore, the rope burning like fire against my wrists, and panic fills my body as I start to tremble.

"No!" I try to yell again as I see my friend struggle. I need to help. I need to get out of here. Oh God, I can't die, what about Mom?

"Help!" I shout, but it does no good.

I struggle. The ropes are too tight, and then I see him. *Hudson.* "Hudson!" I scream, sitting up.

"Lacy?" Hudson's voice is laced with concern from beside me, but my heart thumps so hard in my ears it's hard to hear. I'm sweating, my skin and hair wet.

"Hudson?" I ask, out of breath, as my hand grips on to the sheets. They feel softer than usual.

"I'm here, baby. I'm right here. You had a nightmare. You're safe. You're at my ranch, in my bed. I'm right here." He says the words soothingly as his hand runs up and down my bare back. My breathing slows, heart calms, and my eyes slowly take in the room.

It's dark. But the curtains are open, letting the light from the moon shine in.

"What time is it?" I ask the only thing I can think to ask while I try to settle myself.

"Six a.m.," Hudson says, his hand still running up and down my back. I slowly come back to myself as his lips meet the skin of my shoulder, peppering kisses to calm me.

"Are you okay?" he asks, and I look at him.

"I'm fine." I stiffen a little in his arms as reality seeps in and my cheeks heat. I had a nightmare. In Hudson's bed. Uneasiness fills me. Embarrassment is too light of a word.

"Don't be worried about it. I'm glad I was here," he says like the mind reader he is, and I take a deep breath, wondering what the hell to do. I feel like fleeing. I want to find my clothes and run. But I have no idea where they are and no way of getting home, since he drove me here last night.

"Lacy. Look at me," he says sternly, but I don't want to. Taking a breath, I can't refuse him, so I turn my head slowly and meet his gaze.

"It was just a nightmare. People have them all the time. You're safe. You don't need to worry."

I swallow, trying to moisten my dry throat as I nod. He cups my jaw, his thumb rubbing across my lips before he leans forward and kisses me.

"Hudson..." I whisper. My body calms from the nightmare, now focusing on him as his other hand trails across my body to my lower back and he pulls me toward him as he cuddles me in his embrace.

"This is real, Lacy. You and me. Just concentrate on us," he murmurs against my lips as he soothes me.

I lie in the silent room as Hudson's hand continues up and down my back. His heart thuds at my ear, where my head rests against his bare chest.

"It starts with the smell," I tell him, wanting to open up.

"What do you smell?" he asks, and I close my eyes briefly before opening them again.

"Gasoline. Then I feel restrained."

He kisses the top of my head, letting me talk.

"I then see Victoria and start to panic, trying to get to her. Trying to get out of the rope that holds me." All the while, his hand continues along my back in a steady rhythm. Keeping me calm, keeping me centered.

"I usually wake up then, but it's changed lately," I say, lifting my head and looking at him. The bedroom is still a little dark, but I can see him, the concern etched into his brow.

"Changed how?" he asks as his hand brushes the hair from my face, watching me closely.

"I see you," I tell him and he frowns so I continue.

"I see you at the end. I see you coming for me. Running toward me. Saving me." I give him a small smile.

"The nightmares are horrible, but since you have been back, they don't come as often, and they aren't as violent as they once were." Feeling safe and calm in his embrace, it's easy to be honest.

"Over time, they should dissipate even more," he says, still watching me closely.

"I think they are. I think seeing you again, being with you, I think it all helps." I swallow past a lump in my throat, coming to the realization just now myself.

"There is nowhere else I want to be than with you."

I rest my chin on his chest and look up at him. His eyes are on me, the moonlight streaming in through the curtains, giving a soft glow to his face.

"I have fallen for you, Lacy Jones. Baby, I love you," he says softly, and my heart feels like it is about to explode. The silence sits heavily between us as feelings of longing blanket me in warmth. "You don't have to say it back…"

"I love you," I rush out. "I love the way you remember the little things." I press a soft kiss to his lips, cupping his cheek. "I love the way you didn't take no for an answer when you asked me out." I smile as I say the words. "I love the way you instill so much confidence and positivity into my life when I had very little to give in return. I wasn't looking for anyone. I didn't need anyone. Then you came back. You came back to Whispers."

"I've got you, Lacy. I always will," he says with such sincerity, my eyes tear up as I lie back down. He holds me tight, and together we watch the sun come up on a new day, feeling grateful to have found each other.

But I'm not entirely at ease. His breathing is calm and regular, my body relaxed, but my mind is working overtime. Hudson loves me, my life slowly feels like it is all coming together, yet as I look out the window, I know something is amiss. I can feel it. My life has never been perfect, and while I love Hudson and he loves me, perfect doesn't happen to a girl like me.

40

HUDSON

I'm running around my place, trying to keep busy. If I don't, I will blow a fuse.

"So this is all I need, then?" Lacy asks. Her mom is heading into Williamstown today for her transfusion, and Lacy's nervous, I can tell. She's fidgeting, her shoulders tight.

"Why won't you let me go with you today? I promise I'm a great support person."

"No. It's fine. I know you're busy. Besides, I'll be fine. Mom will be fine."

I feel like she says the words more for her own reassurance than mine. The gate intercom buzzes through the kitchen, and I look at the screen, seeing Connor's truck and who looks to be Sawyer in the passenger side.

"Connor and Sawyer are here," I tell her, Harvey's head pops up from where it's been buried in a book about planes his aunt sent him this week. Having a sister-in-law who owns Bloomers Books is a godsend when it comes to those kinds of gifts.

"Oh? Boys' day?" Lacy asks, her smile small but there, and I sigh.

"Since you won't let me go with you, I need a distraction," I murmur, keen to take the opportunity with Sawyer in town to talk to him about the situation at Lacy's college while she isn't here.

"I will be fine, I promise. Mom is the one doing the hard work today, not me," she reiterates as I see her trimming the stems on some wildflowers that Harvey picked for her. She was only popping in to get the paperwork she needed for the hospital today but took the time to cuddle my son after he presented her with the bouquet this morning, and now she is taking great pride in getting them ready for the vase. I like having her in my house, moving around my kitchen; this whole situation is very domesticated, and it feels good.

"Morning, lovebirds," Connor says, waltzing into the kitchen like he owns the place. Lacy rolls her eyes as I shake his hand and give him a backslap.

"Door was open!" Sawyer says, announcing his entrance. Connor comes and goes from place so regularly he is almost part of the furniture, so I'm not surprised they just walked in.

"Nice flowers. Pick them yourself?" Connor asks Lacy, clearly teasing her, and I see their dynamic now. At first, I was jealous, but now I see them more like siblings. It's hilarious, actually.

"As a matter of fact, they are from Harvey," Lacy says proudly. "Did you tell the boys how much you luuurrved the massage in New York? So much so, you are hiring the therapist and practically dragging her to Whispers?" Lacy teases him, and Sawyer and I cough out a laugh. Connor was less than impressed that he had a sound healing massage when I whisked Lacy away from her work commitments back in New York, but Connor doesn't have a quick comeback like he usually does, which has me squinting at him.

"Are you blushing?" I ask, shocked. Connor doesn't get embarrassed about anything, and now my interest is piqued.

"Shut up," he mutters, before heading to my refrigerator and opening it, grabbing out the juice.

"What did I miss?" Sawyer asks, and Lacy and I look at each other in shock at the coy way Connor is acting. I'm about to push him some more to find out exactly what happened in New York with this therapist, because something clearly did, when my gate intercom buzzes again.

"I'll check it!" Harvey hollers as I look at my best friend. A grin slowly comes to my face at the realization that Connor Whiteman is not as infallible as people might think.

"Who is it, buddy?" I ask Harvey as he walks back to us.

"Ahhh, it's Poppy and Nanna," he says, and I still.

"Who?" Sawyer asks, frowning, and I run my hands through my hair. Of course they didn't tell me when they were arriving. So typical of them to just turn up unannounced.

"My former in-laws," I say as my eyes flick to Lacy.

"Oh shit, I didn't know they were here; otherwise, we

could have come by tomorrow," Connor says, and I shake my head.

"I knew they were coming; I just didn't know it was today. They failed to mention exactly when they might come to town." Seeing them now is one of the last things I want to do today.

"I should go. I'll just get these beautiful flowers in some water, then I will leave you all to it," Lacy says with a tight smile as her movements quicken, clearly uncomfortable with the situation on top of what is already a stressful day for her.

She is beautiful today, even with a million things on her mind. I don't care if my former in-laws meet her. It was bound to happen one day; it might as well be now because she isn't going anywhere. Before I can say anything else, I hear the front door open.

"Anyone home!" my former father-in-law yells out as he walks in like he owns the place. Not that dissimilar to Connor, yet Gordon is no friend of mine. I take a deep breath to steel myself, trying to remain courteous for Harvey's sake.

"Good morning, Gordon. I wasn't expecting you today," I say, letting him and everyone else here know that their visit is unexpected.

"Oh, Gordon, you said you told him we were coming," Gloria, my former mother-in-law, huffs from behind him. "I hope we're not interrupting?" Coming into the kitchen, she sees everyone here. Dressed to impress, high heels on and fully made up, as only a socialite from the city can be.

"Not at all. You remember, Connor. And this is my friend, Sawyer," I say to her as I step forward and kiss her on the cheek in greeting. It hasn't gotten past me that Harvey remains back at the table, obviously not eager to see them either. I don't blame him. He hasn't seen them in a while, and even then, their visits were few and far between, despite them wanting full control and say in his life. They are practically strangers.

"And this is my partner, Lacy," I introduce them, my gaze finding Lacy in the kitchen, but I freeze as soon as I take her in. She's holding the vase of flowers, smiling and looking radiant, but then her eyes lock on my father-in-law, and she goes deathly pale.

"Lacy?" I question, as Connor frowns and takes a small step toward her protectively, and Sawyer looks at my in-laws inquisitively.

"Lacy?" I move toward her and take the vase from her shaking hands, and she clears her throat.

"I need to go," she says quietly, looking at me, my father-in-law, and back to me again. I can hear her breathing quicken, and she seems a little panicked. While I expected meeting my former in-laws may create a little awkwardness, I wasn't expecting this level of fear. She swallows audibly before she gives everyone a fake smile and practically bolts from my kitchen, striding right out the door.

I look over everyone, confused, before I shove the vase of flowers into Connor's hands and run after her.

"Lacy," I call out as I reach her outside my front door. "Wait." Grabbing her elbow, I turn her to face me. My breath catches at the petrified look on her face, and my senses heighten.

"Talk to me, baby. Tell me what's going on," I ask her,

searching her eyes. Clearly, she isn't okay. I can almost feel the unease vibrating from her body, but I have no idea why, and it has my heart pounding.

"It's fine. I need to go and get Mom ready, that's all. I'll talk to you later," she rushes out, giving me another forced smile before she slips from my grasp again and runs to her car, but not before she looks over my shoulder, and her expression falls.

I watch her get in her car and take off down the drive before I turn around and see my father-in-law standing there in the open doorway. He hasn't looked at me once, his eyes still on Lacy's car, even though it's barely visible. I see his eyes crease, and his mouth turns up in a sick smirk, and then it clicks. My stomach drops, and my anger rises.

"Did you tell me you are lecturing at Willowstone at the moment, Gordon?" I ask as I tentatively step toward him, and only now does he look at me, giving me a smarmy smile. I don't know how I know, but I do. I spot Sawyer and Connor, as well as Gloria behind him, probably wondering what is going on.

"I lead their statistic faculty," he says, nodding, pocketing his hands and rocking back on his heels like the arrogant son of bitch he is. I see red.

I stride toward him, and without any warning, I throw my fist at his cheek so hard, I feel like I broke my own hand.

"You sick son of a bitch," I yell as he falls, his knees hitting the ground in front of me as I hear the scream from his wife.

"I'll charge you with assault!" he splutters at me as he tries to get up, and I lunge at him again.

"What the hell?" Connor says, grabbing me from behind, pulling me back. I shout and kick and elbow Connor in the torso, trying to get out of his hold, because I want to pummel this sick, preying asshole into the ground. I can't even see straight, I'm so enraged.

"You're a fucking pedophile!" I yell, feeling like I am out of my own body. I have never been this angry. Ever.

"She was of age!" he barks at me, and I freeze. Gloria gasps in horror. He isn't denying it. I see Sawyer out straighten the corner of my eye, paying very close attention now, the lawyer in him kicking in.

"She was your college student. You groomed her!" I shout or growl; I don't even know what I sound like at this point. I see my mom and dad come out from their place and walk swiftly toward us, hearing the commotion.

"She wanted it. They all do," he says quietly, but not quietly enough, by the looks Sawyer and Connor have on their faces. Connor's grip on me loosens, and while I haven't actually said Lacy's name, it's apparent exactly who I am talking about. Connor steps forward, fists tightening.

"I think you both need to leave," Sawyer says, stepping in between Gordon, Connor, and me, aware things are not going to get any better.

"What is he talking about? What is going on?" Gloria asks as I see my mom rush inside, no doubt going to find Harvey as my father stands watching.

"Do we need to call the police?" my father asks, looking at Gordon. Two totally different men. My father is strong, solid, a workhorse. Jeans and a casual shirt are his daily attire. My father-in-law is in a suit and wouldn't know a hard day's work if he tried. One contributes, one just takes.

"Yes! We do. Your son assaulted my husband!" Gloria screams. The entitlement of these fucking people is astounding.

"No. No police," Gordon says, wiping the blood from his lip, which I busted open. Pity there isn't a doctor in town who will see to his injuries because he sure as fuck isn't welcome at my hospital.

"She doesn't know, does she?" I say, looking at his wife, who looks stricken, but I don't hold back. I can't. "Gloria, your husband preys on college students. Gives them good grades for sexual acts. When they don't comply, he fails them and then stalks them until they agree to come back and make up their grades at a special summer school. It probably makes them a little more accessible, doesn't it, Gordon? Since the number of staff at the school over the summer break reduces quite a bit. Less people. Less eyes?"

Not even acknowledging me, he grabs his wife's elbow and leads her toward their car. His eyes flame as he glances at me, and I can tell I'm right.

"Fuck, how long have you been doing this? How many young women have you assaulted?" I ask, and I see Sawyer on the phone, no doubt to the authorities. We will let them go for now; we can't hold them, but they won't get far. It's all out now, and he needs to be dealt with. His game is up.

"I have no fucking idea what you are talking about,

and if you don't stop with this nonsense, I will sue you for defamation!" he yells, and he knows he's fucked. He knows I will stop at nothing to end him and that I have deep enough pockets to do it.

"Sounds like that will be the least of your problems," Connor says, coming to stand next to me with his arms crossed over his chest. Connor is massive. Bigger than Tanner. Tall, broad, and the one person I don't ever want to get in a fight with. Clearly, Gordon agrees, because his mouth is now tightly closed, and he gets in his car, barking at his wife to do the same. They drive out of my place so quickly their tires almost screech.

"I called the police. He won't get far," my mom says, and I turn, seeing her standing in the doorway. She wasn't here for all of it, but I don't have to tell her. She knows. They all do.

I just hope Lacy will forgive me for what I have done. Because I promised her I wouldn't do anything until she was ready. Now, I've broken that promise.

41

LACY

My cell phone has been ringing off the hook since Mom and I got here.

"Are you going to answer that?" My mom sighs, as sick of the ringing as I am. I continue to ignore it but turn my volume down, not wanting to hear it again either.

"No. It's just Hudson. He is worried," I tell her, plastering a fake smile on my face. My hands won't stop shaking, and my stomach rolls and twists so much that I'm sure if I had eaten breakfast today, I would have already brought it back up.

"Why don't you answer him?" she asks, knowing something is amiss.

"Because I'm here to concentrate on you." I tell her half-truths. She is my priority today, but I'm freaking out about what happened this morning.

My professor is Hudson's former father-in-law. There is no way I can tell Hudson that it's him. No way he can know that man is the same man who groomed me in college.

How is that ever going to work? I don't want to ever see him, but he is Harvey's grandfather, so of course if my life is entwined with Hudson's, then I will see him, hear him, hear of him. But I can't. I can't have that man in my life. He makes my skin crawl, makes me feel pitiful and useless and less than. And dirty. He makes me feel disgusting.

"You really need to stop worrying about me. Maybe Hudson should come and wait with you?" my mom says, worried I'm freaking out, thinking it's all about her. And it should be. All my thoughts should be on her. Yet another thing that horrible man ruins for me.

"I'm okay. Just a little nervous for you," I tell her, putting a fake smile on my face. I'm getting sick of having to fake it all the time.

"It's cold. Are you cold?" I ask Mom as I grab a blanket, my own hands feeling like ice blocks.

"Stop fussing, Lacy," she scolds me, frowning. "You're looking pale. Sure you don't need the doctor?"

I shake my head. I do feel woozy, my body exhausted, a little dizzy, but I'll be okay.

"I'm fine. We're here for you. Not me." I give her a soft smile. We have been waiting in this cold hospital room for what feels like all day, but it's probably only been less than an hour.

"Good morning. How is my patient doing?" Melody says, sweeping into the room, her blond locks tied back into a tight bun, her makeup flawless, even though she is about to operate.

"Feeling great. Ready to get this over with." My mom smiles while I bite the inside of my cheek.

"Great. So just to go over today, we are going to wheel you down now into the theater. We will do a bit of a poke around, using keyhole surgery, inserting a camera into your abdomen and just making sure everything is as it should be. As I mentioned, your red blood count is still low and declining, which I don't like, so if we find a bleed, we will fix it, and then do the transfusion if needed. At this stage, I think it is," she says in a tone that relaxes my shoulders somewhat.

"How long do you expect it to take?" I ask, holding on tightly to my mom's hand as I stand by her bedside.

"It should only be an hour to two, depending on what we find. We should have your mom wheeled back here in no time," Melody says, giving me only a half smile. I don't think she likes me much. Then she sighs and grabs her cell from her pocket.

"Sorry, this has been ringing off the hook all morning." She acknowledges us both before she puts the cell to her ear and walks out of the room, but not before I hear her greeting.

"Hi, Mom," she says, her voice fading as the door closes, and I swallow. Then it triggers in my mind that it's Melody's father. I wonder if she knows her dad is horrible and predatory. I shiver, not wanting to even think about it anymore.

Jolene walks in and gets Mom, ready without even a look in my direction, and I take another deep breath. It feels like the universe is throwing everything at me today, and I'm trying not to buckle, but I'm feeling sensitive to everything. I just want to sit in the corner and hide. I don't want to face the world anymore; it's just too much. All of this is too much.

"We ready?" Jolene asks, and Mom gives her a warm smile while squeezing my hand.

"Good luck," I say to Mom, putting on a brave face. "I have some work to do, so I will stay here and keep busy." I won't move from this room until my mom is back.

"Be back in a flash, sweetheart," she says as some other nurses come in and crowd around her bed, getting it onto the wheels and moving. Then the bed is pushed out of the room, our hands breaking free, and I stand, alone, in the cold space, feeling anxious but positive that she will be back soon and with good news.

Taking a seat on the armchair, I grab my bag, about to pull out my laptop. Might as well try to get ahead with work so there isn't as much to get back to. As I gather my things in my lap, the door to the room flies open.

"I don't know what kind of games you are playing at, but you have some fucking nerve," Melody seethes, and I jolt to my feet.

"What do you mean?" I ask, frowning.

"First, you take Hudson from Amanda, and now you are ruining my father? What kind of sick, twisted bitch are you?"

With my heart in my throat, my eyes are wide as she spits her words so violently, I actually feel her saliva hit my cheek.

"What?" I say on a shaky exhale. I think I'm in a state of shock.

She knows. Which means Hudson knows.

"If I knew that you were this kind of person, I would

never have agreed to see your mom. As it is, I need another donation from you." She stalks to the small trolley that is off to the side, full of needles and other bits and pieces.

"More blood? Why? Is Mom okay?" I ask, starting to panic, even though she was only just wheeled out.

"Oh, your mom will be just fine." I don't like her tone. I remain still, trying to breathe as she pulls the trolley over to take more of my blood.

"Now shut up, sit down, and give me your fucking arm," she demands, all niceties out the window. The last thing I want her doing right now, in her current state of mind, is sticking me with a needle, never mind laying a finger on my mother.

"Why do I need to donate again, Melody?" I ask firmly. My hands are shaking, my vision blurry with the anxiety rushing through me.

"Because the stupid staff at this stupid backward hospital lost your previous donation, so if you want your mom to be without, then I can just wheel her back in here and forget this entire fucking thing. Lord knows, I have other places to be now, since you have ruined my entire family."

I don't like it, but I roll up my sleeve and take a deep breath to calm myself. It's for Mom. I have to. And I have to trust Melody to an extent. She's a medical professional; she wouldn't do this if she didn't have to.

"This is the first and last surgery I will ever do for you," she says before plunging the needle into my arm without a care. It stings so much, I hiss and scrunch my eyes shut. She is taking no care, her movements sharp and angry, treating me like her own private voodoo doll. Once she tapes the needle down, she leaves me to it, pushing out the door with so much force it hits the wall hard before it comes back and shuts out the outside world with a jarring slam.

I only last a few minutes before I'm grabbing a nearby bag and dry retching, falling to my knees onto the cold, hard floor, not able to take it anymore.

42

HUDSON

Today has been an absolute shit show, and if I could rewind it and go back to the start of the day when Lacy was here with Harvey and me at home, with her beautiful smile on me as Harvey gave her the bouquet of flowers, I would.

"This is a fucking hornets' nest," Sawyer says, looking up at me from where he sits with his laptop. He has been busy pulling things together ever since my former in-laws left. Calling in criminal lawyers from his extensive team, pulling evidence and already drafting statements and letters.

"I can't believe it," Connor says with a shake of his head. The two of them know everything I know, and I feel sick for betraying Lacy's trust with the information, but I couldn't keep my anger in check.

"Good thing you have those new security cameras out front; they picked up everything. We have his facial features, his snide comments that he thought only you could hear. Everything. This, along with a statement from

Lacy, will get him, for sure. Not to mention, anyone else who might come forward after word gets out of his situation. The school will remove him, there's no doubt in my mind," Sawyer says, and I sigh. At least I did something right.

I grab my cell and try her again.

"Still no answer?" Connor asks, and I shake my head. I know she is at the hospital because I confirmed they had checked in. I haven't called Melody yet. I have a feeling her mother would do that already, and I need her to concentrate on Lacy's mom.

"Nothing," I say, throwing my cell on the dining table and scrubbing my face.

I hear Tanner pull up, along with Victoria, and I thank God my parents took Harvey to their place. Mom will no doubt have him busy in the kitchen, whipping up some chocolate creation to keep him away from all this today.

"What the hell are you doing here?" Victoria yells at me the minute she and Tanner are inside. Tanner watches me, his gaze almost deathly.

"Trying to get a handle on things. Lacy won't take my call..." I tell her, feeling frustrated.

"Wrong answer. The correct answer is, I'm just grabbing my keys and am driving to the hospital, because I really need to be with the love of my life right about now," Victoria admonishes me as she stands there with her hands on her hips. She's right. I'm worried that Lacy won't want to see me for blowing up her life like I have, but I need to fucking try.

"Fuck," I groan as I quickly grab my cell and keys and stride out the door.

"Fucking love. Who in their right mind would do it to themselves." Sawyer shakes his head, and I don't answer him. I don't talk to anyone, but Tanner pats me on the back and gives me a nod, telling me it is the right thing to do.

"Go get your girl," he says, and I nod to him and run out the door, eager to get to Lacy.

I PACE INTO THE HOSPITAL. I called her another five times on my way here, but somewhere between Whispers and Williamstown, she turned off her phone.

"Doctor Hamilton. Good afternoon," a nurse at the reception says, obviously recognizing me, but I don't recall her.

"Good afternoon. Looking for Veronica Jones' room, please?" I ask, knowing Lacy's mom will already be in surgery and that Lacy will be waiting in her room for her.

"Room twenty-four, just down the hall—"

"Code Blue in twenty-four. Code Blue in twenty-four." We get interrupted, and my chest clenches at the announcement. Without another thought or question, I start running. I sprint down the hall and turn the corner in time to see Jolene push open the door.

"Doctor! It's Lacy!" she says, panicking, and I push through the door and see Lacy slumped on the floor.

"Lacy!" I shout as I dive to her, and I hear others rushing in right behind me.

"What happened?" I bark at Jolene, who looks sick with worry.

"I came to check on her. I wheeled her mom into surgery about thirty minutes ago and, well, I just wanted to see how she was holding up. I found her like this and hit the alarm."

I can tell by the way she's genuinely frightened that she's telling the truth. I investigated Jolene the minute Lacy said she was her high school bully. She's a health nurse, does blood tests, and helps out around the ward. She isn't a seasoned professional, and I dare say has never had to help a patient like this.

Lacy has an IV connected to her arm, her body lifeless and pale, and my whole world crumbles.

"Lacy!" I feel for her pulse, which is faint, and I thank the stars her chest is still rising and falling as I manically start looking her over.

"Lacy!" I yell, as I get to work pulling the IV from her arm. By the look of the bag, she has donated more than another pint of blood, and I'm furious as I try to stem the blood flow while I simultaneously feel her pulse to ensure she is still strong.

I'm breathing heavily, panic crawling up my throat. I'm a doctor, a seasoned professional, but the insane fear and adrenaline that I felt months ago grabbing her from the rafters at Marie's Place comes crashing back to me.

"I have her, Doctor Hamilton," one of my colleagues says, pushing through the door with a team. They know I'm off duty. It's hospital protocol that I step aside and let them handle it, but I don't want to let her go. My heart literally falls out of my chest as they push in front of me and take over. I don't want them to have to restrain me and forget about Lacy, so I step back quickly, moving out of their way, and watch them work on her. I fist my hands. Watching others treat her is the hardest thing I have ever had to do as they try to rouse her, attaching machines to check her heart and pulse. My eyes flick to Jolene, who is standing to the side, shock on her face, and a healthy dose of reality of exactly how precious life is on her mind.

I can barely breathe. I swallow hard, my mouth dry as I look back at Lacy. Her body is still limp, her beautiful hair out, her features softened and her skin deathly pale. She looks rested, at peace, and I look up to the ceiling and close my eyes, praying that this isn't the end.

She will be alright. She has to be, because I'm going to marry this girl.

43

LACY

I hear voices, but I feel like I'm far away, in a tunnel.

"She will be fine. Needs rest. But she has had fluids and an iron transfusion. She will make a full recovery," I hear Hudson say quietly.

"So what, Melody tried to bleed her dry?" my mom asks, and I hear the pain in her tone.

"Apparently," Hudson grits out before I moan, trying to talk.

"Lacy?" Hudson asks, his voice panicked. "Lacy baby, do you hear me?" A grip on my hand tightens.

"Hmmmm, where am I?" I croak out, squeezing my eyes shut, my body feeling heavy, no energy to even move.

"You're in the hospital, sweetheart," my mom's voice comes through again, and I feel her squeeze my other hand.

"Mom?" I ask, wanting to know how she is.

"I'm fine, honey. A bit tender and sore, but fine. My surgery went well and was over quickly."

I try to pull at my memories—her surgery, hospital, what happened before that. *Melody*.

"What happened?" I ask as I slowly open my eyes. I see Hudson's face looking down at me from right above. He is blocking the bright lights, his eyes full of concern. I've seen this before. Months ago, after Marie's Place. We have been in this exact same position, and I try to take a deep breath. His hand cups my face.

"It has been one hell of a day, baby." He sounds a little choked up, his eyes watering a little.

"I'm okay. We're okay," I whisper to him, then another realization hits me with a powerful force as I remember why Melody was so upset. As I remember that Hudson now knows the truth. "The professor?" I ask him quietly, and he nods.

"We got him. I'm sorry I broke my word to you. I'm sorry that I got other people involved in what is your private history, But Lacy, I needed to keep my initial promise to you. I've got you, baby. I've always got you," he says, and I tear up and nod shakily, not confident in my voice right now.

"The professor is being questioned by police," he tells me, and I hear my mom huff.

"I'd like to question him with this walking stick I've got here," she grumbles, and I look at Hudson with widening eyes and a sinking stomach.

"She knows. All our friends and family know now. Victoria, Tanner, and Connor are right outside with Harvey—none of them want to leave here without seeing you today."

Taking that in, I don't feel as badly about everyone

knowing as I thought I would. It's more comforting than anything, having support, not having to keep this secret any longer. I swallow and try to sit up a bit. As I do, I see my mom in a wheelchair next to my bed.

"Mom, shouldn't you be resting?" I ask her. I don't want her putting her own health at risk for me.

"Tsk. I'm fine. Feel a bit like a pin cushion, but otherwise okay. They found a small bleed. They fixed it and I'm all fine now."

I look at Hudson, who nods in confirmation.

"Here, take a drink." Holding a cup of water to my lips, I take a drink, not realizing how parched I was.

"He has admitted to some things. Sawyer and his team are building a case, and they would like a statement from you, if you want to be involved. However, he pretty much admitted to everything on my front doorstep, which was captured all on my security cameras," Hudson says, and my eyebrows rise.

"He will not be a part of our lives, and neither will his wife or Melody. Melody is looking at losing her freedom too after this." Hudson says Melody's name with a bit of a bite and looks at my arm.

"What happened? I remember giving more blood, but I don't remember anything else," I say and I see Hudson's jaw click.

"Melody received a call from her mother just as she was going into surgery. She found out about her father. She thought you were making it all up. That's what her mom told her on the phone. They weren't happy that we were dating. They hated you from the moment they knew about you. I think she acted hastily, being so upset. A spur-of-the-moment decision made her hook you up for another donation that wasn't needed. Your already low iron levels and the few donations you have already given made you weaker than usual. Melody hooked you up to the IV and left you there." He looks like the words he says taste bitter on his tongue.

"Oh my God," I say as my stomach clenches. How could someone do something like that? I could have died.

"Jolene found you. Apparently, she wanted to come and see you and check on you. She was also hanging around outside, wanting to apologize, but I sent her home. Told her that once you are better, you can decide if you want to talk with her or not. But she was a help. She's the one who sounded the alarm so we all came running," he explains, and my brow furrows. Who would have thought Jolene would ever be my savior, yet here we are.

"If I had just gotten my head out of my ass quicker and come sooner, I could have..." he starts to say, frustrated with himself. Head shaking, his eyes search my face. "I don't know what I would have done if you weren't okay."

"You came. You're here now. And I'm okay. More than okay with you by my side," I tell him softly. Even though my strength is almost nonexistent, I grab his hand and squeeze it in mine.

"I'm here, Lacy baby, and I'm not going anywhere. You're stuck with me if you'll still have me?" he says, tone full of regret as he locks eyes with me, and I frown.

"I'm yours," I tell him without an ounce of hesitation, tears pricking my eyes. I can't believe he could think I wouldn't want to be his. "I love you."

"And I'm yours," he confirms, placing his lips to my forehead in a tender kiss. "I love you too, baby. So much."

With those sweet words as my lullaby, I close my eyes and fall back asleep, knowing the two people I love the most are both here with me. And for the first time in a long time, I trust that everything will be okay.

EPILOGUE - HUDSON

"It's so peaceful here," Lacy says from beside me as our feet crunch in the snow. We are in Rovaniemi, Finland, staying in an igloo under the stars, making one of her dreams come true. Harvey was crushed he couldn't come, but we promised him next year and his grandma is making his favorite cake to make up for it. That and the fact that Lacy has been video calling and sending him photos almost every minute of the trip has her smiling and him laughing. The way she has stepped into a parenting role with Harvey is heartwarming. He loves her and she loves him.

"Apart from the drunk Santa at the end." I scoff, laughing. He was an old guy who clearly had a few too many whiskeys to warm up in this weather. Lacy giggles, and I bask in the sound. It has been six months since things exploded. At the time, it was stressful, but I hired good people, good lawyers, therapists, and home help for everyone, because while Lacy and her mom were the most affected, the extended family, Harvey, my parents, and the distillery all needed some guidance too.

It was money well spent as I now hold her close as we walk back to our igloo after dinner at the main hotel.

"He was very entertaining," she says, smiling. Lacy has come a long way in her healing, and I couldn't be prouder.

My former father-in-law was convicted this week in the court of law for the crimes of grooming underage victims, assault, and harassment. He has been dropped from ever working in education again and will serve some time behind bars. Although not enough, in my opinion.

Melody lost her license. Lost her career. She was also tried in a court of law, admitted guilt, and was let off with a hefty fine and a record. Her mother had a fall from grace, the socialite with all the money now no more. I have no idea where they are. They're not allowed to contact us and certainly not allowed anywhere near Whispers, me, my son, my girlfriend, or my other proper-ties. I heard they may have fled to stay with other family in Europe, but I don't know for sure.

"I'm happy to see you smiling," I tell her honestly. There have been a lot of tears, a lot of sleepless nights, but we have come through the other end stronger. Together.

"I feel okay now. I think the worst is behind us," she says, and I hold her tighter.

Once Lacy came forward with the allegations and proof against Gordon, there was a huge media onslaught. While I kept her safe and protected at home, she did make a public statement, and as soon as she did, many other girls came forward. Twenty in total. Their tales were all similar to Lacy's. Some girls fled like Lacy did, but others weren't so lucky.

"I just really want to move forward now, you know. Connor and Victoria have been working hard and I think I might jump back into it. Working a little more will be good."

Tanner, Victoria, and Connor have been amazing through all this. Lacy has had time away from work to deal with everything and they never hesitated to support her.

"Have you spoken to your mom tonight?" I ask her, knowing she already did.

"Yes. She and Jennifer were in Williamstown today. Apparently, they have some new women coming into the group."

When her mother floated the idea of opening a knitting group in Williamstown for other cancer patients, Lacy was a little hesitant, but both Veronica and Jennifer have started somewhat of a movement around the Whispers region. They are often driving here, there, and everywhere, talking to other women who are sick, giving support, and Lacy's mom is thriving.

As we continue to walk, I can see our igloo up ahead. It's cold, and smoke puffs from our hot breaths, but the sky is clear, just as the weather predicted, and full of stars. It's almost impossible not to look up.

"Oh, what's that?" she asks, spotting the large telescope at the door of our igloo that I had brought in for us tonight and we come to a stop in front of it.

"This is for you," I say to her, and she looks at me with a cute pinch between her eyebrows. Grinning, I lean over and take her lips in mine. I will never tire of this, of her. After all that we have been through, it's nice to have everything now falling into place. I feel nervous, because now is the time for my question. I've been toying with it for weeks, wondering what she will say, and I've talked at length with Tanner about every possible scenario. Pulling back, I look into her beautiful eyes.

"So, ahhh, I got you something," I tell her as I pull an envelope from my jacket pocket and pass it over to her.

"What is it?" she asks curiously, eyes widening.

"Just a little gift." I press another quick kiss to her lips, relishing her smile.

"You don't have to buy me gifts, Hudson," she grumbles playfully as she opens the envelope, and I wait as she pulls out the piece of paper.

Her eyebrows furrow before they rise.

"What!" she gasps, her smile now taking over her face.

"I named a star after you." Holding her a bit tighter, she hops in my arms, full of excitement.

"Seriously? You can do that?"

"I called it the Lacy Baby, and its location is just above us here. I brought in the telescope so we can try to spot it," I explain, and her eyes well up.

"Hudson. This is too much." She shakes her head as a tear falls down her cheek, and I lean over, rubbing it away with my thumb.

"Nothing will ever be enough for you," I whisper, and I see her swallow before I continue.

"Hudson, I—" she starts, and I cut her off.

"Lacy, did you know that for most butterflies, finding a mate to share their short lives with is their most important mission. To meet *the one* among a swathe of unsuitable or unwilling partners, butterflies must adopt clever tactics. So..." I trail off before I drop to a knee in this freezing cold snow.

"Oh my God ..." she whispers, her eyes now wide and watery.

"Lacy. When I first laid eyes on you, there was no doubt in my mind that you were made for me. Your smile lights up a room, your humor makes me smile, your intelligence makes me think, and your body makes me crave you incessantly. You are the most beautiful person, both inside and out, and you're the perfect mom to Harvey, stepping into the role of a mother figure for him and he adores you just as much as I do. I want to spend every second of my day with you. Every day of the year with you and all the years of my life with you. I want you in my life for eternity. You and Harvey are, without a doubt, my most important mission in life. We both know exactly how short life can be, but I hope on the ranch, we can live a long and beautiful life, under the stars, together." I'm leaving my heart wide-open for her. "So Lacy, will you make me the happiest man in the entire universe, and will you marry me?" I ask, my heart beating in my ears, my breath nonexistent as I wait.

She sniffs as she takes in everything I've just said. It's been a big week for her, and I really wanted to cap it off with something good, with a new start. I let her take it at her own pace, watching as she takes a steadying breath.

"Yes, Hudson. Yes, I will marry you," she says through happy tears, her mouth curving upward, and I smile. Jumping up before my knee gets frost bite, I grab her around the waist and lift her completely off her feet to kiss her. I kiss her and kiss her and kiss her before I put her back down when we're both breathless, and I take her to the telescope, where we look for the Lacy Baby together.

To find out where Hudson and Lacy are now, grab their bonus epilogue HERE

ALSO BY SAMANTHA SKYE

The Billionaires of Whispers

Tanner

Hudson

Connor

Sawyer

Sutton

Griffin

SCROOGE: A Billionaire Christmas Story

The Baltimore Boys

The Charming Billionaire

The Arrogant Billionaire

The Damaged Billionaire

The Secret Billionaire

The Bossy Billionaire

The Billionaire Babe

Men Of New York

My Legacy

My Destiny

My Fight

ABOUT THE AUTHOR

Samantha Skye is an international bestselling author. A country kid turned city slicker, she writes spicy and suspenseful contemporary romance novels that leave you hot under the collar and on the edge of your seat.

Samantha lives in Melbourne, Australia and when she's not plotting her next novel, she can be found travelling, drinking margaritas and enjoying a sunset or a stargaze somewhere.

To join in the conversation join Skye's The Limit Facebook group here;

https://www.facebook.com/groups/skyesthelimit books

www.ingramcontent.com/pod-product-compliance
Lightning Source LLC
Chambersburg PA
CBHW070822190726
48292CB00006B/2082